APRIL'S FOOL
A Sam Cable Mystery: Book 1
Scott Bell

April's Fool
A Sam Cable Mystery™
Red Adept Publishing, LLC
104 Bugenfield Court
Garner, NC 27529
http://RedAdeptPublishing.com/

For my big sister, Mandy

Chapter 1

"Trouble follows you the way a bad smell trails a fart." —
Captain Les Marshall, Texas Rangers

Sam

I cracked one eye open. A dead woman stared back at point-blank range. Her bloated tongue stuck out, like she was blowing a raspberry from beyond the grave, and both bulging eyes glared at me.

"Gah!" I rolled away, churning out of bed and hitting the floor in a full-body flop with a half twist. Not a proud moment, and not reflective of my normal stoic and firm-jawed reaction to danger. *I hope nobody saw that.*

Clues seeped in by bits and dribbles. Carpet. Tan. Tight weave. Industrial-grade. It smelled of hotel room. Senate candidate April Fortney's hotel room was my guess, since Fortney lay dead less than four feet away.

I was her bodyguard.

And she was dead.

Damn it.

I lay on the floor of the Hyatt, studying the tan weave, trying not to think of my bare junk mashed into a hotel carpet. My stomach churned, and puke threatened to come fountaining up. I swallowed hard and kept it down. My knees hurt from whacking the floor.

How the hell did I get here? What happened last night? I played back last night on the memory screen and came up with a movie called *I Don't Remember.* As in, I didn't remember visiting Mrs. Fortney. Or going to bed with Mrs. Fortney. Or strangling Mrs. Fortney. And... *Oh please, Lord, say I didn't have sex with her.*

One thing at a time.

First, I was naked. Bare butt in the air. Not a stitch on. Naked. Being nude with a dead woman seemed a really bad place to be found.

I shivered, slick-coated in cold sweat. And I was sick as a poisoned dog. Winos in gutters looked better than I felt... *dead* winos in gutters looked better than I felt. Gripping the carpet seemed the only good way to stay anchored and keep the room from spinning. Either this was the mother and father of all hangovers, or my system was working through a heavy-duty, Costco-sized helping of horse tranquilizer.

I executed a clumsy push-up. I reached my hands and knees, pausing in a four-point stance before gathering strength for the rest of the climb. Using the bed for leverage, I took it slow and easy then grunted to a standing position. The room spun, but I held on, arms out like a tightrope walker.

My clothes lay over the back of the easy chair next to the bed. Some care had been taken to set everything out, as if arranged by a loony butler after staging the crime. Even my boxers were folded.

My boxers were folded?

"Well, that tears it," I muttered. "Now I know I didn't undress myself."

Known fact: a man can't think without his pants on. I reached for my underdrawers, but the floor tilted, and I flopped into the chair. The hammer of my gun prodded me in the butt cheek. I dug the weapon out of the cushions, still in its clamshell holster, and set it aside.

Getting dressed turned out to be a pretty big chore, what with the room sliding around. My hands shook so much, I had to feel for the buttonholes with the patience of a bum fishing for a nickel in a storm drain. My Dockers were wrinkled, and my button-down shirt with the Texas Ranger badge looked like the victim of a hard night. I stuffed my feet into my dress boots and tried standing again. Success.

All my gear, including my pistol, went back on my belt, where it belonged. I checked the chamber of my .45. Still one copper-jacketed slug in the pipe and seven of its buddies stacked in the magazine. Good thing I hadn't gotten around to writing April Fortney's name on the tips. Somebody might take that the wrong way.

I left my cream-colored Stetson on the dresser at the foot of the bed. My head didn't want to support the weight. The only thing missing was my cell phone. A quick pocket check, followed by another slow trip to the floor to look under the bed and dig through the chair cushions, confirmed my cell phone was AWOL.

I sucked in a deep breath and examined the dead woman. Mrs. Fortney, former judge and most recently candidate for the US Senate, lay flat on her back. She was naked but for a garter belt with one white fishnet stocking still attached. The other stocking garroted her neck. The bright-white lingerie contrasted with her Starbucks-latte skin in a way that would have been sexy, if she weren't dead.

Her eyes protruded from a swollen face. I leaned over for a closer look and found petechiae—burst blood vessels typically caused by strangulation. Her distended tongue had a blue tinge. She'd been dead more than a few hours.

I was being set up. They—whoever *they* were—had done a good job. I had motive. Probably refugees from Syria and polar bears in Siberia had seen me arguing with Fortney on more than one occasion. Certainly, everybody on the campaign staff had.

I had the means. Whoever had strangled her must have been strong enough to hold her down and twist the stocking around her neck with sufficient force to choke her to death. It would have taken either a strong man or a powerful woman. Given my height and weight, a jury would take one look at me and say, "Yep, he's a big 'un. He must've done 'er."

That left only opportunity. As her bodyguard on the campaign, I had twenty-four seven access to the candidate. By virtue of the job, I had to be close to her. Nobody would question my stopping by her room at any hour of the day or night. I even had a room key.

"Which wraps up the trifecta of criminal justice," I said aloud in the hushed room. "Motive, means, and opportunity."

I knew I hadn't killed her. Even with a blank spot in my memory, the idea of murdering a woman—up to and including someone as disagreeable as Fortney—made me sick to my stomach. *So what happened?*

I anchored my feet next to the bed and captured a mental image of the entire scene before I moved anywhere. Standard Hyatt suite. Mrs. Fortney's room, 1412 from the number on the bedside phone. King-sized bed. Easy chair. Small dresser with white Stetson. Two empty glasses sitting in wet rings. One with lipstick on the rim. Mirrored closet, partially open. Women's clothing hanging there. The candidate's suitcase upright in the corner. A large open area near the window, with a table, sofa, and chairs.

I couldn't see in the bathroom from where I stood, so I watched where I put my feet and circled around the foot of the bed. Nothing in the bathroom except a ton of cosmetics. Wadded towels piled in one corner. The inside of the tub was dry. At the vanity, I used the tip of my gun barrel to push the faucet lever up and drank directly from the spout, sucking down enough water to submerge a whale.

I caught a glance of my reflection and nearly shot myself, just to put me out of my misery. Patriotic eyes—red, white, and blue. Pasty skin. A red crease on my cheek from pressing into the pillow. Sweat-matted blond hair, trimmed short, but long enough to stick up on one side. George Romero would have rejected me for a bit part in *Night of the Living Dead.*

I shuffled back to the bed and continued examining the body. April Maree Fortney, age forty-two. African American female, fit, good skin. Except for the ligature around the neck, I saw no marks on the body. I wasn't about to move her to do a more thorough inspection, as crime scene pricks get fussy about disturbing evidence. Ever since *CSI* came out, they all thought investigators worked for them.

She lay flat on her back, hands by her sides, palms up. Head turned, her brown eyes were focused on the place I had recently vacated. She had a tiny, distinctive mole on the left side of her nose, high up. No mistaking who she was. I lifted an arm, and the elbow joint flexed easily, though her skin was cold. Dead maybe six hours? The bedside clock read 8:22. The red LED was lit next to the a.m. mark. So call time of death between midnight and two o'clock in the morning.

The murder weapon—a white stocking—had bitten into her neck and remained pinched there, twisted into a granny knot at the side. The attacker had been strong enough that the hosiery had squeezed deeply into the flesh of her neck. A small amount of bloating almost buried the material in a ring of flesh.

Several strands of Mrs. Fortney's hair were caught between the stocking and her neck, like the killer had slid it over her head and twisted. Probably held her down with his body weight. Or it was a really big, strong woman. *Modern crime fighters must not be sexist pigs and assume all killers are men.*

I leaned close to inspect the stocking and noted a trace of dark red, almost brown, on one of the loose ends. Blood? That would be a good guess.

The itching on my pinkie finger finally registered, and I held up my right hand. As if splashed with ice water, my face went numb. On the inside of the joint on my right little finger was a small cut.

"How much you want to bet that's my blood on the stocking?" I whispered, awed by the depth, breadth, and width of the pit of shit I was in. "These people don't miss a trick."

My heart thumped in my chest, hard, and new sweat prickled my skin. Swallowing with a dry throat, I checked over the rest of the body, just to be thorough. Gravity had flattened her breasts, but not as much as I would've expected. *Implants? Maybe. Nothing unusual on the ribcage, the stomach...*

"Huh," I grunted.

Judge Fortney had trimmed her pubic hair into a tiny V-shape, clippered close. *Who would have guessed? Then again, who would have guessed she owned a pair of fishnet stockings and a garter?* I would have expected leather and a whip, not something soft and feminine. And where was the matching bra? There didn't have to be one, but its absence seemed strange.

Legs, feet, everything else looked as normal as a dead woman's body could look. I sucked it up and inspected the cleft between her legs, relieved to find no obvious signs of sexual intercourse.

She'd urinated when she died.

I racked my memory to come up with a plausible theory as to how I'd come to be in her suite. The last thing I remembered was having dinner in the hotel bar with some of the campaign staff around eleven o'clock. After that... blank. No little old ladies had carried my six-foot-four-inch, two-hundred-ten-pound body in here. Even one guy would have struggled, considering he would have to knock me out and drag me through a hotel full of surveillance cameras.

"Cameras." *Duh.*

There should be CCTV coverage of every hallway. Whoever entered this room must have passed at least one camera. As the Judge's security detail, I had visited the control room and seen the setup. All digital recording, high-resolution video, with over fifty cameras. Something had to have shown up on one of them.

I had already spent too much time piddling around the crime scene. Calling the local law enforcement types, with me standing there, a finger firmly implanted in my butt, didn't seem the best choice, even though it was the only choice I had available. I wanted at least some clue as to how I got here, but it looked like that wasn't going to happen.

A loud pounding at the door made me jump. A powerful, no-bullshit voice followed. "San Antonio Police. Open up."

Icy spiders crawled over my skin. The killer was being very thorough, getting the cops involved before I could sneak out.

"Just a sec," I hollered. I frowned at the late April Fortney. Things looked bad for me, but still worse for her. Somebody had framed me for her murder, but they'd *killed* her. A woman I was sworn to protect.

A Clint Eastwood line from *Gran Torino* came to mind. I recited it as a promise to the still-unidentified perpetrators of Fortney's murder, whom I had no doubt I would one day meet. "'Ever notice how you come across somebody once in a while you shouldn't have fucked with? That's me.'"

I left April Fortney and reached for the door.

Chapter 2

"*Justice is incidental to law and order.*" — J. Edgar Hoover

Rita

At 8:04 a.m., Rita Goldman, Special Agent of the Federal Bureau of Investigation, crossed the lobby of the FBI's San Antonio headquarters. Her modest heels rapped the faux-marble floor like the beat of an M4 rifle. With guided-missile precision, she zeroed in on the elevators and jackhammered the up arrow. Even when angry, she took care not to chip her red-lacquered nail.

When the elevator failed to appear in a timely and forthright manner, she pivoted and made for the stairs. A janitor swung around the corner, and they each did a skip-step to avoid a collision. Rita skirted past on the right, throwing out an apology.

She mounted the stairs, pounding the treads, legs pistoning, not slowing until she reached the fourth floor. It was a testament to a six-mile-a-day running habit that she wasn't winded when she stuck her ID badge on the reader and slapped open the door.

With its maze of cubicles in the middle, offices around the walls, phones burbling little tones, chatter and hum of voices, all overseen by banks of fluorescent lights, the fourth floor of San Antonio's FBI field office could have been any office in any city in any country. Only two things separated it from corporate America: the workers carried guns, and casual Friday didn't exist here.

Rita cut through the maze without slowing. She failed to acknowledge the rare, brave soul who attempted a greeting. Her eyes focused on the corner office of Jim Whitlach, Special Agent in Charge, her boss and the head of the San Antonio field office.

She planned to rip Whitlach's balls off and feed them to him, salted, with a squeeze of lemon.

Julie Ross, the SAIC's admin, looked up from her monitor at Rita's approach.

"He in?" Rita didn't wait for an answer, wouldn't have heard it anyway, the way the blood pounded in her ears. She marched past the admin's desk and hit Whitlach's partially open office door with both hands at chest height, as if she were passing a basketball. The walnut door crashed against the left wall and bounced back, somewhat ruining her entrance when she had to slap it out of the way again.

"You stole my case," she snapped, coming to a stop an inch away from her supervisor's desk, hands on hips.

"I'll call you back," Whitlach said into the phone and replaced the handset. A well-fed, brawny man, Whitlach had once played middle linebacker for Notre Dame. The SAIC had a Midwesterner's ruddy complexion and cloudy blue eyes. When he got mad, his face flared crimson and his jaw jutted forward, not unlike an Easter Island head hewn from red marble. This time, the flush crept up his face, from neck to hairline.

"What is your malfunction, Agent Goldman?"

"Dobronovich and his goons. That was my case." Rita's nostrils flared. "I worked six months putting that together, but when it comes time to bag 'em, you cut me out. Bialek took 'em down this morning. He's writing up the case. *My* case."

They both leaned over the desk, fists planted as braces. Their faces were inches apart: David versus Goliath, Mighty Mouse against Superman. *Pissed-off Long Island Jew against Porky, the* goy *from Indiana.*

"Goldman," Whitlach gritted out. "Goldman, you are the junior agent in this office. You are not the one who sets policy or decides what case belongs to who—"

"Whom."

"What?"

"The word is *whom*. You were referring to an object."

Whitlach narrowed his eyes as if he were on the firing range. "What. Fucking. Ever. I will decide *whom* gets what case and *whom* will make an arrest and *whom* will get the credit. And if you ever barge in here again, I will be the one *whom* busts you out of this office and out of the FBI and out of the country, if I can so manage."

Rita's heart thudded, more from anger than fear. Whitlach's threats didn't mean much to her. She'd graduated summa cum laude from NYU, had two undergraduate degrees and a master's in forensic accounting. Getting another job would be easy. Getting another FBI job, on the other hand...

A bit late to worry about that. And maybe, a tiny voice whispered, *I'm coming on too strong.*

Whitlach pointed at the door. "What's the title under my name, *Agent* Goldman?"

"Special Agent in Charge?"

"It's the *in charge* part you need to get a reading on."

"I—"

"No, Goldman, shut up now, while you still have a career. Get out of my office before I suspend you pending review of your insubordination. End of fucking story."

Rita burned her boss with a nuclear-powered stare. When he failed to spontaneously combust, she did an about-face and marched from his office, back straight and face heated to solar-flare temperatures. Eyes fixed forward, she cut a path through the pregnant silence of the fourth floor, parting a sea of carefully not-staring agents.

Rita marched to her desk and took refuge behind her three and a half walls. *Well, that was massively unproductive and criminally stupid.* She had accomplished exactly zilch. It was just... she'd worked so hard and so long to bring down Dobronovich... it wasn't *fair*.

She huffed under her breath, arms crossed. "Fair, you wanted?" she murmured a favorite bromide of her mother's. "You want fair, buy a subway token."

She stuck out her lower lip and puffed curly hair off her forehead. *So what did that little outburst get me?*

"Trouble," she muttered under her breath. "Nothing but trouble."

Chapter 3

"*There's only two people in your life you should lie to... the police and your girlfriend.*" — Jack Nicholson

Sam

Two Hispanic cops in San Antonio PD uniforms stood at the door: Valdez and Quintana, according to their nametags. They could have been clones—medium height, stocky build, black hair, and brown eyes. Quintana had a mustache, though, and Valdez did not. Some cops wore an attitude the same way they wore their Kevlar vests. Valdez and Quintana radiated attitude.

I flipped my ID out, showing my photo and accompanying round shield of a Texas Ranger. The real Rangers, my badge proclaimed, descended from the original badass lawmen of the Wild West, memorialized in story and song. Legendary. Stalwart and true. The SA cops held up well under the pressure of being in my presence. Both failed to genuflect.

"Before you boys walk in the door," I said, "know that this is a crime scene. You need to call it in as a homicide."

Quintana and Valdez exchanged a look—a type of cop look that said, "What kind of bullshit is this?" They taught it at the police academy in a class called Everybody Lies.

"Step outside, please," Valdez said, serious as cancer.

Quintana took out his sidearm and went past me into the room, using the hook thingy common to hotel rooms to keep the door open. I did what Valdez wanted, moving slow and gentle. His hand rested on the butt of his sidearm. I kept my hands clear and in plain sight, leaning against the print wallpaper. Valdez settled in front of me, stone-faced.

"Sir, is this your room?" he said.

"No. As I'm sure you know by now, it's Judge April Fortney's room."

"Who are you, sir, and why were you in Judge Fortney's room?"

Rigid sonofabitch. Maybe he was a cybernetic hive mind, part of the Borg Collective.

"You saw from my ID. My name is Sam Cable. I am a Texas Ranger." I spelled it out for him, in case he was a little slow. "Tex-as. Ran-ger. Maybe you've seen the movie? With Dylan McDermott?"

"I did not."

"Just as well," I said. "It was pretty bad."

"Ranger Cable," Valdez droned, as if reading from a teleprompter. "Do you know the name of the homicide victim?"

"Judge Fortney." Maybe if I used sign language?

"And how did you come to be in Judge Fortney's room, sir?"

"I am ... *was* her protection detail."

"Lucky for her."

Very funny. The robot had a sense of humor after all. The blood rushed to my face, and my fists tightened. Valdez was either the kind of cop with a chip on his shoulder, or it was past shift change and he wanted to be somewhere else. His attitude was pegging the meter.

Lucky for Valdez, Quintana came out of the room and saved his partner from getting thrown through a wall. He glanced at me, nodded at Valdez, and holstered his sidearm.

"Female, black," Quintana said. "Possible strangulation. I called it in." He looked back at me. "Who are you again?"

"Oh, for Pete's sake." Railroad spikes pounded into my head, driven by a chain gang of demons. "I just went through this with your partner. Why don't we all wait until a real detective shows up, and I'll give my statement to him? Whaddya say?"

The two amigos looked at each other. Cops loved the chance to pass off work to the detectives. It made their lives much simpler.

"Can I ask," I said, "what brought you to this particular room, at this particular moment?"

They traded another look. Quintana answered me after a beat. "Disturbance call."

"Disturbance call? When did that come in?"

"Thirty, forty minutes ago," Quintana said. He, apparently, was the chatty one.

Thirty minutes ago? I was out cold thirty minutes ago, under the influence of whatever drug that had taken me out. *Which reminds me.* "I need to pee."

That required more telepathic communication between the uniforms.

"Hold it," Quintana said.

"No, you don't understand. I was drugged, which is why I woke up in there." I jerked my thumb at the room. "I need a specimen collected under supervision by an evidence tech."

"Not gonna happen anytime soon," Quintana said, without looking at his partner this time.

"Independent thought has been achieved," I muttered.

"You were drugged?" Valdez asked. "That's the story you're going with?"

"Bite me, Valdez."

Valdez clouded up and put his hand on his baton. He straightened. "You want I should adjust your attitude, Ranger Cable?"

I came off the wall, flexing my hands. "What's your problem, Valdez?"

The elevator dinged, and the first of the paramedics arrived, carrying heavy plastic cases full of medical stuff. Quintana put his hand on Valdez's arm, telling him to cool it. I relaxed.

"Take the EMTs in," Quintana said. "I'll stay with Prince Charming here."

"Valdez," I said, "I want my hat back. It's on the dresser."

He looked at me and enunciated slowly and clearly, "Fuck. You. Texas. Ranger."

The paramedics followed him into the room, and the elevator dinged again. More uniforms got off.

Let the circus begin.

Sam

THEY DROVE ME TO A clinic, where I peed in a jar, which I capped and handed to an Armenian guy in pale-blue scrubs. He sealed the jar, signed off on it, copied the tag number onto the form, and handed the San Antonio PD a receipt after.

My cell phone hadn't been with my things in Fortney's room when I got dressed, so I'd asked Valdez to use one of the office phones when I first arrived at the SAPD station. I'd called my boss, Captain Marshall, who was out of the office. I'd talked to his admin, Janelle, and let her know where I was and to send the cavalry as soon as possible.

I had acquired two new cops by now—a detective by the name of Bernia Woods and a uniformed sergeant named Nguyen. They escorted me to an interview room and invited me to sit in one of the metal-and-plastic chairs next to a card table. Before I could say "Gin rummy, anyone?" they'd left me and closed the door. They locked it.

"So much for trust these days."

A boxy CCTV camera hung from one corner of the room, and the wall across from me featured the obligatory two-way glass mirror. Dust covered the top of the camera, but its little red light glowed with life. I resisted a sudden impulse to pick my nose.

No magazines. No donuts. No bottled water.

To their credit, the SAPD had treated me pretty well so far. No handcuffs. No Taser shots in the back or phone books dropped on my head. All in all, they'd been nice, probably nicer than I would have been, given the situation. I tipped the chair back against the wall, crossed my arms, and tried to catnap. My head hurt like it was clamped in a bench vise, and the room tended to sway and move when I wasn't expecting it.

Two hours later, no one had returned. I waited.

Rita

RITA GOLDMAN REGARDED her desk phone with the same expression she would use if a hissing snake were curled up on her keyboard. The caller ID said WHITLACH, J. in liquid black LCDs. It trilled again, and she picked up the handset with two fingers.

"What?"

"Agent Goldman, what a pleasure. I miss your company already."

"What do you want?"

"I have a case for you."

Rita let that lie there for a heartbeat. "I have cases of my own, thank you very much."

"Not as of now. Turn them over to someone else or shelve 'em. This case is going to take all your time."

Rita fumed, gritting her teeth to keep from screaming. Brought out by stress, her Bronx accent bled through her words. "Tawk ta me."

"A candidate for the US Senate was found dead in a hotel room this morning. In her room was her bodyguard, a Texas Ranger, of all things. You hate cowboys, don't you, Goldman? Rangers are the biggest cowboys of all. Anyway, they found this guy in the room, with the woman he was supposedly guarding. She's dead. He's got no story. It looks cut-and-dried."

"It's a local case. Murder. How does the FBI come into it?"

"She was running for federal office, so we're officially taking an interest. We'll call it a hate crime, Agent Goldman. She's black; he's white. He violated her civil rights." Whitlach chuckled. "He's law enforcement, so it could also have a public-corruption angle."

Rita drew a deep breath and narrowed her eyes. "Why me? I mean, this could be a big deal. Headlines and whatnot. So why give it to me?"

"Simple, Goldman." Whitlach chuckled again. "There are two possible outcomes here. One, you fall flat on your ass and screw the case up. Gives me a good reason to bust you outta here, you and your big mouth. Or two, you win big, and you're a hero. Gives me a good reason to transfer your scrawny butt somewhere else. Somewhere high profile, like Dallas, or New York even. You'd like to go back to New York more than anything, wouldn't you? Get out of this shithole state? Back to civilization?"

Rita held the handset away from her head, frowning.

"Well, Agent Goldman?" Whitlach's voice came out tinny from the handset. "You want it or not?"

Rita clenched her jaw and checked the impulse to throw the phone against the cube wall. She tucked it against her shoulder and reached for a pen. "Give me the address."

Chapter 4

"*Whoever blushes is already guilty; true innocence is ashamed of nothing.*" — Jean-Jacques Rousseau

Sam

Bernia Woods opened the interview room door, jarring me from dozing. A wholesale portion of woman in a casual business suit, blue with a purple blouse, Woods carried a leather portfolio tight to her chest, like a schoolgirl carried her books. She wore her hair trimmed close—more like a cap of tight curls—lightly tinted red.

Another woman appeared from behind Woods, darting around the bigger woman like a sports car zipping around a motor home.

"Ranger Cable." Woods shook my hand and took one of the two remaining chairs. She inclined her head to the smaller woman, who snagged the remaining chair and made it her own. The look she gave me dared me to take it from her. Woods said, "This is Agent Goldman of the FBI. She's here in an"—she traded a dark look with the other woman—"observational capacity."

"My capacity remains to be seen," Goldman popped off.

And they say men have to establish dominance.

Petite, muscular, with frizzy black hair pulled back in a bun, Goldman reminded me of an Israeli gymnast and wore clothing that I guessed cost more than my house payment

Woods folded open her portfolio to a yellow legal pad and took a pen from her jacket. She fussed around, making notes, angling her pad just right, and clearing her throat.

I said nothing.

She cleared her throat again. "For the record, this interview is being recorded. I am Detective Bernia Woods, San Antonio Police Department." She went on to give her badge number, the date, and the time, then she cleared her throat again. "With me is Special Agent Rita Goldman of the San Antonio office of the Federal Bureau of Investigation." She cocked an eyebrow at the agent. "Your ID number, Ms. Goldman?"

Goldman rattled it off.

"Please state your full legal name, Ranger," Woods said.

We went through the formalities of name, rank, and badge number.

"Ranger Cable, you are not under arrest at this time, ergo, I will not read you your rights. This interview is to record your preliminary statement, should you choose to give one. You are not required to give a statement if you wish, although failure to cooperate—"

I held up a hand. "Save it. Let's just get on with it. Okay?"

"Are you willing to answer my questions related to this matter?"

"Sure." *Who am I to argue with someone who could use* ergo *in a sentence?*

Woods started out with a fastball. "Did you kill April Fortney?"

"No."

"Did you have sexual relations of any kind with Mrs. Fortney?"

"No."

"Did you ever make any sexual advances toward her?"

"No."

"Did she ever make any sexual advances toward you?"

"Oh, hell no."

"Ranger Cable, please tell me how you came to be in the room of Judge Fortney."

I looked directly into Woods's almond-colored eyes. "I have no idea. I woke up there."

"Please explain."

I ran her through the whole deal—waking up naked next to the corpse of Judge Fortney, getting dressed, how sick and dizzy I was. Everything. I considered that I could be hanging myself with my own mouth, but the need to tell my side of it was overpowering. There was something compulsive in the need to tell one's story. I'd often taken advantage of that urge—from the other side of the table.

"You suspect you were drugged, Ranger Cable? Is that correct?"

"That's correct. Why else would I still be there at eight o'clock in the morning?"

Goldman squawked a sarcastic laugh, making me jump.

I said to Woods, "Anyway, I have no memory of the previous night. The last thing I recall was having a late dinner with members of the campaign staff."

"Ranger Cable, you are a rather large and muscular man. What are you? Six-five? Six-six?"

"Six-four, but I wear boots to compensate."

"Do you work out? Lift weights?"

"Yeah, from time to time."

"A trained law enforcement officer?"

"Uh-huh."

"Is that a 'yes'?"

"Yes."

"I expect it would be very hard for someone to get the drop on you and dose you with...?"

"Chloroform on a hankie?" Goldman supplied.

"I 'spect so."

"Ranger," Woods said, "please name the campaign staffers with whom you had dinner."

"With whom," Goldman said. "I like that."

I grinned at her. "You with the FBI's Grammar Enforcement Division?"

"I'm with the Bullshit Division. You're playing the amnesia card? That's bullshit. I've seen it a thousand times in the movies: guy gets knocked on the head, loses his memory, can't explain his whereabouts, blah-blah-blah bullshit."

"Which movie?" I asked. "*The October Man* or *The Long Wait*? Both were good amnesia flicks." I shifted my attention to Woods. "Where'd you go to college?"

"Excuse me?"

"You're a well-educated lady. I was wondering where you went to college."

"SMU. On a track scholarship, if you can believe that." For a second. I thought she might flash a real smile, but it died at birth. Her eyes went hard, and her face shut down. "Who was at dinner last night, Ranger?"

I tilted my chair back and looking at the ceiling. I peeled back a finger for every name. "DaShondra Wright, press secretary. Trey Dennison, campaign manager. Moriah Martin, dead weight. And a couple of the local campaign staffers whose names I never got."

"You don't care for Ms. Martin?"

"Why? Is she dead too?"

Woods stared at me like I was a science project gone bad.

"No, I don't think much of Ms. Martin. And if I wanted to blow my brains out, Moriah would buy the bullet and help me load the gun."

"I understand you had words with Judge Fortney, as well." She dropped that one in there very casually. Like I was now supposed to break down and blurt out how I hated Fortney so much that I killed her.

I kept my expression neutral. "Detective Woods, I've been a good boy long enough. This here is bullshit. I didn't kill Judge Fortney. We need to start looking at who might have strangled her and knocked me out."

Woods cleared her throat and flipped back a few pages in her notes. "Ah... let's see." She wore a pair of reading glasses on a band around her neck. She perched them on her nose and peered at her legal pad. "And then Cable said, 'You're about as dumb as a brick and twice as dense.' Or words to that effect."

Woods looked at me over the top of her reading glasses and waited.

My chair squeaked when I shifted. I picked at a thumbnail without looking up. "Yeah. Well, I'm not real proud of that. But—"

The door to the interview room opened, and an evidence tech with a plastic tackle box bustled into the room.

Woods cleared her throat. "Ranger Cable, would you consent to giving us a DNA sample? There was some blood on the stocking used to strangle Judge Fortney, and we'd like to eliminate you as a suspect, if at all possible."

"As if," Goldman said.

I had been expecting the question. The worst thing I could possibly do was hesitate. An innocent man would be eager for a DNA test; the faster it got done, the quicker he could be exonerated. Guilty people would find a way to hedge, or they might stumble or deflect the question.

So when Woods asked if I minded giving a sample, I said "Sure" as fast as I could. Even then, my throat betrayed me by seizing up a little and making it come out "S-Sure."

Woods didn't bat an eye, just waved the tech over and started jotting notes on her pad. "Suspect hesitated when asked for a DNA sample."

The tech did a quick and professional job with the cotton swab, packed up, and left.

When the door closed, Woods said, "Ah-hem. So tell me about the events of yesterday evening and last night, as best you can remember."

"Between eighteen-hundred and twenty-one-thirty, we were at the Four Seasons, downtown, doing one of those political dinners. Thousand-dollar-a-plate type stuff. Nothing much happened there, except I didn't get to eat, so by the time we got back to the Hyatt, I was starved."

Woods stared at me with a frozen expression, slightly robotic.

I leaned back, took a deep breath. "By eleven p.m., I had US Senate candidate April Fortney and her folks holed up in suite 1412 of the San Antonio Hyatt, safe and sound. I checked the bathroom for lurking pervs and toilet-clinging murderers. Without a balcony or an open window to the outside, even a ninja would have a hard time breaking in."

I took a deep breath and recounted the evening in detail...

I was hungry, and missing meals made me crabby. Fortney was safe enough, I could leave her in the hands of her campaign staff and go find food before I started chewing the drapes. The candidate held court at the low table near the window. "The numbers play out, we'll have to win sixty percent of Bexar County—"

"Ma'am," I interrupted.

"I've told you, Ranger Cable, never to call me ma'am."

"Yes, ma'am. I'm out of here. Stay in the room. Don't leave unless you call me first. Check the waiters for bazookas before you let them in."

Fortney twisted her lips into a fake smile. "Have a nice night, Ranger Cable," she said while her eyes said, "Go snort some Ebola virus."

"You too, ma'am," I responded to both messages.

"Hey, Cable." Trey Dennison, Fortney's campaign manager, twisted around in his seat. It took some effort, given he had a lot to twist. "Meet me in the lobby bar in ten, 'kay? We got to plan a strategy."

"Tonight?" I fought back a tired sigh. It has been said I lacked a certain amount of, ah, *team spirit* when it came to the Fortney campaign for US Senate.

"Yeah, tonight. Better nate than lever? Huh?" Trey liked to spoonerize, a habit that twisted my ear canals in knots.

"Come find me downstairs," I told him. "I'll be the one eating my way through the menu."

Of the two others in the room, Moriah ignored me while DaShondra flashed a tiny wave, never lifting her hand from her lap. I touched my hat brim and used my Ranger tracking skills to find the hotel restaurant, which, as it turned out, was closed.

The bar was still open, but they had no food beyond pretzels. In one booth, a couple of Fortney campaign staffers huddled over beers. Three other patrons lingered over drinks and watched SportsCenter playing on the bar TV. I amped up some country-boy charm, laced it with a heavy dose of stoic-yet-heroic public servant, and laid it on the bartender, a white-haired trim man who looked about sixty, wearing one of those purple vests and bowties that hotel purchasing agents bought by the gross. He called the kitchen and ordered up a turkey sandwich for me.

"You may have saved my life," I told him.

"Third one today."

I expected a few cold cuts with a dab of mayo, but when the meal came, I got an open-faced, hot sandwich—a big pile of roast turkey on two slices of white bread, smothered in brown gravy—cozied up to mashed potatoes and steamed green beans.

"On the house," the bartender said.

Apparently, my charm was a powerful weapon. "Obliged to ya."

If heaven had a meal plan, I hoped it included open-faced turkey sandwiches. I closed my eyes and chewed, picturing myself back in Love's Drug Store, where the $4.95 Lunch Special would feed a family for a week.

"Cable, there you are." My dream broke into little bitty pieces on the rocks of Dennison's voice. Bald head atop a round body, supported by short legs, Trey Dennison resembled a snowman in an expensive suit. "C'mere a second, please."

His request sounded more like the school principal's invitation. *Come here, Mr. Cable, and get four weeks' detention. Please.*

Dennison targeted the table he wanted—one surrounded by a moat of empty territory—then he invaded and conquered it. He fortified his position by snagging all the pretzels off neighboring tables. With only six other patrons in the bar, he had little competition for the resources, but with Trey, any competition was too much.

The remaining big chiefs of the campaign staff—Moriah Martin and DaShondra Wright—followed not far behind him.

I took my plate, dropped my hat on a chair behind me, and found a seat at the Round Table of Trey. DaShondra looked tired while Moriah looked like she wanted somebody's guts, fried Cajun-style, with rice. She always looked like that.

Trey looked at my plate and hollered at the bartender, "Hey, three more of these, okay?"

"DaShondra doesn't eat meat," I said. "She's a vegetarian."

"What meat? That's *turkey*."

"How about a salad?" the bartender asked.

"Oh, God bless. And bring me some ranch dressing on the side," DaShondra said. Thirty-five years old and as big as a house, she needed all her extra body mass to hold her heart. Dark complexion with hair lacquered down on one side and tinted, DaShondra had light-brown eyes and wore contacts that changed their natural color to almost purple.

"Okay, okay." On the other hand, there was Moriah Martin. "Thanks, Mike... See you later. Yes, you, too. Bye-bye." Moriah touched the Bluetooth stuck in her ear, laid her glowing tablet on the table, and tapped its screen without acknowledging the rest of us.

Her fingernails protruded farther than some car bumpers—and had more decals.

"Hey, Moriah," I said.

She ignored me. Moriah claimed her official title was Assistant Campaign Manager. She'd gained that position by being the aunt of the candidate and April Fortney's long-time advisor and executioner.

She clung to the campaign, sticky as a booger, with no obvious talent beyond being obnoxious and irritating.

"So," I said to Trey, "what strategy are we fixin' to plan here?"

"Well, Deputy Fife." Trey leaned back and clasped his hands behind his head. "We'll be visiting some pretty shitty—"

"Underprivileged," Moriah corrected.

"Underprivileged neighborhoods. And since you, Ranger, have whined—"

"Expressed my concerns," I stuck in.

"Expressed your concerns about wanting to know these types of things in advance, I'm invitin' you in to hear what we are *fixin'* to do."

"I'll email you the itinerary and addresses of the campaign stops," Moriah said.

"Okay, deal. That's all I need." I mopped up my gravy with a slice of bread. "Usual time?"

"Nah. Late start tomorrow." Trey's tie had worked loose and snaked around his neck like a hangman's noose. "We leave here at nine o'clock, sharp."

"Why so late?"

Trey shrugged. "What's the diff? April's a Democratic candidate in Texas; she's got a snowball's chance in hell of winning statewide office. This is all about getting some name recognition, getting her face in front of the media."

I swore I could feel Moriah's fingernails extend into claws. She leaned forward, and I thought for a second she might come across the table at Trey.

"Don't say that." She enunciated every word with exact precision. "We're going to win this thing, Trey Dennison, and don't ever forget that."

I'd seen evangelicals with less faith.

"Yeah, sure." Trey waved a hand in dismissal. "Hey, barkeep! You wanna bring me a Jack and Coke? What'll you have, Moriah? Hemlock?"

Moriah's eyes narrowed. Without looking away from Trey, she called to the bartender, "White wine."

"Iced tea for me." DaShondra had been so quiet, I'd lost track of her.

"So that's it?" I asked. Maybe I could get away long enough to catch the basketball scores.

"Just be ready to, ah, to do your thing, you know." Trey waved again, already forgetting me.

"You mean that thing where I jump in front of some crazy-ass with a gun?"

"Yeah, that thing. I knew you was good for something."

I snorted and stood up. "Okay, I'll try to stay awake for the whole day."

"Cable"—Moriah looked at me for the first time since she'd sat down—"don't ever forget. April has a lot of enemies. Lots of people want to pull that girl down." That spooky Holy Grail light remained in her eyes. Whatever else anybody wanted to call her, Moriah was a true believer.

"Yes, ma'am." I picked up my hat and went to the bar for a beer to go.

Chapter 5

"*The lamentation of the African American community at yet another injustice, the surprise and disgust of others who understand, stand against this pseudo-god of capitalisms and incarceration that threaten to take over our nation.*" — Anthea Butler, July 2013

Sam

"After that," I told Woods, "I took my beer up to my room. The memories seem to fade out somewhere around the elevator."

Woods flipped a page in her legal pad. "All right. Ahem. Okay... ah, Ranger, let's go over it again."

The door slammed open, and a tornado in boots blew in. Captain Les Marshall stormed the room as if he were taking a German gun emplacement on D-Day. Old enough to have been a cabin boy on Noah's ark, Captain Marshall stood five-eight in boots and weighed about as much as a bantam rooster. But I would rather have gone up against a room full of Hell's Angels than a pissed-off Les Marshall.

"Who's in charge of this here clusterfuck?"

Bernia Woods looked taken aback for a moment, but she didn't get to be a detective in a tough city by being a wuss. "Who the fuck are you, and what the fuck are you doing in my interrogation room?" Her voice went from educated SMU grad to street cop in a heartbeat.

"Captain Marshall, Texas Rangers... ma'am." He didn't get to be captain in the Rangers without having been down the creek a few times, as well. Even so, Les couldn't overcome years of good manners;

he had to add the *ma'am* at the end, even if it killed him. "And this here dumb shit belongs to me."

"Ranger Cable—"

"Is mine. Interview's over. Charge him or cut him loose."

"Wait just a second." Agent Goldman popped up. Her dark eyes flashed. She looked ready to go to war. "I'm with the FBI, and the interview's over when *I* say it's over."

The resulting shouting match registered on earthquake monitors in Beijing. I'm certain they were within seconds of emergency sirens as the tiny FBI agent went up against the tiny Ranger captain. Jurisdictional territories were marked, agendas bared, and metaphorical dicks measured.

Captain Marshall ended it when he barked, "Are you arresting him?"

Woods and Goldman exchanged a look. I held my breath as the seconds crawled by. With a microscopic slump of her shoulders, Bernia Woods said, "Not yet, Captain Marshall." The words broke off one by one, with crystalline clarity. "Not. Yet."

"C'mon, boy," Les said. "Your day's not over. You get to explain all this shit to me."

I nearly asked Woods to throw me in jail right then and there.

Rita

RITA FUMED WHILE THEIR prime suspect followed his captain through the door, resembling an ocean liner following a tug. The door swung shut and latched with a click, leaving her and Detective Woods alone in the interrogation room. The air smelled faintly of disinfectant and testosterone.

"Well," the heavy-set detective said, "that went well."

"You think he did it?" Rita's right hand tapped her leg with a staccato beat. Damn cowboy. God, how she hated the type—tall, blond-haired and blue-eyed, shoulders wide as a doorframe. With this one, it was hard to tell whether he was a cornpone hick or just pretending to be one. The way he talked... Rita shuddered. *Was that English?*

Woods had taken several pages of notes on a yellow legal pad, folding each page carefully back. She took her time flipping the sheets into their original position, page by page. She capped her pen, tucked it in the loophole in the portfolio's inner spine, and folded it shut. Woods took her glasses off and considered them with a squinted eye. She pursed her lips. "He looks good for it."

"I know, right? But why'd he hang around? Time of death was what? One a.m.? Why does a LEO hang around the crime scene after he's killed somebody?"

"Law enforcement officers are people, too." Woods shrugged and dropped her glasses to dangle from the chain. "Maybe he passed out, drunk or high. Or he freaked out and went into a funk, trying to think of a way out."

"And that disturbance call. What's up with that, huh? Call comes in on a burner cell—"

"We don't know it's a burner."

"Oh, come on, Bernia, it's a prepaid cell number."

"Doesn't mean it's a throwaway. We'll have to find out if the owner paid cash or bought it with a credit card. Haven't had time to run that down yet."

"But if the disturbance was in a hotel, why call from a cell? And why wait six hours after the disturbance?"

"I got a quick listen at the 9-1-1 call tapes. The guy—and it was a guy—said he heard the argument last night, but was too scared to call it in until this morning."

Goldman shook her head. "That don't feel right."

Detective Woods picked up her notebook and pushed past on her way to the door. "Well, if Cable's DNA comes back a match on that stocking, I'm taking it to the Grand Jury. You can count on that."

Rita scowled while the door closed and latched for the second time. In the end, Woods was probably right. The big cowboy had to have lost his mind, or something, then killed Fortney in a drunken rage before passing out. That wide-open Boy Scout face had to be an act. Nobody could be that sincere and be for real.

Sam

THE INSIDE OF CAPTAIN Marshall's car smelled of spilled coffee and stale cigarettes. He drove an old Crown Vic with mushy suspension, cruise-liner steering, and a driver's seat contoured to fit his butt and no one else's. I knew that because I'd driven it once, and my rear end had taken a day to recover. The captain lived in his car, ate takeout food every meal, smoked more than a creosote bushfire, and had his admin print all his emails rather than learn how to use a PC. Dinosaurs were more progressive than Captain Marshall.

"You mind tellin' me," he said "what that *bull*shit back there was?"

"Which bullshit was that?" *When in doubt, ask a question back.*

"You talked so much, Detective Woods must've paid you by the word. That's what bullshit."

"I thought it best to appear cooperative. I mean, I didn't kill the woman, so why shouldn't I get my side on record?"

"Boy, ain't you never seen a perp hang himself by running his mouth? Don't think anymore. You ain't no good at it. Let me do the thinking."

I swallowed back what came to my tongue. He was probably right. About the saying too much part, not the thinking part.

Marshall started the car to get the AC blowing, rolled down the window, and lit a cigarette from a disposable plastic lighter. Smoke jetted from his nostrils. He turned right on Frio from the Central Substation parking lot, the car squatting through the dips like the shocks were made of cotton candy. Marshall handed me a cell phone. "Here."

"What's this for?"

"Call your momma. She's worried sick about you."

"How'd she find out so fast?"

"You're big news now. All over the country. You think the scum-suckin' media *wouldn't* find out you was shacked up with a big-time politician? One who gets murdered?"

"I wasn't shacked up with her."

"According to CN-and-N, y'all had to be fuckin' like bunnies on Viagra. Then you killt her in a fit of rage. They ain't sayin' it, but they're *sayin'* it, if you know what I mean."

The cell phone weighed heavy in the palm of my hand. Call Momma or jump out the window of a moving car? I tested the electric button on the armrest, and the window stayed up.

"I already called her once." Marshall palmed the wheel in a fast left turn and headed for the I-35 entrance ramp. "I told her I'd come and see what's up myself. When your daddy died, I promised her I'd look out for you."

"I remember."

He flicked his butt out the window and hit the switch to roll it up. We zoomed up the entrance and blasted onto the interstate at Warp Nine.

"Where are we going?" I asked. *Mars? Pluto? Somewhere without cell reception, please.*

"Well, the San Antonio police done taken all your stuff. Their propeller heads are going over it, looking for evidence and shit."

I swallowed that bug and let it sink to the bottom of my belly. The cops were digging through my things, trying to pin a crime on me. The bug crawled around my gut and went for a tour of my insides. I read the billboards flashing by on I-35 without recording what they said.

"So I'm takin' you to a motel near the Ranger office south of town," Marshall said. "Keep you out of sight, at least until tomorrow morning. Them shit-eatin' reporters find you, they'll tear you a new ass."

"This ain't right." I crushed the bug of dread under a big can of anger. Somewhere past my headache, dry throat, and nausea, Bruce Banner started to Hulk out.

"Ease back on that armrest, son," Marshall said. "You're about to squish the stuffing out. Now listen up. Tomorrow morning, the Internal Affairs slimeballs from the Inspector General's office will be in the office. You get in there, you give 'em just the facts, you hear? Don't you go in and make their tiny pea brains hurt no more'n you have to."

I grunted something like a yes.

"Now," the captain said, "in betwixt now and tomorrow morning, you better tell me what the Holy Jesus, Mary, and Joseph happened last night."

So I told him. By the time I finished, we'd pulled into a Holiday Inn Express.

"Well, boy, that's one hell of a story." Marshall pulled the Crown Vic under the awning over the circular drive and switched off the engine. He looked directly at me, holding my attention with gray eyes that were outlined in a field of crow's feet. "You know the San Antone PD like you for this. They's just itching to put the cuffs on you.

FBI, too. That Washington crowd would do a happy dance all over your grave, boy."

"What stopped 'em?"

He shook his head, holding his fingers like he was pinching a grapeseed. "They's about *this* far from being sure you done the deed. That little bit right there is the only thing allowed me to get you out. Only reason they let you keep your gun and badge, just on the off chance you might've been in the wrong place at the wrong time. Bein' a cop, you get the benefit of the doubt. That benefit is mighty slim these days, with all the shit's been stirred lately about black folk and cops." He looked out the back window then back at me. "You know they followed us, don't you?"

"It's what I'd do."

Marshall jacked open the door on his side. "Fuck it, boy, come on. They're close, but close only counts in horseshoes and hand grenades, right? Horseshoes and hand grenades."

Captain Marshall checked me in under his own name and handed me the room key. "Now, don't order any of them porn-o-graphical movies on your TV. Sit tight, don't move, and I'll come get you in the mornin'. We'll sort this shit out."

He left, and I bought toothpaste, a toothbrush, deodorant, and a razor in the hotel's little travel store. I added three bottles of chilled water from the cooler and drank one while I waited for the clerk to total my order.

"Eighteen dollars. Ninety-two cents," he said.

"Charge it to my room." I took the stuff and went for the elevator.

Showered, shaved, and wearing a towel, I downed the second bottle of water while lying on the bed, flipping channels. I froze when I hit CNN.

A black man with his hair worn tight to his scalp in rows that dangled down his neck stood at a microphone. Middle-aged, he looked prosperous in a dark suit and conservative tie. I recognized him immediately. Jawn Calvin "JC" Fortney, husband of the deceased, was as full of human warmth as a dead Eskimo.

"My wife," JC intoned, "may God rest her soul, was brutally murdered today. Brutally murdered." He paused and looked down at the podium, apparently too distraught to continue. The crowd moaned in response. "The poh-leece," he said, uttering the word as though it made him physically ill. "The poh-leece, they say they don't know who done it."

The crowd jeered and shouted. The camera zoomed out, showing the packed bleachers of a high school gym. Fortney stood at single microphone set up on a stand in the middle of the jump circle on the basketball court.

"*They say...*" He emphasized the words with sarcasm, and his audience jeered again. "*They say* they have to process the *scene...*" Fortney paused again, and the mass of faces nodded and shouted catcalls. "They say... they say they have to *weigh* the *evi-dence.*"

The crowd followed his remarks like a snake following a charmer. Some preachers could induce that kind of hypnosis on their congregation, but not many. Fortney had mastered the skill somewhere, though I didn't believe he'd ever preached a day in his life. One thing was for sure—he'd gotten over his grief mighty fast.

"Even though..." He paused for effect. "Even though they caught a *white pohhh-leeece officer* in her room."

The audience grumbled and shouted, right on cue. My balls tried to crawl up and hide in my belly. Not every day did I manage to get an entire race of people after my hide. The anger I'd used earlier to kill my anxiety dribbled away, leaving a hollow feeling behind.

"Now we know..." Fortney leaned close to the mic and pitched his voice to a deep rumble. "Now we know, if a *black man* had been found in that room, even a black *poh-leeceman,* we know where that black man would be, don't we?"

Scattered calls of "Yes, we do" and "Amen" answered him.

"He'd be in *jail*!" Fortney shouted the last word into the microphone and raised a shaking finger. Sweat beaded on forehead.

"Screw you, Fortney," I told the TV. "I didn't kill your wife."

"I ask you," Fortney said. "Is this justice?"

"No!" the crowd shouted back.

"My wife. The mother of my children. A judge who fought for the right of our people to live like decent human beings. A woman who challenged the establishment and made them afraid. That woman! April Fortney. Killed by a white cop."

My face burned, and I looked for something to throw at the TV. The man was inciting a mob, trying to start a race war for something I hadn't done.

Fortney mopped his forehead with a white handkerchief. His eyes watered, and he stared at the mic for several long seconds.

"He's gonna cry," I said.

"I ask you again," he nearly whispered. "Is that justice?"

"No."

"Is that justice?" Louder this time.

"No!"

"Is that *justice*?"

"No."

"Is. That. *Justice?*"

The crowd screamed its answer, one large, angry roar: "No!"

Holy Mother of God. I turned off the TV and stared at the ceiling for a long time.

Sam

I WOKE UP ON TOP OF the hotel bedspread, still wrapped in a towel. The lights were on, and the AC hummed in the corner, but the room had that dead feeling that comes from the silence of the wee hours. An elevator dinged from somewhere down the hall, its bell muted. Voices and footsteps followed, then a room door shut with a thunk.

My feet were cold. The bedside clock read 1:16 a.m., making it somewhere around twenty-four hours since April Maree Fortney had died of strangulation. Fifteen hours since I'd woken up next to her. Still clueless.

I got up long enough to drink more water, latch the door, and turn off the lights. Sliding under the covers naked reminded me of how I'd woken that morning. I punched up the pillows, got my head angled just right, closed my eyes—and promptly did not fall asleep. Clear-headed for the first time since the night before, my thoughts raced around like blind squirrels in a nut factory.

How did I wind up in Fortney's room? Drugged? If so, by what? Rohypnol would've done the job, but its most common form was a tablet dissolved in a drink. It would've taken a few minutes to work, which meant somebody must have dropped it in my beer last night at dinner. It would've taken a magician to pull that off, since I'd only had the two beers, and both of those never left my sight.

The bartender? That would take a conspiracy on the level of an Oliver Stone movie. I'd decided to go to the lobby bar at the last second, so if the bartender dosed me, he would have needed standing orders from the beginning of our stay there. I couldn't rule it out, but the scenario didn't seem likely.

There were other possibilities besides a roofie. Ketamine and GHB were two common date-rape drugs readily available to street crooks. GHB hit pretty fast and cleared the body within hours. All those drugs affected memory, which was why testimony by victims of a date rape was problematic. GHB and Ketamine could be consumed orally or injected.

I lay awake, staring at the clock and thinking about injections for ten minutes. Then I gave up and went into the bathroom. Under the stark glare of the bathroom light, I twisted into pretzel shapes, looking for needle marks, examining places best left in the dark. The results were inconclusive. I had a number of bruises and sore spots, any of which could have been a puncture site. I'd accumulated some bumps and bangs over the past few days, so there was no telling—to my untrained eye—if any were new.

I turned off the light and went back to bed. I flipped the pillow over to the cool side and stared at the clock. *Bruises. Which ones did I get from Randall Berkley and John David Szankowski? Was it only three days ago? No, today's the seventh, so that makes it four now. Tuesday, April third.*

Four days had passed since my one heroic defense of Candidate Fortney, single-handedly fighting off three attackers at once. *High Noon* in Jacksonville, Texas. *Well, kind of...*

Chapter 6

"I *don't call myself a white supremacist. I'm a civil rights activist concerned about European American rights."* — David Duke

Sam

Four days earlier, the humidity in Jacksonville, Texas, would have made a preacher condemn his momma to hell just to get a cool breeze. Heavy clouds refused to rain, blocked the sun, and trapped sweat close to the body. The candidate, Judge Fortney, stood at the lectern inside the air-conditioned chamber of commerce office, delivering a speech. The topic? Pick one: creating jobs, improving education, or balancing the budget. The speeches were all canned; just the names of the towns were changed. The choice of which shrink-wrapped speech to use depended upon the audience, the day's headlines, and polling data.

Jacksonville, Texas—"Tomato Capital of the World"—was south of Tyler and north of Houston, deep in the piney woods. The mosquitoes could suck a man down to a husk in seconds, leaving nothing but a skin sack behind.

The Jacksonville Chamber of Commerce was located, aptly enough, on Commerce Street and resembled a strip mall with angled-in parking next to the building. The lot on the west side was packed. Fuel-efficient economy cars stickered with Democratic slogans shared space with dusty farm trucks and modern SUVs.

I stood outside, under the awning, watching the traffic. Cars inched to a stop at the corner and made the turn onto Austin Street, where Commerce dead-ended. Directly across Austin, a set of stairs led up a short hill to a stadium called the Tomato Bowl.

When Trey Dennison heard the name of the stadium, he laughed. "You gotta be shittin' me," he said, shaking his head. "Goddamn hicks."

He had disappeared inside, giving last-minute instructions to Fortney. Like a pack of ducklings, Moriah and the rest of the crew trailed along, straining to hear. The machine of politics rolled along, speech to speech, town to town, collecting votes and money like a big, sticky ball of greed. Fortney was no different—no better, no worse—than any other politician I'd ever come near. She followed the money, and the money followed her, all in a big circle.

I'd long since had my fill of political speeches—from either side—preferring to see their actions rather than hearing the words. Even the sweltering weather was more pleasant than listening to another hour-long heaping of horseshit. So I put a couple of Jacksonville cops next to the candidate and stayed outside. I tamped a can of Skoal and took a dip, squeezing the flavor onto my tongue. My last dip in my last can. *For real this time. Seriously.*

I tossed the can in a trash bin and stifled the impulse to go after it.

Nothing moved in the west-side parking lot, unless I counted the grackles skittering and pecking at the ground, so I moved over to the Commerce Street side. A couple of old geezers in cowboy hats sat on a bench next to the building. We nodded at each other, and they went back to comparing liver spots and surgery scars.

Across the street, three men weighed down the tailgate of a truck. They sucked Miller Lite from blue aluminum cans, looking as if they'd missed the exit for the fishing demonstration. Dressed in camo pants and cut-off tees, wearing a variety of oil-stained gimme caps, the trio could have posed for *Probation Magazine*. They yukked around, talking too loudly and laughing too hard. Nervous laughter.

I angled for a better look at the Three Stooges. My instincts tingled. *Rednecks lingering in front of the Chamber of Commerce, drinking beer out in the open? What was wrong with this picture?*

About that time, Fortney and her entourage bubbled outside in knots and clusters. They bunched up near the exits, a beehive around the queen. One citizen after another besieged the candidate, either to make a point or just make noise. Fortney listened to them all, nodding and touching their arms in a warm and sympathetic way. Had I not seen the way she acted in private, I would have bought the entire act and come back for seconds.

"Cable!" Trey Dennison bustled over, mopping his face with a handkerchief. "Get in there and get her out. Let's roll! C'mon, c'mon."

Part of the protection detail involved playing the bad guy and ushering the candidate away from the unwashed masses and into her limo. Fortney stood among a cluster of citizens, trapped just outside the door by the earnest expressions of her prospective voters. She listened to an old white guy in a straw hat tick off one point after another on his fingers, her face serious, as if she wanted to hear every word he said.

The limo idled at the curb, parked lengthwise, blocking three angled spaces, a few steps from Fortney. I cut into the crowd around, digging my way toward the candidate, thinking only about getting her moving toward the car. Bodies pressed in close, laughing, happy—everyone thrilled to be near a political superstar.

Motion from the street caught my eye. The Three Stooges came fast. Two circled behind the limo, one around front. All three vectored straight at Fortney. A half dozen blue-haired grandmothers stood between me and my protectee. The mathematics of converging bodies played out in my head in fast-forward. I was too far away to intervene; I had to get closer.

"Move! Police!" I plowed through civilians like a halfback. Clusters of little old ladies flew apart with shrieks and squeals. My right hand swept my sport coat aside and locked on the butt of my Kimber .45. I broke it free and drew, all with one motion. With my left, I pushed the women aside with enough force to move them, but not enough to injure them. I hoped. My mother would whip my ass if I hurt an old lady.

I shoved myself between the candidate and the threat, scattering the crowd. Stooge One had scraggly red hair trailing out from a baseball cap bearing a Chevy logo. Long-limbed and bony, he came around the back of the limo. A heavyset black couple blocked my view of his hands. The couple stood rooted, frozen to the ground.

"Move!" I shouted and lunged, aiming for the middle. They broke apart at the last second, splitting an instant before I barreled into them. Stooge One was only a couple of steps away—laser-beam focused on Fortney, behind me and to my left. Wild gray eyes glinted. His lips curled back over yellowed teeth. Metal glinted from his hand.

I stuck out my arm and clotheslined him as he went past. He never saw me coming. His eyes bugged out in surprise. Stooge One hit my arm at neck height, and his feet ran out from under him. He squawked like a ruptured duck and hit the concrete sidewalk on his back.

As soon as he crashed, I remembered to yell, "Stop! Police!"

Stooge Two saw what had happened and came straight at me. He dove into my midsection like a linebacker. Whatever he'd been carrying dropped to the ground with a clatter. He wrapped both arms around me in a bear hug. I staggered back a step.

This guy was shorter, but heavier than the first, with a Dodge logo on his cap. His legs pistoned as he tried to drive me backward and tackle me to the ground. I slapped the side of his head with my pistol. Then did it again. It was neither fair nor sporting, but it knocked the fight completely out of Number Two. He dropped to all fours at my feet.

My brain finally processed the image and translated it to a definition of the object the first two carried. Three Stooges was right. All three clowns were armed with cream pies. And one pistol.

Stooge Three dropped his pie plate and dug at his waistband. The butt of a blocky semi-auto pistol jutted from his pants. Cream pie splattered on the ground. The circle around Fortney cringed and screamed. Stooge Three snarled and tried to dodge away.

I leaped and snagged the last guy's collar, jerking him forward. My grip slipped, and his shirt tore, but it was enough to spoil his coordination. He sprawled at my feet. His pistol pinballed through the scattering crowd.

One guy squalled, "Get back! Get back!" He danced away as if the gun would bite him on the foot.

Stooge Three came off the ground swinging. I blocked a couple of shots with my arms, then he hit me a solid lick on the shoulder. That one stung.

"Goddamn it, quit!" I hammered the guy across the bridge of his nose with my fist. Something crunched. He grabbed his face and shrieked like a cat in heat.

The Jacksonville police officers showed up about then and jumped all over the trio of nitwits. I snagged Fortney and shoved her into the limo. When I slapped the roof to signal the driver, he shot off from the curb, missing my toe by an inch. Good man, but he must have thought he was taking Reagan to the hospital after Hinkley tried to kill him. The limo screeched around a corner and disappeared.

Jacksonville Police Sergeant Delroy Johnson appeared at my elbow when I turned. Delroy led the police contingent assigned to the event. He was a large, round man, one of those fellows with a wide body, big butt, pumpkin head, and a frizz of hair about one molecule long. He had a country-boy way of speaking, but he seemed to be hiding a pretty sharp mind behind his Oakley sunglasses.

"You all right?"

"You know these jokers?" I pointed at the trio his boys had cuffed. They sat on the curb, a miserable collection of stooges arranged in a row. Cream pie filling melted into sticky goo.

"Yeah, I know 'em." Delroy toed the last guy in line, shoving him in the back and getting a glare in return. "This ol' boy you neck collared, his name's Peacock. Daniel Peacock. Local boy with no ambition, but he makes up for it with an extra helping of stupid."

Peacock sneered at me and rasped out, "I'm gonna sue you, cowboy." For some reason, he seemed to be having trouble with his throat. "You done fucked up my civilian rights."

"Shee-it, boy," Delroy said. "If you had a civil right, you'da eaten it by now."

I had no idea what that meant, but I laughed anyway.

"The other two, I know by sight," the big sergeant told me. About then, a couple of Jacksonville patrol cars whipped up, LED light bars flickering passionately. "They all live off in the woods with a bunch of survivalists, playing with guns and their peckers. They preach white supremacy and the coming race war. Call themselves...What do y'all call yo'selves, Daniel?"

"Soldiers of Jesus," Daniel bit out the words, looking truculent.

"Seems kind of a juvenile stunt for a bunch of bigoted assholes," I said. "Smacking a Senate candidate with cream pies."

The leader, the last guy I'd tackled, craned around and spat at my feet. His words were hard to make out, given his swollen—and hopefully broken—nose. "It's a polididal point, ya dumb sunna bitch. Fordney's a clown, a big-lip nigger adding like a trained monkey. Nobody can'd say nuddin' again 'em, you know, 'cause the media calls you a racidst."

"Calling you a racist?" I said with a deadpan look. "How dare they."

Sam

I STARED AT THE BEDSIDE alarm clock in the Holiday Inn Express. *Could the Soldiers of Jesus be sharp enough to arrange all this? Pay me back and get Fortney out of the way at the same time?*

"Not freakin' likely," I muttered. If I counted up the IQ scores of the three I'd met, I would have fingers left over. No way they could have set up the scene in Fortney's room without getting caught.

At 2:16 a.m., I was no closer to figuring out who might have dumped me in this mountain of shit. I not only had to defend myself against a murder rap, but also dispel the image of me as a racist. I had no idea how to do that.

I got up, took a leak, and drank a glass of water, then I tried to get comfortable again. I really wished I hadn't given up tobacco. The inside of my lip ached, missing the burn of Skoal.

One thing was sure. If I didn't get some sleep, then the IA people would eat me for breakfast. I rolled over and closed my eyes. Images of April Fortney's bloated face and distended tongue popped into my head. It creeped me out to think I'd been sleeping next to a dead body, voluntarily or not.

More importantly, it pissed me off that somebody had killed her. I may not have liked her, but it was my job to protect her. I'd failed. She was dead on my watch. Somebody was going to pay for that.

Chapter 7

"*Around here, the fuzz are trouble, no matter which end of the stick you're holding. You call them in because somebody busted your legs with a baseball bat, and the next thing you know, you're the one being sent to jail for bleeding on the sidewalk.*" — Ed McBain, *Hail to the Chief*

Rita

Rita Goldman rocked in her office chair and considered Ranger Samuel Duncan Cable's service record. At six in the morning, she had the fourth floor to herself. The overhead lights were off, and only the fluorescent under her cubicle's storage compartment gave her reading light. She sipped from a paper cup of coffee—black, no sugar—and reviewed her notes.

The Rangers were part of the Texas Department of Public Safety, headquartered in Austin. Rita had figured a visit in person would do more good than a phone call. The drive from San Antonio, mostly on a toll road with a posted limit of eighty-five miles per hour—one thing Texans did right—took an hour. She had made it to the DPS offices at two o'clock yesterday afternoon.

The battleaxes manning the personnel office had closed ranks and refused to give up their fair-haired boy's jacket. Rita called Whitlach—the man was good for something, anyway—and Whitlach called his boss in Washington. That wheel rolled and tipped a bigger wheel, which then rolled over somebody in the governor's office. And since the governor had gone on record pledging full cooperation, that person kicked off a whole new chain of calls. By the time that tsunami of momentum hit the personnel office, it had gathered enough power to shake the building.

At 5:05, Rita took the file and beat it out of the building without looking back. Behind her, the ladies in personnel no longer needed air conditioning; their glares were enough to frost the windows. The spot between Rita's shoulder blades remained tight and itchy all the way to her car.

After a dinner of microwaved Lean Cuisine, she had spent a couple of hours on web searches related to Fortney's campaign, then she gave the personnel folder a quick scan. She slept poorly, woke early, and went to the office to get started.

A few cubicles away, the network printer hummed and chuckled, churning out the witness statements Woods had scanned and emailed to her. Rita sipped from her coffee, leaving a red lipstick stain on the white plastic top. The cosmetics company called that shade of red Crimson Fire, but Rita thought of it as Vampire Mouth.

The file in her lap told her a lot. Samuel "Sam" Cable. Thirty-two years old, with a bachelor's degree in criminology from Sam Houston State, achieved while a rookie trooper in the Texas DPS. Graduated the academy in the upper third of his class. Expert shot, handgun or rifle. Some unknown person had scrawled "best natural pistol shooter I've ever seen" in the margin of his qualifying results.

He'd signed up for the Troopers at twenty—the minimum age—and been assigned to a field trainer officer at graduation. Cable served ten years as a trooper before applying for and being selected for the Texas Rangers at thirty-one.

"Hmph," she grunted. *Young for a Ranger.* Rita suspected he had a godfather somewhere higher up the food chain.

She read the rest of the file and found nothing remarkable: glowing evaluations from superiors and the normal supply of complaints any cop would pick up, given time. Citizens complained about every damn thing; even great cops had complaints in their jacket. Cable had no more and no less than one might expect for twelve years of police work. More importantly, though, he had only a couple of minor complaints from African Americans. It weakened Whitlach's hate crime theory right off the bat.

Rita tossed the file on her desk and locked her hands behind her head. She studied a brown spot on the overhead acoustic tile. The big amoeba of a stain saturated most of one square. The stain had a vaguely yellowish tint.

"Probably Whitlach peeing on my head," she muttered.

Rita crimped her mouth in a sarcastic smile and trekked to the printer to gather the witness statements. Maybe somebody had seen something that would make sense of how Big Tex went nutso and killed his protectee. So far, all she had was a decent cop with no history of psychotic episodes or serious anger issues.

When she was ten steps away from her desk, her cell phone rang.

"You're kidding me." Rita ran to her phone and answered it. "Goldman here."

"Goldman, it's Woods."

"You're up early, detective."

Woods sounded grim when she said, "Crime Scene people brought Cable's things back here from the hotel. I thought you should know they found something."

"Something?"

"Something bad," Woods said. "We got him."

Sam

"HELLO?"

My grip on the cell phone tightened. "Hi, Mom."

"Samuel Duncan Cable." Three magic words turned me four years old again.

"Yes, ma'am. I'm sorry. I didn't mean to worry you."

"Worry me? Why would I be worried? My youngest boy is all over the news, found in a hotel room with a dead woman. Why would I be worried? I've had reporters traipsin' up to the front porch all day. I finally let the dogs out on 'em, so they ain't bothered me much lately."

"I didn't do it."

The cell phone crackled, and I couldn't hear what she said. I moved to a different spot in the hotel room and angled my head around, looking for a clear signal.

"What was that, Mom? I couldn't hear you."

"I said: Of course it wasn't you!" Momma huffed into the phone. "I didn't raise you thataway."

"Yes, ma'am. I mean, no, ma'am, you didn't." I was freshly showered, the motel room AC was on frigid cold, and *still*, beads of sweat rolled down my back.

"If only your daddy or Luke was around. They'd know what to do."

Luke was my eldest brother, or he had been until he died in Afghanistan. They'd said it was a helicopter accident. Luke was Special Forces, deployed in deep, dangerous places of deniability, so I smelled a government bullshit story. My father was killed when I was sixteen.

"I actually am a professional crime fighter, Mom. Got a badge and all. I know what to do."

"What? Get caught with dead bodies?"

"No, ma'am. Investigate crimes."

"Call Matt."

My brother Matt was a Dallas County Sheriff's Deputy. Two years older than me and two inches taller, he'd worn me out between the ages of seven and seventeen. I had scars from those days.

"Yes, ma'am, I will," I said with as much sincerity as I could muster.

"Don't you bullshit me, Sam Cable. I'll come down to San Antonio and blister your ass for you. You call your brother, you hear?"

My sincerity needed work. "Yes, ma'am. You want I should call John also?"

"John? He's a doctor. Why'd you want to call him? Are you hurt?"

"No, ma'am." John, the black sheep of the family, had gone off to be a pediatric oncologist in Houston instead of going into law enforcement.

"Well, don't be silly then. Little John won't help you much at all." Little John stood six-eight in his socks. He could scare cancer into remission with a threatening glare.

"Yes, ma'am. Hey, I gotta run. Captain Marshall's here to take me to the office."

"All right, baby. You take care now, y'hear?"

"Yes, ma'am, I will."

"I love you, baby." She sounded close to tears. I hadn't heard her like that since Luke's funeral. "You call me if you need anything. Anything at all."

I gripped the phone and stared at the wall. "Yes, ma'am, I will."

Sam

THE INTERROGATION STARTED at nine in the morning. I was convinced there was a school, run by the descendants of the Spanish Inquisition, who only granted admission to applicants who'd made a pact with a minor demon from the fourth level of hell. Graduates from this school, a sort of Jesuit Academy of Torture, went into the internal affairs divisions of law enforcement departments across the country. Or they became fourth-grade math teachers.

Ibanyez—a short, dark-haired, and intense Hispanic in a blue suit, light-blue shirt, and red tie—took a seat directly across the conference room table. Johnson, a tubby white guy with mean eyes, sat to his right, clicking a ballpoint pen like a metronome. Captain Marshall sat at the end of the conference table.

They asked me if I wanted my union rep present, and I declined. We got the preliminary questions out of the way, then they dug into me with hot pokers and thumbscrews. Ibanyez did the talking, Johnson did the staring. I suspected he was trying for intimidation, but he wound up looking constipated. We went over the basics, then Ibanyez took off into uncharted territory. I signed off on the transcript when the stenographer handed it to me.

Q: How would you describe your relationship with Judge Fortney prior to 7 April?

A: Strained.

Q: Why?

A: Judge Fortney was... very outspoken in her opinions of white law enforcement officers.

Q: In what manner?

A: On one occasion, Mrs. Fortney claimed that the original purpose of the Texas Rangers was to oppress the Indians—Native Americans—and Mexican citizens of Texas.

Q: Anything else?

A: In late February, or early March, I advised her against making campaign stops in a high-crime neighborhood in Houston. Judge Fortney stated that I wouldn't say that if it was a white neighborhood. She also told me at that time to stop "eyeball frisking" every black man who came up to her.

Q: And the outcome of that conversation?

A: I told her the only racist in the room was her.

Q: And she said?

A: Something like "Black people can't be racist, not after hundreds of years of slavery and oppression."

Q: So you argued.

A: I wouldn't say "argued." More like, we had some heated words.

Q: What's the difference?

A: It was just a quick exchange, and I dropped it after that.

Q: Why do you think she kept you on the detail? I mean, knowing how she felt about you, personally.

A: I don't think it was personal for her. I think she would've seen any white cop the same way.

Q: Question stands. Why didn't she have you removed and a, an, uh, African American officer assigned?

A: Honestly? I think she got a kick out of having a cop do her bidding. I couldn't prove it to you, but I'd catch her smiling this wicked little smile whenever she got to tell me to do something.

Q: Were you angry at her for it?

A: Angry? No, not really. Annoyed occasionally. Not angry.

Q: Did you kill her?

A: No.

Q: Threaten her in any way?

A: No.

Q: Any idea who'd want to kill her?

A: I thought at first the Soldiers for Jesus, but then I figured they'd be too stupid to lay out the scenario.

Q: Anybody else?

A: Not a clue. I mean, we got the usual bunch of morons at campaign stops. Hecklers. Haters. And as I understand it, she was a pretty controversial figure in Dallas politics. But nothing comes to mind.

Q: Is there any reason you can think of that your blood would be on the stocking used to kill Fortney?

A: Yeah. Somebody's setting me up to take the fall.

Q: Setting you up? Like framing you?

A: Yeah.

Q: You think this is some kind of James Bond movie?

A: No. More like a Freddy Krueger movie.

Q: Who?

A: Nightmare on Elm Street? You know?

Q: Don't be flippant, Cable.

A: No, sir.

Q: Anybody have it in for you? Enemies? Anybody you've put in jail?

A: Dozens. Nobody smart enough to put this together.

Q: So nobody could have done it, but somebody did it?

A: Obviously. I didn't do it to myself.

Q: So Fortney doesn't invite you to her room for a little hanky-panky, a little fun and games? Things don't maybe get out of hand? Get a little rough?

A: No. I mean, she never gave off a single sexual vibe in the entire time I was around her.

Q: And did that piss you off?

A: No. Hell no.

Q: I mean, think about it, Cable. If she didn't like you in some way, why'd she keep you around? Maybe all that public bickering was just to throw everybody off, and the two of you were getting it on when nobody was looking—

A: No. Didn't happen.

Q: Sit back down, Cable.

A: What about the surveillance cameras? Didn't they see anybody?

Q: Well, that's the problem. The camera on the fourteenth floor points at the elevator. Seems like everybody had a reason to be on the fourteenth floor that night. Half the campaign staff and a bunch of other folks got off the elevator. And you.

A: My room was on the fourteenth floor.

Q: Exactly.

A: And the door's key access?

Q: One entry. 10:26 p. m.

A: Prints, fibers, trace evidence?

Q: It's a hotel room, Cable. The problem isn't lack of evidence, it's too much evidence.

A: (Silence)

Q: How much did you drink that night?

A: Two beers.

Q: Two beers? Seriously?

A: Two beers.

Q: Were these beers ever out of your sight?

A: No.

Q: Anybody give you any little white pills?

A: Hell, no.

Q: With no drugs showing in your system, how do you account for your statement of being left unconscious in the Judge's room?

A: No drugs? At all?

Marshall: Slightly elevated for GHB.

Q: Slightly. Inconclusive.

A: I can't explain it at this time.

Q: All right, Cable. You are dismissed. Remain in touch.

Sam

CAPTAIN MARSHALL BOUGHT me lunch at a Red Robin just off the interstate, near Ranger Troop F Headquarters. Patches of sweat were still drying under my arms, and after two days, my shirt gave off a gamey smell.

"Well," Captain Marshall said, "that coulda gone better."

"I told the truth, Captain."

"This is one of those times where the truth may not set you free."

"I understand that." I sipped my tea.

A TV in the corner of the bar caught my eye. I couldn't make out the words trailing across the closed-captioning. Fortney's press photo flashed on the screen, followed by shots of protestors marching in the street, holding signs and chanting. I couldn't read the words on the signs any better than the text scroll, but I had a pretty good idea whose head they all wanted on a pike.

Marshall followed my eyes to the screen. "Don't worry about it. Nothing but noise."

"For now," I said. "For now."

Chapter 8

"*As proof of the reality of this declaration I have determined to augment at my own private expense the company of men... for the defense of the Colony against hostile Indians. I therefore by these presents give public notice that I will employ ten men in addition to those employed by the Government to act as rangers for the common defense.*"
— Stephen F. Austin, 1823

Sam

Captain Marshall and I returned to Company F HQ, on New Braunfels Avenue. The Rangers were organized into companies, the tradition dating back to when the Rangers were a quasi-military force, more like a militia than a police department. A good chunk of Central Texas fell under Company F's jurisdiction. The force had one hundred Rangers and a proud tradition of being relentless lawmen harder than battleship steel, with more grit than a case of sandpaper. Like the FBI, but with style.

Company F shared space with a half dozen state agencies. Everybody from the Forest Service to the License and Weight Office crowded into a building designed by Frank Lloyd Wright's LSD-addicted second cousin. The collection of rectangular building blocks looked like a fourth-grader had run out of blue Legos and finished the construction with tan ones.

Television vans lined the outskirts of the parking lot, creating a forest of satellite dishes.

"Aw, dogshit," Marshall said. He zipped the Crown Vic into the parking lot with a sharp right, tires squalling and suspension thumping. "Maybe they won't see you."

Wannabe drivers lined up, waiting their turn for a driver's license test. Before we could dash around the front of the building, a test-taker in a brown Acura pulled in front of us. Marshall stomped the brakes and screeched to a stop, inches from the lady's bumper. She kept starting and stopping, unsure which way to go in the milling crowd of reporters.

One of the news people swiveled at the scream of Marshall's brakes. Spotting us immediately, he pointed and shouted. A dozen of his colleagues swiveled in unison. They reminded me of a gopher colony, the way they all turned as one.

"Move it, Gidget!" Marshall blipped his lights and siren, spooking the poor woman so much, she froze in front of us. She threw up her hands and grabbed her hair. The examiner in the car made calming gestures, and the woman jerked the Acura forward enough to leave a gap. Captain Marshall hit the gas and bolted past. As we blew by, the woman was in tears and shaking. *Probably never drive again.*

The posse of reporters trailed behind, one long media conga line.

The captain squealed left, the Vic sagging and shoving me against the door, then he shot straight through an overhang that looked like a bank drive-thru, slewed left again, and jolted to a stop in a reserved parking slot near the back door.

We piled out and made it inside before the herd of reporters cleared the corner. The back door was a badge-access door, not open to the public, so I was relatively safe for the moment.

"Come with me," Marshall ordered.

We followed institutional halls to a borrowed conference room Marshall had commandeered. He took a seat and pulled out his phone while I sat across from him. A painting of beech trees, their leaves turning color, hung on the wall over the captain's head. The office air conditioning struggled to keep up with the muggy air, making the conference room stifling and close. The combination of warm room and full stomach left me struggling to stay awake.

"There you are." A squawky voice spiked my drowsiness and killed it flat dead. Rita Goldman, the head of the FBI's Elfin Enforcement Division, leaned in the doorframe. "I thought I'd find you here."

"What do you want?" Captain Marshall snarled.

"Keep your panties on there, Roy Rogers." Rita Goldman closed the door and took a seat at the table. Her cream-colored pantsuit flowed when she walked. "I had a couple-a follow-up questions for Trigger, here."

The captain swelled up like Spindletop ready to blow a gusher. Goldman stuck out a traffic-cop hand. "Hold it. Hold it. Peace out, Boy Scout. I'm from the government, and I'm here to help."

I snorted a laugh, and Marshall cocked a fishy eyebrow and tilted his head to the side, studying the strange, alien creature with the Gilda Radner hair and silver hoop earrings who had materialized in his conference room on a beam of light.

"Fire away," I said. "You can't make it any worse."

Marshall glared at me. "You wanna bet?" He leaned back, patted his pocket for cigarettes, and tossed the pack on the table. "Well, Goldman, go ahead. Let's hear it."

Up close, I noticed the FBI agent had olive skin and dark, liquid-brown eyes. The black of her pupils blended into chocolate irises, and she enhanced the look with laser-applied eyeliner and maybe a touch of shadow. A fingernail-sized Star of David hung on a monofilament chain around her neck.

"So okay," she said to me, "you know they found white supremacist stuff in your bag, right?"

"Say *what?*"

"Siddown, siddown." Goldman patted the air. "I had a hard time buying that myself. It seemed a little too... easy, you know what I mean?"

"Easy?" I fired back. "Nothing about this is easy."

"Siddown, already. You're giving me a crick in the neck. I'm looking up at you all the time."

I picked my chair off the floor and set it upright. Planted my butt in it and sent Goldman an expression sweetened by sucralose.

"What I'm saying here," Goldman continued, "is that little detail seemed one straw too many, you know? None of that jives with anything from your record, so I'm... willing to explore some other avenues, cowboy."

How nice. I felt so much better.

"What I'm wondering is this," she said. "If you didn't kill Fortney, who did? I mean, you were her protection detail, so... were there threats?"

"I don't know," I told her. "Most days, all I did was open doors and look tough. The only time I broke a sweat on this detail was when the clowns showed up in Jacksonville. Brains the size of boogers."

"No active threats?"

"None."

"Threatening emails?"

"None that came to my attention."

"She have any family?"

"Two people that I know of. JC Fortney, her husband, and Moriah Martin."

"Tell me about her husband," Goldman said. "Statistics show that if the wife is killed, good odds are the husband did it."

"You must have caught his speech on TV?"

"I did. Seems he got over his grief awfully fast."

"But what does he have to gain?" I said. "Life insurance? I never got the impression that either of the Fortneys were hurting for money."

"I'll check their financials," Goldman said. "What about Martin?"

"Moriah? April Fortney was her meal ticket. Moriah is a professional hanger-on, part of her niece's posse. Without April, Moriah will have to go back to painting nails for five bucks a finger."

"So maybe somebody from Fortney's past?"

"The woman was a civil court judge. She heard tort cases, land disputes, injunctions. Like that. No murderers, rapists, or secret agents armed with knockout drops on her docket."

"You keep eliminating suspects, cowboy, you're going to put yourself behind bars."

"I picked a bad week to give up dipping Skoal."

"What?"

"Never mind."

We went around and around for a while, talking things out but getting nowhere, then Goldman gave me her card and told me to keep in touch. She left behind a floral scent.

"Okay, listen up." Captain Marshall reached for his cigarettes, started to shake one out, then stopped. "Goddamn anti-smoking Nazis. Hate 'em." He tipped his hat back and looked at me. Crow's-feet tracked around his tea-colored eyes. His weather-hardened face, tanned from the hat line down, made it look as if he'd stepped out of a Zane Grey novel. "Here's what we're gonna do. I'm bringing Dusty and Kent down from Company B. Stan Coats owes me some favors, so he's gonna give me room to run with this."

Captain of Company F, Stan would ordinarily have jurisdiction in San Antonio. Randall "Dusty" Boots and Kent Erikson were Rangers from my home company. Good men. I felt better having them on my side.

"I'm makin' a pain in the ass outta myself down at the San Antone PD until they let us in the door on this one," he said. "If they don't, well, fuck 'em. We'll conduct our own investigation."

"So when do I hook up with Dusty and them?"

"Never."

My hands curled into fists. "So you're shutting me out?"

"Cable, you're suspended until this little goat rope is over."

"It's my ass they want to hang," I told him.

"Which is just why you're stayin' out."

"This is bullshit, Cap."

"I know, son, but they ain't no help for it. Now sit down, and I'm gonna tell you what you *are* gonna do."

I stopped pacing but didn't sit down. *That'll show him who's boss.* "Tell me."

The captain tipped back in his chair and hooked his thumbs in his belt, cocking an eyebrow at me as if I were a steer he wanted to buy. Or cook for dinner. "What you're gonna do is take a pool car and get outta sight for a while. And I don't mean go to Mexico or any other dumb shit like 'at. I want you outta sight of the press pussies but available to me. Don't go home and see your momma. Don't go back to your place in Longview. I'm approvin' your per diem for lodging at one a them extended-stay places. Do not bring any women back to your room. Last thing I need is some reporter catching you out cattin' around. Just stay away from this investigation and away from the media."

"Just hide?"

"Yep." He nodded. "That about sums 'er up."

"While half the state wants me hanged and the other half wants me in jail? And Black Lives Matter wants to burn me at the stake?"

He nodded again. "I know it's a raw deal, son, but keep your powder dry. Dusty can track a mouse fart in a monsoon. He'll find out who done this to ya."

I nodded and got directions to the washroom. I didn't want to hang around the cagey old lawman too long, or his cop radar would pick up what I was thinking. *Whoever did this to me is laughing somewhere, fat, dumb, and happy, thinking they put me in a noose and stood me on a three-legged chair. What a surprise it's gonna be when I punch a .45-caliber hole right between their eyes.*

Chapter 9

"*A few years ago, [Barack Obama] would have been getting us coffee.*" — quote attributed to Bill Clinton in *Game Change*, by Mark Halperin & John Heilemann

Rita

Rita Goldman pushed through the gaggle of coiffed and powdered reporters waiting in the parking lot of the Rangers' local HQ and found her car in the lot. None of the press people gave her a second glance. Reporters fell into a special category she called "Pretty People." Tall, good-looking, and well-groomed, Pretty People were the show dogs of the world. AKC-registered versus her common breeding.

She grinned. *Junkyard dog, that's me.*

During her short time inside the DPS building, the dingy-gray clouds had swollen with rain, turning black. Rain threatened, and she had no umbrella. With all the moisture in the air, gills would have been good. *Texas. Damn state. Pfft.* On the rare days it wasn't hot and arid, the place was hot and humid. Winter lasted a week. And fall? Forget about it.

In her car, Rita tilted the vents and let the cool air roll over her neck and face. She belted up, put the car in gear, and floored it out of the parking lot, nearly scorching the jet-black loafers of one of the Pretty People.

"Damn, I missed," she told the rearview mirror. "Maybe next time."

Rita hit traffic on I-37, so she took the shoulder and blew down an exit ramp to a side street. Better to keep moving—at least a little—than sit in traffic and waste time. She caught two green lights in a row, which made her happy. She piloted her two-seat lemon-yellow Solstice through the afternoon's accumulation of cars without conscious thought, her mind focused on their main suspect in the Fortney killing—a big, square-jawed Texas Ranger. A Pretty Person, if ever there was one. The man was Randolph Scott, Jimmy Stewart, and Gary Cooper all rolled into one. A clean-cut, American country boy. Captain of the football team. Blond hair and blue eyes. Way fucking broad shoulders and powerful hands. Big, strong hands.

Rita blinked and hit the brakes, a second away from zipping through another red light.

"What are you, Texas Ranger Samuel Duncan Cable?" she muttered. "Cowboy cop or deranged, racist killer? Are you all rotten on the inside of that pretty shell?" She shrugged. Her instincts said he had more depth of character than someone who got by on looks alone. Drumming the steering wheel, she waited behind a Honda minivan with stick figures of a family of four, plus dogs, plastered on the back window. "You're kiddin' me. A mommy taxi?"

The devil's advocate in Rita wouldn't let her settle, either for or against Cable's guilt. The Ranger exuded a primal, male power that could easily have broken loose and wreaked havoc. She could almost picture him going full King Kong, climbing the Empire State Building, and swatting at pesky planes. Had he lost his temper? He'd jumped up damn fast when she mentioned the white supremacy literature. Was it possible Judge Fortney had pushed the right buttons and set him off? Everything she'd heard so far indicated Fortney was a royal bitch to underlings, and Cable had been an underling to her for a couple of months, taking a lot of needling. *Or is his crazy story possible? Did somebody drug him and stage an elaborate setup?*

The light turned green, and the mommy taxi failed to move. Rita blipped the horn and shot around the Honda the second she had clearance.

One thing was as sure as sunrise: if somebody set the Ranger up to take the fall for murder, the answer would be found in the money. Passion wouldn't account for the deliberate, cold-blooded nature of the false trail laid directly at the big cowboy's feet. On her desk waited a stack of campaign finance documents, which would need hard scrubbing to uncover anything hinky in the politician's honey pot. After she dug through the campaign finances, she would have to forensically examine the woman's personal accounts.

"And won't Whitlach shit a brick when I ask for *that* warrant?" Rita grinned. "I can't fucking wait for that conversation."

Sam

I SNUCK OUT THE BACK door. A line of thunderstorms swirled up from the Gulf, and bruised clouds covered the sky. The first heavy drops of rain splattered the pavement as I found the pool car and adjusted the driver's seat to fit my length. The clouds let loose about the time I hit the interstate, rain sluicing across the windshield in time to the thumping of the wipers. Traffic slowed to a crawl then halted. Brake lights painted a red, watery kaleidoscope on my windshield.

"Where am I going?" The question had been chewing at the back of my mind for an hour. At the moment, I had no plan beyond simply moving. For two days, I'd followed someone else's lead, like a good little doggie. First the San Antonio PD then Goldman, Ibanez, and Marshall. Things had been happening to me, rather than *me* making things happen. I was still dancing to whatever tune the mystery assassin had dreamed up, two-steppin' my way into a jail cell.

"So what now?" I asked myself.

A *crack* of lightning, close enough to feel like a personal assault, whitened the sky; a long rumble followed.

"Was that a message, God? If so, I need you to be a little more clear."

The pool car was a 2014 Taurus with over a hundred eighty thousand miles on the odometer. The cloth interior had worn so thin, a loud fart might tear it. Accumulated coffee stains, grease, and sweat had baked into the interior. Moisture in the air helped bring the gamey smell of the car to life. The wipers smeared more than cleaned the windshield, and the radio crackled and fizzed with every lightning strike. But I was moving. Kind of.

I wanted to go back to the Hyatt and see the video footage of the fourteenth floor, talk to the gray-haired bartender, walk the hall again, and retrace the route I'd taken from the lobby to my room that night. Maybe something would jar loose. Every time I tried to bring up those memories, I hit a brick wall.

But...

Going the Hyatt would be a bad idea. No doubt SAPD would still be all over the place. Not to mention it would freak out the hotel staff to have the "crazed killer" show up at valet parking.

The captain had given me a cheap prepaid cell phone. All of my contacts were listed in my personal phone, which was still missing, presumably being held by the SAPD as evidence. I made a mental note to ask about it next time I talked to Captain Marshall. As a result of having to rely on memory, I dialed two wrong numbers before I hit the right combination for my fellow Ranger, Dusty.

"Boots."

"Dusty, it's me."

"Sssh! Hold on a minute."

Some shuffling and bumping came through the earpiece, followed by some distant voices, then Dusty came back on the line. He sounded like he was in a barrel. "It's okay now. I'm in the john."

"When do y'all get to San Antonio?"

"Already here, buddy. Me 'n Kent smoked out of Garland first thing this morning. Kent must've lit up every radar gun between Dallas and here. Like a cruise missile on crank."

"So where are you now?" Traffic bunched up, and I had to hit the brakes hard to avoid smacking into the guy in front of me. The Taurus had the stopping distance of a cruise ship.

"At the Hyatt," Dusty said. "We're goin' over the videotapes from the night Fortney... from the other night."

All the cameras in the Hyatt were recorded digitally, not taped, but I didn't bother trying to correct Dusty's impression. He thought a toaster with a bagel setting was high-tech.

"Perfect," I said. "I need you to do me a favor."

"Favor? Favor? Dang, boy, I can't be doin' you no favors. Be worth my ass, the captain was to find out."

"I need you to burn me a copy of the CCTV footage y'all are watching. All cameras from, say, ten... no, make it nine p.m. to the time when the SAPD showed up."

A long silence came back. Nothing but breathing, then he said, "Sam... Shit, Sam. You know I can't do that."

I sighed. "Okay, Dusty. I understand." I put a chipper note in my voice. "How's Randy doing? He make all-state yet?"

More silence. I let it hang there and ripen for a while.

"Goddamn it, Sam." Dusty breathed hard into the phone, air blowing like a rumble of thunder. "For a Captain America type, you can be a real bastard sometimes."

"Hey, Dusty. It's my ass that's hanging over the edge right now. Last I looked, we still have the death penalty in this state. You and I have sent a couple of ol' boys to meet Jesus by that route."

I had an ace in the hole with Dusty. Three years ago, he and I were on the trail of two bad asses wanted for killing a cop in San Saba. We'd tracked them to a small wood-frame house on the outskirts of Marfa, in a working-class neighborhood gone to seed. Long story short, things went bad. I had the back door, but I got hung up navigating around the neighbor's pit bulls, and it took me longer than expected to get into position.

Dusty didn't wait. His war cry and the sound of the flimsy front door shattering froze the blood in my veins, as I was just then coming over the back fence, having detoured around two houses. By the time I crashed through the back door and found Dusty, he lay on the living room floor, bleeding from a scalp wound, staring at the muzzle of Emilio Lantana's shotgun. The room was small, no more than ten or fifteen feet across. A painted mural, a modern cityscape, covered one wall. Well done, too. Professional quality. It was like looking out a window at a distant city.

Emilio grinned, his meth-rotted teeth gray and nasty. He appeared from nowhere, riding a busload of chemicals, a cocktail of crack, meth, and a heavy dose of Miller Lite, all loaded atop his natural mad-dog crazy. His eyes said he was going to do it. He was aching, itching, *needing* to blow Dusty into little bits with one tiny squeeze.

Three years later, in a smelly Ford Taurus, I inched through traffic and waited for Dusty to say something. He blew out another hard breath, a sigh of defeat.

"I still wake up at night," he said, "in a cold sweat, seeing that damn shotgun bore. What was that you said after you shot him?"

"I don't remember."

"I do. Just like Clint Eastwood. You said, 'I painted the town red.' Couldn't figure out what the hell you meant until I saw that picture on the wall. Painted the town with Emilio's blood." He blew out a lungful of air. "All right, goddamn it. I'll cut you some tapes. Or have Kent do it. He knows them computers 'n shit."

"Great, Dusty, thanks. I'll owe you one."

"Naw, Sam, ain't no way you'll ever owe me nothin'. Is that it?"

"Well, now that you mention it, I need a couple of other small things."

"Holy fuck, you're killin' me."

"The disturbance call," I said. "The timing seems… it was too convenient."

"Yeah, that bothers me, too." A door squealed in the background. "Hold on."

I listened to several minutes of Dusty's heavy breathing in the foreground and somebody else's urination, flushing, and handwashing in the background. Traffic on I-37 started to loosen up, and the rain dropped off from a deluge to a downpour.

When the door squealed again, Dusty said, "Anyway, yeah. That was weird. Fortney died around midnight or so. This guy calls 9-1-1 from a throwaway phone at ten 'til eight in the morning, says he heard some fighting and swearing in 1412 around midnight. Says he didn't want to get involved, but his conscience got the better of him. Then he hung up."

"Can I get a recording of the call, too?"

"Jesus, Sam. What else you want? My wife?"

"At least she'd be happy for a change."

"Hardy-fuckin'-har. Look, brother, I gotta get back. Is that it?"

"Well," I said. "There's one more little thing… I need to locate somebody."

Chapter 10

❝ *Confusion never stops,*
    Closing walls and ticking clocks." — "Clocks" by Coldplay

Sam

According to Dusty, Moriah Martin had moved to the Hilton Palacio del Rio a few blocks away from the Hyatt. Lucky for me, I found her at an outside table on the patio next to the River Walk. Tourists ambled past, wandering along the San Antonio River, sampling the shops and bars lining both sides of the muddy canal. Brightly colored flat-bottom boats filled with sightseers on bench seats paddled along the waterway, guides cracking the same stale jokes they'd used for the last ten years.

Moriah had a frozen, pale-green drink in a salt-rimmed glass in front of her. An empty glass next to it indicated she was on at least her second of the day. Knowing Moriah, it was probably her fourth or fifth.

The rain had passed, leaving everything soaking wet and the air steamy and sticky. The sun hid behind choppy clouds, rays breaking through at odd intervals. Emerald leaves dripped water on the paved walk. I still hadn't recovered my hat from police evidence, so I winced when heavy blobs of water fell on me from the trees along the River Walk. Puddles rippled when the wind blew and drops spattered across the pavement.

Moriah remained immersed in her iPhone, clicking at it with her long nails and frowning at the screen. Her eyes were puffy, and her cheeks sagged. She wore no makeup, which for Moriah, meant the next thing to naked. She looked up when she sensed me standing across the table from her. Her eyes grew wide, and she sucked in a deep breath, preparing to either scream or run—I wasn't sure which. I held out my palms, down and flat.

"Hold on, Moriah, calm down. We're in a public place, so nobody's getting hurt here. I just want to talk a second." I kept my voice pitched low, as the tables around us were occupied and pedestrians jostled back and forth behind me.

"Can I sit down for a second?" Without waiting for a reply, I stepped over the rope stanchion separating the Hilton's tables from the tourists and flipped a chair around so I could rest my arms across the back. Maybe the psychological barrier of the chair back would make her feel safer.

It might have been because of that or my boyish charm, but Moriah didn't scream. Her nostrils flared, and she narrowed her eyes at me. If her glare had been a gun, she would have killed me, my brothers, my mother, and all my living relatives.

"What do *you* want?" she hissed.

"First off, let's get something clear." I held my eyes level with hers, unblinking. "I didn't kill April Fortney."

She squinted and looked as if she'd found a worm floating in her margarita.

I continued, "You said something the other night. You said a lot of people wanted to tear April down. Do you remember that?"

All the hatred and the venom seemed to drain from Moriah as if somebody had opened a valve and let it all flow out. Moriah prided herself on her looks. She'd always been meticulously dressed, made up, and had her hair professionally styled. A well-built woman, not fat, not skinny, Moriah was fifty-two but could pass for forty-two. Now she looked eighty-two.

"I don't know wha' to think anymore." She sipped from her drink, and judging by the way she slurred her words, I upped my estimate from five drinks to eight. "So many enemies."

"Who?"

She glared at me through reddened eyes. "You, for one. You always hated her, and don't deny it."

I held my peace, sensing she wasn't done.

"The entire... All you white people hated my girl." Moriah raked salt off the rim of her glass with one finger and painted it across her lips, tasting it with her tongue. She sipped more margarita, getting down to the bottom and making a slurping sound. A waiter must have heard her, because he arrived promptly with a refill.

"And for you, sir?" he asked me.

I shook my head, and he went away.

"Any particular person, Moriah? Anybody who wanted her dead?"

"Lots of enemies, that girl." Moriah stared into the distance, not seeing me anymore. "I thought she got away from all that. I thought she left all that behind. But the past, it don't never go away."

"She got away from what?"

Her eyes focused back on me. She blinked, and I could see her physically force herself into the present.

"Fuck you, Cable," she spat. Wherever the venom had gone, it returned with a vengeance. "Fuck you and all your white police brothers. Y'all gonna sweep this under the rug."

Her voice climbed higher as she went along, her anger stoking the heat in her words, her well-honed diction disintegrating to street lingo in a hurry. "Y'all is all the same! You ain't gon' do one day in jail, Mr. Texas-fuckin'-Ranger, are you? Y'all is gonna make it disappear. Ain't no justice in this world!" Moriah's rant climbed the decibel scale, and heads turned. Passersby circled wide of the table, stepping dangerously close to the bank of the river to avoid the confrontation.

"My beautiful baby girl, my darlin' April—you had no idea wha' she hadda do, climb outta the trash. No idea at all. Well, fuck you,

Texas Ranger! Fuck you, and I hope you happy now. She dead. She dead, and you all can res' happy now!"

The last part she shouted at my back as I walked away. The scene was already out of hand; my staying would only make it worse. I told myself I wasn't running away, that it wasn't cowardly to walk away from a bad situation.

I found steps leading up to street level and took them two at a time. Traffic noise blanketed some of Moriah's words. I could hear her voice but not make out what she said. Thankfully. At street level, foot and auto traffic jammed the downtown business district. I got my bearings and took off toward the lot where I'd left Wonder Car. As I weaved through the pedestrians, something Moriah had said stuck in my head.

April Fortney had climbed out of the trash and done awful things to get out. It was the first inkling her past may not have been as squeaky-clean as her public image portrayed. She had done... things.

What things?

Sam

MY FAITHFUL STEED AWAITED. All the other cars were ashamed to be next to my Chariot of Fire; it squatted, alone, in the middle of the lot like the kid not picked by either team. Black clouds crowded the sky again, threatening to dump another prodigious round of rain, and gusty winds blew stray droplets sideways.

I pulled off my sport coat and pitched it in the back seat. Sweat-soaked armpits reminded me I didn't have a clean shirt, pants, or underwear to my name. I settled into the wheezing driver's seat of the Taurus, and the smell of ancient vomit and old socks puffed from the upholstery.

The temptation to head for home pulled at me. Fresh clothes, my personal vehicle, and a bed I hadn't seen in a few weeks were all in Longview. About six hours away by car.

The dashboard clock worked, at least. It read 6:26 p.m. If I fueled up on gas and coffee, I could make it home around one in the morning, get a few hours of sleep, and head to my next stop, in Dallas, first thing in the morning.

Would reporters be hanging around my house at one in the morning? It didn't seem likely, though if I turned out to be wrong, I would make the early-morning news shows, and the captain would go ballistic. Best case, I would avoid the reporters and make it home unseen. What would that get me? Clean undies and a late start to Dallas.

I drummed my hands on the steering wheel. Time was squeezing my chest. All day, I looked at clocks compulsively. I had no way of knowing when I would find myself behind bars. The real bad guys did such a good job, Vegas oddsmakers would have me as a lead-pipe lock to be indicted, and indictment was the greasy banana peel positioned at the top of a long slide to prison. Wal-Mart was open twenty-four seven, so I could pick up clean clothes along the way rather than detour out to Longview. I needed to be moving, not sleeping.

I cranked up Ol' Bessie and followed the signs to I-35. Raindrops splattered my windshield as I coaxed the tired engine to freeway speed and headed north for Dallas. At the entrance ramp, the dashboard clock turned over to 6:42.

Rita

ISOLATED IN HER SMALL part of the cubicle maze in the FBI office, Rita Goldman ignored her environment, eyes fixed on the task in front of her. A vacuum cleaner hummed and whined somewhere on the floor. Phones rang, and voices murmured in the background.

She piled paper into stacks, collated documents into chronological sequence, and built a castle of paper towers: six stacks on the floor, three on her desk, and four balanced on top of the eye-level credenza mounted on her cubicle wall. Her phone was plugged into its charger, and white earbuds connected Rita to her favorite playlist. Eighties pop. Her secret weakness. The same tunes her mom played while doing housework: the songs Rita had grown up humming while studying, driving, or doing anything when her mind went into analytic mode.

She was in hyperdrive analytic mode at the moment. In addition to financial data, Rita wanted to create a paper trail of April Fortney's life. If something from her past had killed April, Rita would find it in the documents. Everyone scattered footprints on paper—or on digital media—on their journey through modern America. It was unavoidable. Birth certificates, school records, traffic tickets or other arrests, DBAs, Uniform Commercial Code filings, credit reports, civil judgments, marriage licenses...

Fortney's candidacy complicated the investigation in a number of ways, beyond the media hype. Not only did Rita have to examine the woman's personal finances, she also had to take a serious look at her campaign's contributions and expenses. *And* her joint finances with her husband, a very successful businessman who owned several used-car lots. Used-car dealerships were a notorious pain to audit.

Rita's instructor at the academy had once said, "The documentary evidence of a person's life is astounding, especially for a politician. You get onto a public-corruption case, go for the paper trail. Nine times out of ten, the evidence will jump off the page. These people aren't subtle."

She swiveled in her chair, adding more Candidate/Office Holder forms to a stack growing from the floor. A pair of black Oxford shoes appeared next to it. Scanned up from the shoes to the navy pinstripe suit, jacket slung over one shoulder. Briefcase. Beefy face. One eyebrow cocked. Jim Whitlach. Rita pulled her earbuds free, and Madonna's tinny voice piped "Like a Virgin."

"Jim, what's up?"

Whitlach scanned the stacks of paper as if her cubicle had been invaded by the Mafia, or, even worse, a budget committee. "What... are you doing?"

"What you pay me for. I'm investigating."

"The cop?"

"The Ranger, yes. Samuel Cable." Rita passed a hand over the paperwork. "Honestly, I'm taking a look at the victim, see if there's anybody else might have wanted her dead."

"Wanted her dead? Who cares who else wanted her dead? I mean, the cop killed her, right? And besides, it's the SAPD's job to investigate the murder. You're there to make sure we look good."

"But what if the Ranger didn't do it?"

Whitlach double-blinked, and his mouth gaped. "Didn't... Of course he did it. They found all that racist shit in his luggage. He was in the room. His blood—"

"It could be a setup."

"A setup?" Whitlach walked away a few steps then came back. "Goldman, you're cracked. You know that? Cracked."

"But—"

"No fucking 'buts,' Goldman. You're not a homicide investigator—you're an FBI agent. A computer specialist, at that. Let the SAPD do their job, and you do yours. Convict this bigoted asshole of a civil rights violation. If the black community thinks the FBI is trying to clear this guy, Stable—"

"Cable."

"—rather than bury him..."

"Is that all you care about?" Goldman fired back. "What the black community thinks of us means more than a man's innocence?"

Whitlach shook his head. His jaw stood out of his brick-red face, and he spoke with the careful diction of the very angry. "You see all the shit going on in this nation right now? Or are you oblivious, as always? Last chance, Goldman. Last chance. Pull your head out of your ass and do your job!" He stalked away, stiff-backed.

Goldman dropped the sheaf of papers in her hand to the top of the stack without seeing it land. She stared at the spot her boss vacated. *Was that a dream?* she wondered. *Did Whitlach really just say what he just said?*

"Cable, I hope I'm right about you," she said under her breath. With the click of a mouse, she sent another set of documents to the printer. "If not, you're spending a long time in prison."

Chapter 11

"*A wise man makes his own decisions; an ignorant man follows public opinion.*" — Grantland Rice

Sam

Thunderstorms trailed from northeast to southwest, perfectly aligned with the I-35 corridor from San Antonio to Dallas. The rain varied in intensity from heavy to biblical. At times, even with wipers on max, visibility dropped to about a car length. Spray from a passing eighteen-wheeler blinded drivers entirely.

With an eighty-five-mile-per-hour speed limit, the Austin bypass road was a super-fast shortcut around a real traffic nightmare. Except when there was a wreck. Or rain. Streams of red brake lights flared, and traffic came to a standstill. Nobody moved.

I dialed Matt's number from memory.

He picked up after a couple of rings. "What the hell, bro? What's this bullshit you got yourself into now?"

"Look, man, I need some help."

"Du-uu-uh."

"Stop bustin' my chops for a minute and listen. I need somebody to analyze Fortney's docket, check out what she was into as a judge. Maybe something reared up out of that swamp and bit her."

"Already on it, Peanut."

"That nickname stopped being funny in fourth grade."

"You're the smallest. You get to be called Peanut."

"You have time to make a visit with me tomorrow?" I asked. "I have to go see one of the campaign staffers, and she might freak out if I just show up on her doorstep."

"I'll make the time," he said. "Hey, did you hear the news?"

"I've tried to avoid the news lately."

"JC Fortney is politicking to take over his wife's candidacy for Senate."

Traffic inched forward. I topped a rise, and the lights of the emergency vehicles flashed about a mile ahead. The heat of the phone made my ear warm. I finally asked, "Can he do that?"

"Don't know. But he says he wants the job."

The wipers thumped back and forth.

"Maybe," my brother mused, "we should go have a talk with him first?"

"I dunno, Matt. I go try to interview the husband of the woman who I'm accused of—"

"Gotcha. Where're you staying?"

"I'll find a place south of Dallas for the night."

"Bullshit you will. Get your ass over to my house."

"Have the reporters found you yet?"

Matt said nothing for a couple of beats. "Yeah, we've had a few. I wanted to shoot BBs at 'em as they came across the lawn."

"Well, I'm getting in late anyway. I don't want to wake Darla."

We made plans on when and where to hook up, and I ended the call. One thing about brothers like mine: they might ride their little brothers' asses day and night, but when a brother called, they answered.

It was quarter after nine when I passed the wreck. At the rate I was moving, archeologists would be digging up parts of Dallas before I got there.

The rain stopped about forty-five minutes later. A whipped dog had more spunk than I did by the time I made it to Waco, which is pretty close to the halfway point between Austin and Dallas. I passed a road sign that said FOOD, with a collection of company logos on it. One of them was for Whataburger, so I pulled off the highway to find a men's room, some food, and a whole gallon of coffee. And a tankful of gas for the Rolling Wreck.

After a long run down the access road, I made a right into the restaurant parking lot and found a spot near the front door. Out of the car for the first time in hours, I stretched, and my back popped in three places. I twisted the other way, and a flash of headlights swept the lot, nearly blinding me. A black Nissan Altima turned in then went left, to a far corner of the lot, before it parked.

I took my time pulling on my sport coat, but nobody got out of the Altima. The headlights stayed on, and vapor trailed from the tailpipe. The engine was still running. Why were they sitting in a car in a parking lot? No interior light, so the driver wasn't reading a map or programming the GPS. What bugged me the most was I'd seen a similar car where I'd parked in San Antonio.

Would the SAPD put somebody on me to make sure I don't run?

The Altima was about the most popular car in America; the odds of two black ones intersecting my life in the last few hours were pretty good. *No need to get worked up every time one shows up.*

I pushed through the glass doors of the Whataburger. Halfway to the counter, I stopped in place, frowning at the Formica floor. If anybody had a reason to be paranoid, it was me. Somebody had gone to the trouble of framing me for murder and doing it in a fairly sophisticated manner. It wasn't much of a stretch to believe they were keeping an eye on me. Muttering a curse, I pivoted and beelined for the door. I slapped it open, and muggy air swamped me the second I stepped outside. The Nissan had not moved. Its lights were still on. I crossed the walk and strode into the parking lot, bearing down on the black car. I pushed my coat back behind the butt of my holstered Kimber and held it there.

The driver hit the gas and pulled away—at an angle so I couldn't get a good read on the tag. It hit the access road and accelerated north. With the tinted windows, I couldn't tell how many people were inside.

Interesting. Was I being followed, or did I just scare some poor citizen by charging at them with my gun showing?

"Hell with it," I muttered.

It was 10:24 p.m., and I had an hour, maybe two, of driving before I could find a place to sleep. No time to worry about black cars following me. Eat, drive, sleep—those were my priorities. Then I would go see DaShondra in the morning.

Sam

TALK-RADIO STATIONS out of Dallas blew their signal almost all the way to Austin, especially after six o'clock, when they were allowed to hit the juice. I needed the noise more than anything. My eyes were sagging, and my brain kept trying to cat nap for a few miles at a time. The traffic was relentless, fast and unforgiving. I punched the radio buttons until I found something with a voice and cranked the volume. Even with the lever pushed to Max A/C, I had the window cracked enough to keep a strong breeze across my face. The news shifted into commercials, then went to the talk-show host.

"And we're back. Jack Armstrong here with my guest, Dr. Cal Newton, Professor of Political Science at UT Arlington. Dr. Newton—"

"Call me Cal."

"Okay, Cal. What is it about this case that's made so many African Americans angry? You're African American. What makes you angry?"

"Oh no," I told the radio. "Please, not this."

"Well, Jack, take a look at how the San Antonio police are handling this case. What people see from the outside, the outside looking in, is a double standard. Or at least, what they perceive is a double standard. White man allegedly kills a black woman—why isn't he in jail?"

I hit the seek button.

"...people don't seem to be getting that this is not just a black-white thing. It's a violence-against-women thing. Toxic masculinity, alive and well. Do you know that more than—"

Seek.

"But—"

"No, hang on a second. Ask yourself this question: What if the man found in her room had been black? Or Hispanic? Or anything besides a white cop? Would they get the same treatment? No. The answer's no."

Seek. Tejano music. Seek.

"...outside DPS headquarters, the reverend led the crowd in a chant—"

Seek.

"...I say, 'Way to go, man!' Texas Rangers did us all a service—"

"Oh, no," I groaned. "Shut up, dude." I tapped the FM button, and Foghat's "Slow Ride" came on. "Well, that's appropriate, at least."

A glow on the horizon, reflected light from a padding of low clouds, indicated Dallas wasn't far. My foot squeezed a little more speed out of the Taurus, and I zoomed northward, another pair of headlights in a steady stream of traffic.

Sam

I CAUGHT A FEW HOURS of dead-to-the-world shut-eye at a LaQuinta in DeSoto, south of the Dallas city limits. My alarm woke me at six in the morning, then I got a shower and dressed. I was out the door by six thirty and met my brother for breakfast at the International House of Pancakes a few blocks away.

I found Matt drinking coffee at a table next to the front window. He was easy to spot: the only six-foot-five guy in a tan uniform in the place. We hugged and slapped backs.

Matt held me at arm's length for an inspection. "Man, you look like shit. You just buy those clothes?"

"Last night. I had to. All my stuff is in the hands of the SAPD."

"You didn't need to buy stuff. I bet some of my old baby clothes will fit you."

"Bite me."

We sat at the table, and the waitress appeared with a cup and a glass of ice water. She filled the cup from a tan carafe on the table and asked if we were ready to order. Matt said he wanted a three-stack of pancakes with sausage and eggs.

"Make it two, please," I told the waitress.

"Are you two related?" the waitress chirped.

"No, but we have the same parents," I told her. Matt and I looked very much alike, except for a few pertinent details. My hair was wheat blond, and his was almost completely brown. The shade of my eyes leaned toward blue versus his aquamarine. Other than that, we couldn't deny being brothers.

"Uh..." She tilted her head and touched an index finger to her lips, pretending to think. "You're both cops?"

I pointed at Matt. "Not him. He's a deputy sheriff, which is to cops like monkeys are to astronauts. On the other hand, I'm a Texas Ranger."

"Really? Cool." She posed there in a waitress uniform, twenty-something, country cute with dark hair pulled into a ponytail. Her name tag read "Chrissy." She got all bright-eyed with excitement. "Texas Rangers? I love baseball. What position do you play?"

Matt laughed so hard, he pulled a muscle. The waitress flashed a gotcha smile then went away to put in our order.

"She loves you, bro," Matt told me after wiping his eyes with a napkin.

"Yeah, I can tell," I said. "The way she swooned all over me."

"The smell of dumb overcame her senses. It's pretty strong. So, what's your plan, oh mighty Texas Ranger?"

"The plan? Well, here's how I see it." I took a sip of coffee. *Not bad.* "Dusty and Kent are digging into the video and whatnot in San Antonio." I held up a finger to forestall protest. "There's a wolverine of an FBI agent *supposedly* pulling Fortney's financials."

"One Feebie? Oh, brother, you're in deep shit. You're going to need a whole team of people digging at that. We're talking campaign contributions, property records, everything. Shit, dude, her hubby made a fortune sellin' used cars to poor people at high interest. A used car lot and money laundering go together like ducks and fucks."

"Real good." I stared out the window. Bright sunlight reflected off windshields in sparkling flares of white. "I feel like I swallowed a bowling ball. This sucks."

"Cheer up, Peanut." Matt shifted from lounging to sitting upright.

Chrissy brought breakfast and set the plates in front of us, bubbling with down-home charm. "Y'all need anything else?"

Her green eyes promised a lot, but I had a feeling a man would have to ante up a wedding ring to get in the game.

"More coffee, please. Pot's empty."

"Sure thing, sweetie." She took the carafe and left.

"See, Peanut," Matt said, eyeing the syrup selection. "Stick around town, and you might get lucky there."

"Might come down with a case of marriage, you mean."

"There's pills for that now."

"Anyway." I snatched the maple syrup before he could claim it. "What I need to do is find out about Fortney's past. I don't know anything about her except what I've learned while playing bodyguard. That and what I read in her press clippings."

"Which is what?"

"Forty-seven, married. She has two kids I've never met—boy and girl, ages eighteen and twenty-one. Says she pulled herself up by her bootstraps. Worked her way through college then law school. Made her bones as a tort specialist. Or ambulance chaser, if you read between the lines."

I took a forkful of pancakes, speared a bite of sausage, and swirled the chunk in a puddle of syrup. I shoved the whole thing in my face before any drips came loose. Matt and I chewed together in holy reverence of pancakes and syrup.

"Elected to city council," I continued. "Then to county commissioner, then judge at thirty-two. Been there for ten years, until she decided to run for state senate. A few years in Austin, and she caught the politics bug. Jumped into the race for US Senate first time she was eligible." I shrugged. "That's about it."

"And you spent *how* long with her?"

"Shut up, dickhead." I cut into my eggs and let the yolks run into the slurry of syrup, then I piled egg, sausage, and pancake onto my fork and navigated it home. Bliss.

"Who's this campaign staffer you need to see?"

"DaShondra Wright. Personal secretary. She kept Fortney's calendar. If anybody knows what the judge was into, it'll be her."

"You think she's gonna talk to you?"

"Hope so."

"Because you are pure at heart and clear of brow."

"'Cause I'm a real live Texas Ranger and shoot silver bullets."

"If you show up on her porch, she's liable to shoot first."

I nodded and swallowed another giant bite. "Have to risk it."

"So who wanted Fortney dead?" Matt took smaller bites but motored through his plate with speed and efficiency. He was almost finished.

"She was a righteous bitch to me, but I need to know if anyone else got the Fortney treatment the way I did."

"Well, then, I 'spect we best get to it. Finish your breakfast, Peanut, before Chrissy gets mad and takes your plate away."

"She'll have to pry it out of my cold, dead fingers."

My borrowed cell phone chose that moment to buzz in my pocket. I wiped my hand on a napkin—*how is it you can eat pancakes with a fork and still get sticky hands?*—and plucked it out with two fingers. "Cable here."

"Sam, it's me. Dusty."

"Talk to me, Dusty. Whatcha got?"

"Bad news, bud." He hesitated, and I tensed up like I was about to take a punch to the gut. "I got in close with the SAPD detective, you know, Barney Woods?"

"Bernia," I corrected. "Yeah."

"Well, it don't look good, man, I gotta tell you."

"What, Dusty? Spit it out."

"They found some stuff in your luggage. Some literature and pamphlets and shit." He paused again. "It was all Nazi and anti-black propaganda and books."

"I know about that. It's not mine, Dusty."

"Shit, I know that, boy. I been around you too long to believe that shit. But you know how it looks, right? Woods and them, they all set to light a fire under you and toss on the gasoline."

"Anything else?"

"Yeah, the bartender cleared a poly. We can't find a connection between him and the Fortney people, either. He looks clean."

"Thanks, Dusty. Keep me posted."

"You got it," Dusty said then hung up.

Chrissy came with the fresh coffee pot. "Sorry I took so long. We had to make a new—Are you okay, honey? You look like you've seen a ghost."

"I have." I pushed my plate back, my appetite gone. "The ghost of Sam Cable, killed by lethal injection."

Rita

AT EIGHT IN THE MORNING, the San Antonio office of the FBI transformed from a quiet haven to a bustling maze of chatter and movement. Her earbuds plugged in, Rita remained oblivious to the racket around her as she clicked and moused from screen to screen on a pair of side-by-side monitors. She tipped her cup of dark-roast coffee and drained the last of it. Finding it had cooled while she worked, Rita pulled a face.

She downloaded the last of April Fortney's C/OH filings from the Texas Ethics Commission's public website and copied it into a spreadsheet. The stack of PDFs she'd printed the night before contained more detailed information, but the spreadsheet format could be analyzed for trends and anomalies much faster than she could correlate data manually from PDFs.

She quirked an eyebrow at the totals. April Fortney's campaign had raised a little over one-point-two million dollars in the six months since she announced her candidacy. Rita checked a few other candidates for the same office in different parts of the state, and the amount, though large, wasn't out of the ordinary.

Saving the spreadsheet, Rita took a peek at her email and found the Dallas office had sent a copy of April Fortney's birth certificate. April Maree Haddock, born to Jeanie May Haddock forty-seven years ago on April sixteenth. The father was listed as Martin Barber, no middle name given.

She logged into NCIC, the FBI's repository of crime-related information. With roughly twelve million active records, if the National Crime Information Center didn't know about a crime, that was because it hadn't been reported. She tapped some keys and ran a search on Martin no-middle-name Barber and came back with too many hits to weed through without more information, like, say, a blazing-red arrow pointing to which Martin Barber had fathered April Haddock.

The mother, Jeanie May, came back blank. No criminal records. Same thing for Jeanie Barber and May Barber. Or, at least, none of the hits that came back were in the right age range or race to be April's mother.

"So she was raised by decent people," Rita said under her breath. "Or at least not by criminals."

Judges and political candidates received intense background checks. April Haddock, April Fortney, and Jawn C. Fortney would have been researched as far back as kindergarten. No chance that the deceased or her husband would have a record not already unearthed. She checked anyway, and found nothing.

"I wonder..." Rita typed in "April Maree Barber" and hit Enter. The screen refreshed, and a record appeared. Rita clicked to open it. "Well, well, well. Lookit what we have here."

Chapter 12

"*Time spent with cats is never wasted.*" — Sigmund Freud

Sam

Matt and I left the IHOP and drove directly to DaShondra's in Matt's F-250 diesel pickup truck. The thing was a monster, even bigger than my Expedition, and it could have pulled the Queen Mary across dry ground. I spotted six black Nissan Altimas along the way, but none appeared to be following us.

Fortney's secretary lived in a modest three-bedroom brick house in Duncanville, on the south side of Dallas. If the IHOP in DeSoto was at the six-o'clock position relative to Dallas, Duncanville would be at the seven. The houses in DaShondra's neighborhood looked like they'd been built by a government contractor on a low bid. Carbon copied out of cheap brick, each home differed only by the number of plants, toys, or cars scattered around the front yard.

We found DaShondra's place, and Matt cut the engine. I climbed down from the big pickup and took a look around. Weeds split the front walk of DaShondra's place, and a dog ran loose across the street, no tags or collar visible. The number of cars per house seemed disproportionately large; the street was impacted with more vehicles than a parking garage.

The plastic center had worn out of DaShondra's doorbell, leaving only a ring to push, but it worked. Faint chimes rang from inside the house, and I stepped off the porch. I didn't want to loom over DaShondra when she opened the door. Matt stood next to me. The situation could go several ways to hell when DaShondra Wright saw me. Every possibility, from a shotgun in the face to a screaming fit like Moriah's, crossed my mind. What I didn't expect was for her to give me a big hug and invite me in.

But that was what she did. A hefty woman, DaShondra. When she puts a hug on somebody, they'd better suck in a deep breath and hold it or risk cracked ribs.

"Sam Cable," she said. "Oh my, you are the last person I expected to see. C'mon in here and have some iced tea."

I hesitated. "DaShondra, you got to know something first. I didn't kill April Fortney."

"Oh, Sam, I know that." She waved a hand as if batting away a fly. "You're not a killer. No way, blessed be the Lord."

"Oh, and this is my brother, Matthew."

"Of course," she said. "Matthew 7:1."

"Judge not, that ye not be judged," Matt said with the most serious look I'd ever seen. I had to catch my jaw from falling open. There were times my big brother could still take me by surprise.

"Amen," DaShondra said with a sigh. Not much ever seemed to make that woman frown, but her eyes were puffy and reddened, and she moved with the slowness of someone in physical pain. "Y'all c'mon in. It's hot out here."

DaShondra had a tidy home scented by Glade and Pine-Sol. Living room in front with an adjoining kitchen, separated by a counter. Hallway on the right going toward the bedrooms. Two cats, an orange tabby monster and a smaller black-and-white short-hair, lounged on the sofa. Another furry critter blurred down the hall to our right as we came in.

"Y'all sit down. I'll bring some iced tea." DaShondra shuffled to the kitchen. She wore a knee-length black house dress and fuzzy brown slippers. I'd never seen her so... disheveled. Fortney's death must have hit her hard.

Two chairs flanked the sofa, a cushioned guest chair that matched the tan sofa and a La-Z-Boy recliner, well-worn with a half-full glass of tea resting on a side table next to it. Matt grabbed the guest chair, leaving me a spot on the sofa with the cats. On the side table next to DaShondra's recliner, a Sudoku puzzle book lay open. I glanced it; she was working on one of the hard ones. She did those puzzles religiously every day and could finish the hard ones faster than I could write my name.

The big yellow tom stood, stretched, and promptly wandered over to stand in my crotch, offering me the opportunity to rub his head. He was big enough, I was afraid not to do it. The cat purred like a rusted washing machine.

Ice rattled and clinked, and DaShondra came back in the room with two glasses and a plastic pitcher. "Y'all like it sweet?"

"Yes, ma'am."

"Well, that's good, 'cause that's what this is." She pulled two coasters from a drawer on the table, set the glasses on them, and filled them with tea. The coasters were white ceramic with pictures of roosters in blue. DaShondra took the jug back to the kitchen then reclaimed her chair with a sigh of effort. "Now, Baby, don't you bother Mr. Sam. Throw that old fat creature off you, Sam. He won't leave you alone, you give him any attention at all."

"His name is Baby? There was a Kathryn Hepburn, Cary Grant movie with a leopard named Baby. It was about the same size as this guy. We're good as long as he doesn't plan to eat me."

"Ah, Sam, you and your movies. I bet you've watched every movie ever made."

"No, because," Matt butted in, "Momma won't let him see the R-rated pics yet."

Baby butted his head into my hand and flopped into my lap, accepting a chin scratch with eyes closed in ecstasy. It was like having a fuzzy bowling ball drop into my crotch.

"So, D, here's the thing," I said. "Somebody killed April Fortney and set me up to take the fall. I'm hoping you might know who'd want to harm her. Was anyone mad at her, or did she have a fight with anyone in particular?"

"Oh, Sam, you know I don't like to gossip."

"I know you don't, but I really need your help. If you don't think I did it—"

"I don't."

"Then I need to know who might have wanted to."

"Did she get along with her husband?" Matt asked.

DaShondra shook her head and frowned. "Not for a long time." She paused, and we let the silence grow.

I sipped some tea and nearly choked. DaShondra liked a little tea with her sugar.

"They always fightin', lately."

"Lately?"

"It's not like it was in the beginning, you know? When they first married, they were as happy as any couple. I've been with April for a long time. I was her admin at her law firm, back in the day. I knew her before she got married to JC. So sad." DaShondra snatched a Kleenex out of a box next to her and dabbed her eyes.

"But what happened to change that?" I asked.

"Jealousy," she said then blew her nose. "Just plain ol' jealousy. April kept gettin' elected to this and that. She got big into politics, and she was the popular one. JC, he didn't like being number two, you know? Even though he was making money like crazy, selling cars, opening his own business, he still gets introduced as Mr. Fortney, husband of Judge Fortney. I don't think he liked that at all. It led to a lot of bickering between them."

"Bickering," Matt said, "or outright fighting?"

"Arguing, you know—shouting and like that."

"Ever come to violence?"

DaShondra shook her head. "Not that I ever seen, no. April wouldn't have put up with that, not for a second, I swear. She was a tough little woman, let me tell you."

A picture of Jesus on the wall regarded me with a gentle expression. Now that I looked, I noted crosses and other religious-themed decorations dotting the living room walls. DaShondra was a woman of strong faith.

"Moriah said April had a past." Baby had curled into a long-haired diesel engine in my lap, eyes closed, and was vibrating with a steady rumble. "That she's been through some tough things."

"I wouldn't know about that." DaShondra sipped some tea and set the glass back in the wet ring on the coaster. Water pooled and dripped onto the table, and DaShondra mopped it with her tissue. "When I started with her, she was a lawyer and all. Where she came from, she never said, and I never asked."

"Anybody else not like her?"

"Hah!" DaShondra barked a laugh loud enough to startle Baby into stabbing my leg with prickly claws. The cat twisted around to find a better position and settled. The heat of his enormous body made my legs sweat. "Oh, sugar, you don't have the time to hear about all the people didn't like my little girl, April."

"What do you mean?" Matt scooted forward in his chair. He hadn't taken more than one sip of his tea, either. Our glasses sat next to each other on our side table, dripping beads of moisture, barely touched.

"Oh, April," DaShondra said, tearing up and smiling at the same time. Yet another cat, a gray tabby with green eyes, sauntered from the hall and yowled a word of command. "Not now, Brutus, I'll feed y'all in a little bit. No, April, she made everybody mad. She made white people mad. She made Mexican people mad. She made Jewish people mad... She was an equal-opportunity aggravator. But she has—had—a gift with people, too. She wanted to, she could turn on the charm and make those same people love her."

"Anybody in particular?" I asked.

DaShondra shook her head and sighed again. "No, Sam, just the usual kind of things come out of politics, you know?"

"D, what I'm gonna ask you next, I want you to understand is probably not right to ask, but I gotta know something. Can I get a copy of the judge's appointment books for the last six months or so? And her email, too? I'm sure the police took all the originals, but I know you kept copies of all that stuff backed up somewhere."

DaShondra leaned back in her chair and stayed silent for a long time. She stared at the cross on the wall over the TV, maybe praying, maybe just thinking. Maybe a combination of both. I held my breath and waited. Brutus yowled and jumped onto the arm of the recliner, tail up in the air like a flagpole. DaShondra stroked him absently.

"Okay, Sam," DaShondra said at last. "I know you're a good man. I don't want to see you get sent to jail for something you didn't do." The recliner squealed as she gathered herself to get up. With a shove and a woof of breath, DaShondra came out of the chair. "Y'all hold on a second while I feed these cats, and I'll get it for you."

Brutus jumped down, and the cat on the sofa joined him. Even Baby showed an interest, standing in my lap and stretching. When DaShondra went to the kitchen, all three cats followed, tails in the air. Baby left me without a second glance.

I sipped another tiny bit of tea and made a face. Matt's look agreed with my assessment. He left his untouched.

Thirty minutes later, we left with a flash-drive copy of Judge April Fortney's Outlook calendar from November through the day she died. Outside, the sun had burned off any stray clouds, and the intense light smacked me in the face. I squinted and cringed away like Bela Lugosi in *Dracula*.

"I miss my hat," I said.

"You say hat or cat?" Matt grinned and hooked a thumb over his shoulder. "'Cause your cat's inside."

"You don't go making fun of Baby. At least he likes me."

We made the climb into the cab of Matt's Ford Space Shuttle, and my brother ignited the engine. Ten minutes later, he swerved onto the entrance ramp of I-20 and achieved escape velocity.

"We're not going back to the IHOP for your Taurus," Matt said. "We're going straight to my place, get you fixed up. You can use my Mustang."

"Your *Mustang*? Jesus Christ, you really do love me."

"Scratch it, and you're dead."

Matt dug in the center console and pulled out a Bluetooth earpiece, which he switched on and stuck in his ear. I held back telling him how much he reminded me of Moriah Martin.

"Call. Darla." He enunciated each word clearly then waited. "Hey, sweetie, it's me. What's up? No, I said what's up with you?"

As he made small talk with his wife, I tuned him out and watched the scenery blur past. The wing mirror on the passenger side had a small, inset wide-angle mirror. Made for hauling trailers, the little mirror reflected a large swath of road behind us. Traffic was middling-heavy for a weekday morning. Cars jockeyed around behind us, most falling behind as Matt cruised past them. One seemed to be...

I leaned forward for a closer look. A black car followed us, about six cars back. It looked like an Altima.

Chapter 13

"*We must learn to live together as brothers or perish together as fools.*" — Martin Luther King, Jr.

Sam

The car behind us *looked* like an Altima, but it was hard to say from the tiny image in the mirror. I squinted, which only made the view smaller.

Matt continued talking to his wife, oblivious. "So anyway, darlin', baby brother's coming back with me... I'll ask him." To me he said, "Darla wants to know, can you still eat a cow down to the hooves?"

I grunted without taking my eyes from the mirror, and he said, "That's affirmative, honey. You, too, sweetie... bye-bye." Matt touched his ear, ending the call. "Darla says hey."

"Hmm." The black car kept pace with Matt, shifting from lane to lane, staying about six or eight cars back.

"It's gonna cost you, Peanut. Darla's gonna want to yak all about the baby and being pregnant and morning sickness and the nursery. Be prepared to discuss breathing exercises and... What the fuck you looking at?"

"See that black car behind us?"

He squinted into his rearview. "Yeah."

"What is it?"

"Some kind of Nissan. They all look the same to me. It's got that round thingy in the front, though. Definitely a Nissan."

I told Matt about the car in the Whataburger parking lot. "I couldn't say if I was being followed, or what."

"No shit," he said. "Well, let's find out."

The Interstate 45 overpass crossed the horizon about a mile away. Matt signaled right and started moving over, taking it slow and careful. I lost sight of the black car in my wing mirror, so I had to wait for Matt to tell me what was happening. My neck itched with the urge to crane my head around and look through the back window. I fought it off and held still.

"Yep," he said. "They're moving over with us."

A Christmas-morning charge of excitement tingled my heart. Santa had laid a big, fat present under the tree, just for me. "Oh, thank you, Lord," I breathed. "Let's not lose them."

"Lose them? I'm driving a goddamn red bus the size of Rhode Island. How're they gonna not see me?"

We took the ramp to the northbound side of I-45, an arrow-straight superhighway aimed directly at downtown Dallas. The skyline stuck out of the flat horizon like a growth of crystals in the middle of a petri dish.

Using the curve of the overpass to conceal my movement, I took a quick glance through the back window. Another charge of excitement tickled my chest when the Nissan took the ramp about thirty seconds behind us. Christmas and birthday together. A blue Pontiac from the mid-eighties lagged behind us, blocking the front grill of the black car.

"We need to find a place to take him," I said. "Get the jump on this guy and take him down."

"You're thinking like a lone Ranger again, little bro. You forget, I have lots and lots of police-type friends around here. We'll just have him pulled over."

"No," I snapped. "No, no, no. You pull the guy over for what? Speeding? What do we get from that?"

"His name and address. DL number. With that we get a criminal history."

"Yeah, true. But I want to look this guy in the eye and find out who he's workin' for."

"What are you gonna do when he says 'Fuck you'?" Matt flicked glances in the rearview mirror. I ached to get another look.

"You gonna beat the crap out of him?" Matt continued. "You want to, that's okay with me. I'll hold your coat. But think a minute, bro. Say you beat a confession out of him; you know you can't use the information in court. You're a Texas freakin' Ranger, for God's sake. You go pounding on a suspect, and they'll crucify you for sure."

My jaw clenched tight enough to snap a tooth. I really wanted to open that Christmas present in the Altima, and my big brother wasn't letting me.

"Let's get him pulled over," Matt said. "Then you can walk up to this guy and look him in the eye. Maybe you'll recognize him, and it's game over, right there."

"Fine." I hated when he turned reasonable and logical.

"What?"

"Fine, I said!"

"Okay, no need to shout."

Matt spoke to his Bluetooth again. "Call. Sandra."

I tuned him out as he talked to somebody in his office. The Dallas city limit was coming up fast. Getting this guy pulled over safely would be easier away from the maze of highways converging among the skyscrapers, and we were running out of space to do that.

Damp, clammy sweat plastered the back of my shirt. My heart rate had doubled in the last five minutes. Stopping this guy and finding out who he was might mean the end of this entire mystery. I could maybe get out from under the crushing weight poised above my head.

The Nissan remained locked about a quarter mile or less behind us. I turned sideways, like I was talking to Matt, and kept the trailing car in my peripheral vision. It made my eyeballs hurt.

Traffic thickened as we neared downtown. Interstate 45 ran through the middle of one of the poorest neighborhoods in Dallas. Metal reclamation plants, liquor stores, car lots, and trucking companies lined the sides of the road, all of them fenced in with concertina wire, including around their rooftops. Air conditioner theft prevention.

April Fortney had once lived not far from here.

"Here we go." Matt looked in the mirror.

Coming up fast from the south, a black-and-white Dallas County sheriff's car sliced through traffic, its LED light bar flickering red and blue, headlights flashing. He zoomed up behind the Nissan and squatted there.

"All right!"

The Altima signaled and moved to the shoulder of the highway, the deputy right on his bumper.

"Pull over, Matt."

My brother worked his way to the shoulder, stopped, and threw the big Ford in reverse. He twisted around, one arm over the back of the seat, and accelerated. We had traveled a good half mile past the Altima before we stopped, so Matt had to do a lot of backing.

Traffic blew past us, the pressure waves of big trucks buffeting the F-250 as Matt negotiated the shoulder.

From this distance, the deputy wasn't much bigger than a stick figure, but I could see him approaching the driver's side, one hand on his gun butt. As he reached the rear quarter panel, the black car shot away, tires churning. The deputy jumped back, an inch from being run over. The Altima smoked off the shoulder and onto the highway. Directly into traffic.

Cars smacked together, brakes screamed, and metal crunched with a series of dull thuds and tinkling glass. Demolition Derby in Big D. The black car punched it hard, going for liftoff. He avoided a crash by some miracle of physics. The vehicles behind him weren't so lucky. At least six cars crunched bumpers as they tried to avoid the maniac in the Altima.

"He's running! He's running!"

"I see it!" Matt skidded the big truck to a stop, slapped the shift lever into drive, and jammed his foot on the accelerator. The Nissan shot by us.

I snapped a look at the deputy, who'd made it back to his car door and was piling into the driver's seat. The Altima would be in Oklahoma before the deputy got his cruiser out of park.

"He's gettin' away," I shouted. "Move this piece of junk!"

"I've got it floored, goddamn it!"

Diesels weren't built for acceleration. The pickup had a massive engine, but it was geared for pulling, not speed. The Altima was almost out of sight before we hit sixty.

I pounded the dash, willing the truck to go faster. The once-distant skyline had grown to a forest of concrete and glass. Freeways converged and merged, and traffic flowed along the way traffic does, fast in some places, slow in others. The black car dodged and weaved through it all, finding gaps, cutting people off, and bullying other drivers into giving way. As the seconds clicked off, the gap widened.

"Goddamn it," I gritted. "He's getting away."

Matt had the Ford up to ninety, swaying between lanes like a pregnant hippo.

"It's like chasing a speedboat with the Titanic," I griped. "Remind me to never buy a fucking diesel pickup, ever."

Matt didn't respond, but his face grew as red as the hood of his truck.

The Nissan hit the entrance ramp to I-30 and had to tap his brakes to avoid rear-ending a beer truck, but a second later, it shot into a narrow gap and floored it, heading east. By the time we made the curve, he was gone. The deputy's squad car wailed past us, getting into the game late. Too late.

"Well, shit! That sucked." Matt brought the pickup down to a reasonable speed, and we stayed on I-30 all the way to Mesquite. Neither of us saw a black Nissan Altima for the rest of the drive.

Matt took the Galloway exit off I-30. His brick ranch-style in the suburbs looked a whole lot like DaShondra's, only in a better neighborhood, a few blocks off the freeway.

"Get down," he said before we turned onto his street. "In case there's any reporters hanging around."

I slunk below the dash and stayed there until Matt docked the rumbling diesel inside his garage. The overhead door clanked down, shutting us in the gloom.

My brother switched off the engine and looked at me. "One thing we know, Peanut."

I scowled, doing my best to burn him down to his shorts. "Great idea, pulling him over."

He just sat there and grinned, unfazed. "At least we know you're not just paranoid." A smile tugged the corners of his mouth. "They really *are* out to get you."

Tony & Danny

AT NINE THIRTY IN THE morning, the driver of the black Altima parked beside a nightclub on Greenville Avenue. In the light of day, the street showed the world an ugly face; the neighborhood needed the cover of night to hide its scars. Bars and restaurants that looked trendy and cool at night looked sad and worn out in the morning. He slid the window down and lit a cigarette. Holding it outside, he blew smoke into the sky.

"Like waking up next to a coyote-ugly girl, this place," the driver said to his partner. The Irish-whiskey sound of South Boston flavored his speech. "And would you look at these people? Vampires."

A scattering of young people with moppy hair and thrift-store clothes slouched along the street. They all seemed to have tattoos, piercings, and a fuzzy grip on reality.

"Hippies," his partner grunted, as if the word meant cancer.

"Asswipes, more like it. Save me from trendy asswipes."

"You're stallin'."

"Well, no shitski, I'm stallin'."

"I'm just saying, you gotta call him."

"I know I gotta call him. You're such a tough guy, you call him."

The driver's partner shrugged and looked out his window. "Not my job. You're the boss."

"So I'm the boss, as long as it suits you." The driver took another drag, keyed the speed dial on his phone with a thumb, and waited for the hello.

"Hey," the driver said. "It's me."

"Why are you calling? What's going on?"

"The cop made the tail."

Silence.

The driver took another hit on his butt and flicked it into the gutter. "We bailed out, but he knows we was on him. Or that somebody was. On him, I mean."

A sigh. Patience stretched to the limit. "Ditch the car. Wipe it down and leave it. Walk a couple of miles away before you call a cab. Come back here while I source another vehicle. You got all that?"

"I got it."

Dead air indicated no one was on the other line.

Source another vehicle? What the fuck does that mean? The driver pocketed the phone, looked at his partner and said, "He's pissed."

"Wouldn't you be?"

Chapter 14

"*Love is all fun and games until someone loses an eye or gets pregnant.*" — Jim Cole

Sam

Matt and I entered his house through the laundry room then the kitchen. A digital clock on the oven read 9:42 a.m. I checked it against my watch and found the clock was two minutes fast.

"Darla still teaching?" I asked.

"Substituting. With the baby comin' and all, she didn't want to take on a full-time assignment. She works about three days a week."

"She's close now, huh? To delivering?" I continued through the kitchen, past a small dining area and into the living room.

"Yep," Matt said. "Middle of May."

People called Darla "striking" instead of pretty. Strong cheekbones, laughing eyes, and what I guessed I would call a generous nose. Darla could have played an Amazon warrior on TV. After she got too big for barrel-racing, Darla was a hellraiser until she got drunk and drove her car into Lake Ray Hubbard on New Year's Eve two years ago.

On patrol in his black-and-white squad car the night it happened, Matt had witnessed Darla's Pathfinder go off the road. When he reached the spot where she hit the water, her taillights were going under. Matt dove into the frigid lake, pulled her out of the car, and gave her CPR until the paramedics arrived. Breath blowing white clouds, shivering with the cold, he worked on her for way longer than he should have before she coughed up a lungful of water and started breathing on her own. He'd told me later, the entire time he was doing chest compressions, hands clamped between her breasts, he kept thinking: "Man, it'd be a shame to lose a woman like this."

At the hospital the next day, he asked her out, and she said, "Well, you've already kissed me and felt me up. Least you can do is buy me dinner."

A year later, they were married.

I pulled the flash drive from my pocket and waggled it. "I need a computer with Outlook so I can read these emails."

"In the office." Scrolling through his cell phone, he didn't look up. "You know where it is. I want to call Pete, find out what he saw."

"Pete the guy who pulled the Nissan over?"

"Uh-huh. You want coffee?"

"Does a cat have a climbing gear?"

Matt and Darla's office was the smallest of three bedrooms. I'd slept on the futon in there last time I visited. The second-largest bedroom was well on the way toward becoming a nursery. Darla had sold off all the old furniture, including the queen bed, and started painting and redoing the room about six minutes after the test came back positive.

I fired up the computer and got to work. Going through somebody's email felt sort of like going through my mother's underwear drawer. It was creepy and turned up things I really didn't want to know. But people recorded the dumbest things in email. Reveal confidences, talk dirty, plan crimes. It never ceased to amaze me, the sheer volume of evidence people left behind in their email.

Sadly, Judge Fortney had exchanged a *lot* of email. And I couldn't read just the first email; I had to read through every email chain, some of them a mile long. Often, they referred to events, places, and people of whom I had no knowledge, making my comprehension less than total.

Matt brought a cup of coffee soon after I got started, but it went cold before I noticed.

He dragged me away from the screen at noon to eat. My eyes watered, and I had to blink a few times to refocus on the outside world. Politics and attorney speak rattled around my head in a convoluted knot of people, places, and events. I'd tried keeping a log of who was who but had given up after the third full page of notes.

Lunch was frozen pizza baked in the oven. Matt could do a lot of things, but cooking wasn't on the list. We ate at the kitchen table, and he brought me up to speed on what he'd learned from Pete.

"No go on the license plates," he said. "Stolen off a Dodge Neon from a San Antonio car dealership three days ago."

I bit off a chunk of pizza. "Shiah!" Mouth open, I waved my hand in front of my face. "Hah."

"Hot? Blow on it first, dummy. Anyway, Pete said two people in the car, probably male, but it was hard to tell. Heavy tinting, and the driver never rolled down his window. He said they transported three people from the car wrecks this asshole caused. One critical. A little boy, four years old. No car seat."

I stared at my plate and said a silent prayer for the child to be okay. That was another debt these people needed to pay. One for Fortney, one for me, and now one for a little boy whose life had changed forever, if not ended.

"Anything in the email?" Matt asked.

"Hmm? No, nothing." I waved a hand in front of my face. "I mean, not nothing, but more like too much of something. A thousand needles in that haystack, and I have no idea which one is the right one. I've barely made it back to the beginning of March. And that's just the email. No telling what's in the calendar."

We chewed in silence. The pizza cooled off enough to taste, which was unfortunate. At least it had a lot of saturated fat and calories.

"Hey, wait."

Matt looked up, a string of cheese hanging between his mouth and the slice in his hand. "Wha'?"

"You said the Neon's tags were stolen from a car dealership. Who do we know owns a bunch of dealerships? And is connected to the victim?"

Matt's eyes got big. "Duh."

"Can you find out which dealership?"

"On it." My brother wiped his hands on a paper towel and dug in his pocket for his phone. I listened to his side of the conversation and read the answer from his expression. He said thanks and hung up.

"No go, Peanut. The lot belongs to a local guy."

"Of course. Couldn't have been that easy, right?"

"Don't worry about it, baby brother. We'll figure this thing out, if we have to kick ass from here to the Gulf of Mexico. Ain't nobody whipped this pair of Cables since you were six years old. Back when those twelve dudes jumped us behind the school. Remember?"

"It was four dudes."

"Yeah, well. They were big."

Sam

I WAS BACK IN FRONT of the computer in the spare room when my borrowed cell phone rang. I answered, and without preamble, Agent Goldman said, "Hey, Lone Ranger, did you know Judge Fortney was busted for prostitution?"

"For what?"

"You know, being a prostitute? A person who sells sexual favors for money."

"I know what a prostitute is, but Fortney...?"

"Yeah, Fortney. Although when it happened, she wasn't a Fortney. She was a Barber."

"A barber? Like a hairstylist?"

Goldman sighed. "Keep up with me here, cowboy. I'll try to use small words. Her father's name was Martin Barber. Little girl April used her mom's name through school, then she disappeared for a few years, until she shows up in college, with no income, no job, and no tax returns. However, April *Barber* was busted outside an SOB in Dallas. SOB means sexually-oriented business, in case you didn't know. And before you ask, I looked it up; the club was owned by D-Max Entertainment, which owns a number of similar sexually orient-ed businesses in Dallas. That type of SOB would be known to you as a 'titty bar.' You with me so far?"

"Yes."

"Just making sure you're keeping up."

"Give me the details on the arrest."

"Well, first you gotta know, it's a sealed juvie record. I'm not even supposed to have it, so you can't say shit to nobody about nothing. We clear? Two, the case was never adjudicated. Looks like it just... fell through the cracks."

"How'd you get it?"

She paused, and I shifted the phone to my left side so I could write on my notepad. Matt's voice rumbled from somewhere in the house; he was on the phone, as well, from the sound of it.

"The FBI knows all, Kemo Sabe," Goldman said after the hesita-tion. "Now shut up and listen."

Goldman told me April Barber was picked up in front of a gen-tlemen's club for soliciting an undercover agent. Arrested with her was her "business manager," Damian Maxwell Ford, who had nego-tiated the terms of the act of oral sex Ms. Barber was contracted to perform. "So she got popped for a forty-dollar blow job in the park-ing lot of a strip club" was how Goldman summed it up.

"This is pretty big stuff," I said. "How come the news people haven't dug this out?"

"Well, first they'd have to find it, which wasn't easy. Then they'd have to get the record unsealed, which would take a court order. Not for nothing, but I put in the papers to get the records unsealed."

"Are you sure it's the same person?"

"Oh yeah. Booking photo matches, all the way down to the mole on her face. The report also states she danced at the club under the stage name April Showers."

I toyed with my pen, doodling on the pad where I'd written the details of the arrest. "This is good stuff, Goldman. I'm not sure if it helps me, since it was so long ago, but it's... interesting. What kind of determination does it take to go from an exotic dancer to a Senatorial candidate?"

"A lot," Goldman declared. "Not for nothing, but something like that, if it hit the papers... well, she could kiss politics goodbye. However..." She paused here for emphasis. "It doesn't explain how you got to be in her room. Maybe you found out about this and decided to get your kicks with her. I'm still not swallowing your Gary Cooper act. You could've killed her for real. I'm just not a hundred percent sure."

"Uh. Thanks?"

"You bet. Anytime. I'm going to hang up now because I don't want to know if you, say, decide you want to see this guy, Damian Ford, and follow up on this angle from the vic's past. Were you to do that, and they found out I told you to find him at D-Max Entertainment on Harry Hines Boulevard in Dallas, I could lose my job."

"Why *are* you telling me this?"

She hesitated again, and her voice turned serious. "My gut tells me this means something. I can't follow up because my boss is, like, breathing fire over me for looking at the vic instead of the killer. Which he thinks is you, by the way. And because, you know, I pulled in a favor to get the info on her record, so it's kind of illegal. If you find something that has bearing on this case, you get it to me, understand?"

It was my turn to hesitate.

"Understand?" she repeated.

"Yes." Goldman was putting her ass on the line. The least I could do was keep her in the loop. Eventually.

"Can your cell receive pictures?" she asked.

"Where'd you get this number, by the way?"

"I called your captain. Duh. Now, can I send you JPEGs, or not?"

"Uh, I think so."

"Technology is our friend, Cable. I'm gonna send Fortney's mug shot to your phone. You didn't get this from me, either."

She hung up, and I went to look for Matt.

Sam

"I *know* this Ford guy," Matt said. "He's a scrotum-sized pus bag. Runs girls and dope out of his clubs."

I showed him the picture on my phone of a younger version of April Maree Fortney-Barber. Shorter hair, tinted blond and styled in a pageboy cut, she stared at the lens with the sullen boredom typical of a thousand other mugshots.

"Damian Maxwell Ford," Matt said. "Goes by the name of D-Max. Keeps an office in a place called Skinny Dippers."

"Lovely. Goldman said Harry Hines Boulevard."

"That's the one." Matt stood and grinned. "You wanna go see Mr. Ford?"

"Yes. I do."

"Let's roll. Skinny Dippers is way the hell on the other side of town. Traffic will be a bitch."

I followed him to the garage. Something clicked, and a memory shook loose. "I remember her campaign literature said she worked her way through college waiting tables."

"Looks like she was slinging more than drinks." Off a hook in the laundry room, Matt grabbed a windbreaker that said Sheriff's Deputy in bold yellow letters on the back. "Maybe she was strippin' and hookin' her way through college."

"And when she gets busted, she uses her daddy's last name."

"One name for under-the-table hanky-panky and the other for legit stuff."

"Hanky-panky?"

"Law enforcement term. Being a baseball player, you wouldn't understand."

Chapter 15

"*Have you ever wondered if those dollar bills in your wallet were ever in a stripper's G-string?*" — Anonymous

Sam

Matt was wrong. Traffic wasn't a bitch. It was a double-bitch and a half. A wreck in a downtown tangle of interchanges forced us off the highway. We crept along side streets between the tall buildings down Main Street. Near the west side of town, Matt cut over a block and took the Commerce Street viaduct, passing what had once been the Texas School Book Depository.

"Always gives me a shiver," Matt said, "driving past the place where JFK got shot."

"You weren't even born when Kennedy got shot."

"Still."

"Idiot."

"Jackass."

Interstate 35 saved him from my witty comeback as he had to navigate the big diesel into a narrow slot between a Prius and a Mercedes-Benz at sixty-seven miles per hour. Matt took the Inwood Road exit, passing Parkland Memorial Hospital and turned left on Harry Hines. The businesses lining the road soon changed from hospitals to wholesalers, with signs in Spanish and Korean. Every block had a heavy sprinkling of nightclubs. We passed modeling studios, strip clubs, and a few adult DVD stores.

"Here we are," Matt announced, signaling and turning into a trash-strewn parking lot.

A dingy square building made of bricks painted flat brown sat in the middle of the lot. Skinny Dippers had a sign out front with changeable plastic letters, like the kind they once had on movie theaters. The top two lines read TUES NITE DINK SPECALS 2 FOR 1 WEL DRIKS NO COVR.

"Classy place."

"Hey," Matt said. "Don't knock it. We could get a real buzz on after twenty or so 'dink' specials."

Six cars shared the lot with Matt's steroidal pickup. At 3:42 p.m., Skinny Dippers had few customers. My chest vibrated with the thump of heavy rock and roll as we got close to the club's red door. Matt pulled the handle and gestured me in first, bowing like a doorman at a fancy resort. Cold air laced with beer and stale sweat, overlaid by an industrial cleaner smell, puffed into my face. A short hall led to an empty podium then cut left. Past the podium, behind the wall, the space opened onto the main club floor.

Only one of the three stages was lit and occupied. In the center of a pool of light, a striking blonde with iron-hard breasts leaned back from the stripper pole. Her hair touched the dance floor. Steppenwolf's "Magic Carpet Ride" throbbed from the million-watt speakers.

Four guys ringed the stage, spaced wide apart, nursing bottles of beer and watching the blonde do her limbo act.

"I'm already getting a headache!" Matt yelled in my ear.

I nodded and motioned toward the bar. At its far end, a hallway led toward the back of the building. A neon sign over the hall spelled OFFICE in red letters.

"Helpful," Matt said.

The bartender gave me an eyeful as I snaked my way through the tables. A black man big enough to bench-press a Volkswagen, he wore a tight maroon T-shirt over rock-hard muscles. His biceps bunched into footballs as he wiped out a glass with a rag.

I made sure he was properly intimidated by pushing my sport coat open enough so he could see the silver glint of my Ranger badge. He failed to dive under the bar. Maybe he was made of sterner stuff than I imagined.

"Hey," I shouted over the music. "D-Max here?"

The obsidian mountain stared back without answering. He stopped polishing the glass, though, so maybe I was making progress.

Matt came up to the bar next to me and clapped me on the shoulder. "Don't he remind you of something scary? What was that thing from *Lord of the Rings*? Wore black, rode ghost horses?"

"A Ringwraith?"

"That's it." To the bartender, Matt said, "You speak English or Elvish? Damian Ford. Where is he?"

The song ended, and a DJ—I think they cloned the same one for every strip club—came on to say, "Ashley, gentlemen, give it up for *Ash*-ley! Now on the main stage, the lovely and talented Karen! Let's hear it for *Karen!*"

"I'm Too Sexy" started pumping through the club.

The Nazgul behind the bar worked on his impression of a sneering statue. "You gotta warrant?"

"You hear that?" I asked Matt. "All I asked was where is Damian Ford, and this guy wants a warrant."

"I blame it on too much TV."

"Y'all funny as shit," the Nazgul rumbled. "Go fuck yo'selves. I don't gotta answer any your questions, Wonder Bread."

In any closed system, when too much pressure builds up without a release valve, an explosion was sure to follow. Inside my chest, something flared to life, and fire trickled through my bloodstream, swelling muscles, pressurizing my system. Every detail of the bar, the bartender, the glasses, and the bottles aligned into sharp focus. I breathed in a cleansing draft of fresh air, expanding my lungs and supplying my inner fire with enough oxygen to burn bright and hot. Blood thundered in my ears, and my face heated.

"Uh-oh." Matt must have sensed something, because he put a hand on my arm and said, "Whoa, brother. I've seen that look before. It comes on right before you lose it and start tearing shit up. Don't do it. You fuck up, it could be your badge."

"I'm cool, Matt. Don't worry." I picked up the barstool and threw it against the rows of liquor bottles behind the giant bartender. He ducked.

The enormous explosion of glass sent jagged, glittering shards showering over the barman, who covered his head with his arms. The music screeched to a halt, and the silence was jarring. Inside my chest, I held on to a tornado with a fraying rope.

Matt stepped back out of the way. "You know what Momma always said about that temper, Samuel."

"How much more trouble can I be in?" I said without looking at him.

"Okay, good point."

My rational brain flatlined.

Stinking of liquor and trailing glass, the bartender shouted, "You motherfuckah!" and vaulted over the bar at me. He planted a hand and cleared it with one jump.

Or he tried to. I punched him in the throat about halfway through his leap, turning a graceful, acrobatic move into a disaster. The Nazgul came down in a heap on my side of the bar, choking and gasping.

"I don't think he wants to fight no more, Sam."

"Too bad." Putting one knee in the giant's chest, I knelt into his sternum, grabbed the man's chin, and pulled his face around until he looked me in the eye. His were red-shot and panicked as he tried to breathe with two hundred and ten pounds kneeling on his chest.

I spoke loud and clear. "Where. Is. Damian?"

Another voice shouted from behind me, "I'm here, motherfucker. Who the fuck is you?"

At the end of the hallway stood a smaller version of the guy on the floor—better dressed, too, in pleated slacks, a trendy button-down shirt, and expensive shoes.

"You D-Max?" I asked.

"And I say again: Who the fuck is you?"

"Texas Ranger."

"Shee-it," he drawled. "Texas Ranger?"

I came off the Nazgul's chest, fists tightening into knotty clubs.

Matt grabbed my arm and jerked me back. "We just want to talk, D-Max. Don't we, Sam?"

I took a couple of deep breaths and blew them out. It was like letting steam pressure escape from an overloaded boiler.

"Yeah," I admitted when I could speak again. "Just talk." I held out my hands, fingers spread, to show everything was cool, and Matt let me go.

The front door squealed, and I flicked a glance over my shoulder. The last of the patrons had fled, and the place was deserted but for Karen. Leaning against the stripper pole, she stood in her G-string, arms crossed under her boobs. She looked annoyed.

Ford shook his head at the door closing behind his escaping customers and looked back to me. "Why the fuck not? It's not like I got anything else to do." To the guy on the floor, he said, "You gonna live, TJ?"

TJ coughed and wheezed, tears in his eyes. He nodded and scooted himself into a sitting position, his back against the bar.

"Well, clean up this mess then," Ford said. "It stinks like a Mexican toilet in here."

Ford looked at me. With a dark complexion and acne-scarred face, Ford was older than fifty, younger than sixty, with a frosting of gray at the temples. He had to look up to meet my eyes. "C'mon then, Big Tex, let's go have us a talk."

Ford's office reeked of pot smoke. Big as a medium-sized bedroom, painted yellow, with a wooden desk and a round card table, the office spared every expense on décor and fixtures. A shredder sat next to the table, a stack of loose papers on top. D-Max had been doing a little house cleaning. Ford claimed the only nice piece of furniture in the room, his chair behind the desk, and poured himself a glass of vodka topped off with cranberry juice.

"You all want some o' this?"

Matt and I said no. We snagged chairs from the card table, which was littered with partially consumed liquor bottles and a collection of sticky glasses.

"So then..." D-Max's eyes flicked to the shredder then back to me. "Whyn't y'all get to the point, and then we can discuss how you gonna pay for my inventory you done fucked up."

"Yeah, good luck with that," Matt said.

I settled my chair in front of his desk and leaned forward, blocking his view of the shredder. "Let's talk about April Barber."

"Who?" He took a sip of his drink, looking away from me.

"Also known as April Fortney. The judge. One of the underage girls you turned out, back in the day."

Ford leaned back in his chair and steepled his fingers in front of his lips, trying out a thoughtful look.

"April Barber... April Barber..." He rocked while he mused, his chair creaking slightly. Ford shook his head. "No, can't say as I remember no April Barber."

"First dumb thing you've said, D-Max. You should have gone with 'Yeah, I remember her, but I haven't seen her in a long time.' That would have played better."

"Huh?" D-Max didn't seem to be the brightest bulb on the circuit.

"Maybe he remembers her stage name," Matt said. He sat behind me, at the card table. "April Showers."

"How about it, D-Max? Ring a bell now?"

He nodded slowly, tipped forward in his chair, and reached for his drink. "Yeah, come to think of it, I do remember her. But it's been a long time. Since I seen her, I mean."

"Tell me what you remember," I said. "From a long time ago."

"What's to tell?" He shrugged and sipped on his drink. "She a dancer. Dime a dozen."

"She turn tricks on the side?"

"Some do. Some don't. How'm I suppose keep track?"

"You pimp for her?"

Ford leaned back again, chair creaking. Papers rustled from behind me, where Matt had claimed a seat. "'Pimp' is a harsh word, Big Tex. I sometimes might help a lady with her business, but I don't be a pimp—" Ford snapped out of his seat. "Hey, watchu doin' back there? You can't be goin' through that stuff. That's personal."

"Well, lookie here." Matt held a sheet of paper in one hand and flapped it around like it was hot. "You been to the Hyatt in San Antonio in the last few days, D-Max?"

"Nah, man, that's not me." Ford came around the desk, but I stepped in front of him, and he bounced off my chest.

"Who was it then?" I asked.

"A friend o' mine, y'know. Yo," he said around me, looking at Matt. "Y'all got a warrant and shit?"

"Don't need a warrant for things I observe in plain sight," Matt told him, digging through the papers atop the shredder one at a time. He came up with a wrinkled scrap. "Like this. Parking receipt for the Hyatt where Mrs. April Fortney was found dead. And on the night she died, as well."

"The fuck you say? I didn't kill no April nobody." He took a good look at my face. "Fact is, you the one capped her off. I saw you on the news."

I picked up Ford by the collar of his fancy shirt and planted him against the wall. "Here it is, you little dipshit. I ain't playin' cop right now. I'm being framed for that woman's murder, so I got nothing to lose. I'll turn you into a grease spot and never look back. Now tell me what you were doing in that hotel."

Ford made a choking noise, and his face twisted up.

Matt said, "I don't think he can talk. You might want to ease up, just a tad."

I let Ford drop. "Talk."

He sat on the floor by his desk and held out one hand in a wait-a-minute gesture.

When Ford kept silent longer than I thought he needed, I cocked one foot back, setting up practice field goal kicks on his stomach.

"Wait, wait, wait!" Ford held out both hands, palms up. "I was just... just reacquaintin' myself with April, y'know. Seein' an old friend."

"She know you were coming?"

"Sure, she know." His face took on a sly look. "I been seein' her off an' on for years."

"Seeing her?" Matt asked. "You mean sexual relations?"

Ford rocked his head from side to side. "Yeah, maybe like that."

"You're telling me you've been having an affair with April Fortney for years." The stockings and panties came to mind. *Could he be telling the truth about an affair? Why else would she get dressed up in lingerie?*

"This relationship," Matt said. "Did she have a choice, or did you threaten to expose her if she didn't go along?"

Good question.

Ford's eyes shifted, as if seeking an answer from the corners of the room. "April, see, she always had an... an affectionate nature toward me, y'know? She couldn't let on, on account of her being married and all, but she still had a thing for me. She always made time for D-Max."

"She made time whether she wanted to or not," I said. "What else were you blackmailing her for? Money? She was a judge; maybe you used that?"

"Hah!" He sneered. "I don't need blackmail to get what I want."

"She stop paying you?" Matt asked. "That why you killed her?"

"I didn't kill nobody, I'm tellin' you." He looked more defiant, nostrils flared. Ford got to his feet. "Yeah, I went to see her, but she never answered the knock on her door, so I left and shit, y'know?"

"What time?"

"'Bout twelve-twenny, twelve-thirty."

"In the morning?"

Ford nodded. He found his office chair and sat back down, looking much older than before.

"You know, there are cameras all over the hotel. If you went there, you'll be on tape."

"Check it, man," Ford said. "I was there for five minutes, tops."

I made a mental note to call Dusty. He and Kent should have reviewed all the tapes by now. If Ford had visited, Dusty would know. Matt and I went through the questions again with Ford and got nothing else.

"What do you think, Matt? We have enough to arrest this piece of shit?"

Matt scratched his jaw and looked thoughtful. "I don't think that'd be wise, little brother. Best leave it to your pals doing the investigation. If he was there, he'll be on the tapes, right? But still"—he held up the papers in his hand—"we'll hold on to these for the time being."

Damian Maxwell Ford was a pimp, a strip club owner, and probably a blackmailer. I had my doubts he was bright enough to arrange a scene as complex as the one in Fortney's room, though.

"Look at me, Ford," I said. When I had his full attention, I leaned both hands on the desk and put my nose a few inches from his. My voice went *Godfather* quiet. "If I find out you lied to me here, I'll come back one night. Should that happen, you will not walk upright again. We clear?"

Ford's eyes narrowed, and some of his fire came back. A little fear, too. He moved his chin in a microscopic nod.

As we were on our way out, Karen danced to "Simply Irresistible," working her hips for three new customers clustered around the main stage. Her eyes were focused in the middle distance, and she swayed completely out of time to the music. Her audience didn't seem to mind at all.

The bartender, TJ, leaned on a mop behind the door as we passed and said nothing.

"Hey, Ringwraith," Matt quipped, "how'd it feel to get your ass kicked by my hobbit brother?"

"Shut up, Matt," I told him.

"What? What'd I say?"

"Nobody likes a wraith-baiter."

Chapter 16

"*There's no great, white bigot; there's just about two hundred million little white bigots out there.*" — Julianne Malveaux, *USA Today* columnist, author, and economist

Rita

Rita tracked down Richard K. Dennison III—aka Trey Dennison, aka April Fortney's campaign manager—at a yuppie sports bar a couple of blocks off the River Walk in downtown San Antonio. The noise inside the club registered on seismic monitors in California. A dozen different sporting events flickered on TVs spotted along the walls and hanging from the ceiling. Dark paneling gave the place a cave-like feel.

A Danny DeVito lookalike stuffed in a white dress shirt and a blue-striped tie, Dennison had a table in an alcove near the bar. Two younger guys in rough clothes sat across from him, expressions frozen in boredom. Dennison waved a long-neck beer to illustrate a point in the story he was laying on the two guys, neither of whom seemed to care.

"Hey, look, Agent Goldman of the FBI!" Dennison shouted when Rita reached the table and flashed her creds. Sweeping a hand at the two guys with him, Dennison said, "Agent Goldman, I'd like you to meet my associates, Tyler and Snake. This is Tyler, and this is Snake."

The one called Tyler raised an eyebrow and straightened up, not bothering to offer a handshake. Rita estimated him at six feet and a bit. He had hard, dark eyes, rough skin, and scruffy hair. She cataloged a razor-wire tattoo circling his bicep and another curl of ink peeking from his collar. And he was the nice-looking one.

"If he's Tyler," Rita said to the bald guy next to him, "you must be Snake."

With a forehead ridged in scar tissue and prominent brows, Snake would scare spiders. *Drop him in the ocean,* Rita thought, *and he'd be a natural shark repellent.* Snake's biceps challenged the cuffs of his polo shirt. A tattoo of a cobra coiled up from his forearm, its hooded head spread across the man's bicep, baring its fangs. Snake leered at her with crooked teeth.

"You wanna know why they call me Snake?" He waggled his eyebrows. "I can show you."

"Will I need a magnifying glass?"

Snake's brow ridge collapsed, and a muscle twitched in his jaw. He oozed off his barstool and faced Rita square-on, looming over her. Glasses clinked, and conversation hummed. People laughed and shouted in the background. Normal bar noise. Oblivious and involved in their own lives.

Rita was used to being the shortest person in the room, but the guy towering over her would have given Ranger Cable a run for his money. Snake was a killer, hard and true. She could read it in his eyes—anger had wiped away the leer. Her foot twitched, and she ached to step back and give herself room. Instead, Rita willed herself to be still and let her hand creep toward the holster on her hip. *What the fuck were the academy shooting drills again? Sweep the coat back, grab the butt firmly. Draw, aim, fire. Breathe. Don't forget to breathe.*

She was too close. She would never clear the holster before Snake twisted her head off. Heart thudding, she held her stance and lifted her chin. She locked eyes with the thug, and she froze, a mouse caught in the eyes of a predatory owl. Or snake, in this case. Rita held her ground, more from locked-up muscles than bravado. Her skin felt ice cold in the air-conditioned room.

The man named Tyler laughed and joined his partner, slapping him on the back. "She got you that time, buddy, and you deserved it. Hey, let's roll on outta here. Leave these two to their business."

"Sure." Snake remained rooted in place for two long seconds. He smirked and showed his pumpkin grin. His voice had a rusted-metal scratchiness, and his teeth were gray with rot. "Till next time, Miss FBI Lady."

Tyler and Snake plowed through the crowd, the average citizens parting unconsciously, like bait fish giving way to a pair of sharks swimming past.

Rita tried to swallow, cleared her throat, and tried again.

"Who were those two charmers?" she asked Dennison.

"Those guys?" Dennison shrugged. "Who knows? We were just having a beer. Watching golf." He jerked a thumb at the TV nearest the table, where somebody in silly pants and a white cap teed off. The camera focused on blue sky, following the ball. Rita lost interest a half-second later. Her insides were shaking, and she wanted a drink.

"What can I do for you?" Dennison asked.

Rita took the chair vacated by the Neanderthal, Tyler. She tucked her hands under the table to hide the shakes. For the first time since... ever, really... she'd come up against someone who had scared the absolute living shit out of her. If Snake had decided to kill her with his bare hands, he would have done it. She had been utterly defenseless, and there was not a thing she liked about that thought, at all. Rita took a deep breath and replayed Dennison's words in her mind. *Wahkinn-I-do-for-uzz?*

"Jersey?" she asked. "Brunswick, maybe."

"Close. Trenton."

"Hey, practically neighbors here. Bronx."

"I thought so. You miss it?"

"Every day I'm in this hell hole."

"Hah! Me, too." Dennison signaled the waitress with his empty beer bottle. When she came, Rita ordered a vodka martini. "Make it a double."

"What is it about this place?" Dennison waved a hand, encompassing everyone in the bar and the State of Texas. "A bunch of hillbilly, gun-totin' Bible-thumper dumbfucks. And the Mexicans? Shit, history lied. It says we took this state away from them. Little brown fuckers are everywhere."

The Hispanic waitress set their drinks on the table and gave Dennison a glassy professional smile. "Will that be all?"

"Yeah, sure." Dennison waved her away and faced Rita. "So talk to me. You wanted something else? I thought you and Woods got everything outta me you wanted the other day."

"Tell me about April Fortney."

"What's to tell?" Dennison shrugged and sipped his beer. "A chip on her shoulder, on account of being black and all. A good candidate. Articulate. Smart. Charming when she wanted to be, but behind closed doors... whoo-wee."

"Hard to get along with?"

"Grade-A bitch. Probably why Cable killed her. Couldn't take any more of her bullshit."

"What kind of bullshit?"

"She had him do petty stuff, you know? Step 'n' fetch. Or try to. Gotta say one thing for Cable—big dumb hick that he is, he don't take shit from nobody. Said he was there to stop a fucking bullet, not play butler. Cable don't swear much, him being a good Christian boy and all that, but April could make Jesus wanna choke a puppy."

"What else? Any chance they were having an affair?"

Dennison snorted in the middle of swallowing, choked up, and pounded his chest with a fist. "Are you kidding me? Nah, no way. They'd have to be the two greatest actors since Liz Taylor and Dick

Burton. But, you know, stranger things have happened, so I suppose anything's possible."

"What about racism?" Rita took a microscopic sip of her martini then took another right after. "You ever get the feeling Cable hated blacks?"

"Hah! Don't all these Southern hillbillies hate blacks?" Dennison knocked back more beer, tipping the bottle all the way up.

"Anything in particular stand out? Remarks?"

"Nah, nothing specific. But you could tell he hated her ass, big time. You gotta unnerstan, April made her bones as an anti-essab... anti-es-tab-lish-ment type." Dennison appeared to be one beer over his speaking limit. His speech had taken on that overly precise cadence of the nearly drunk. "Whitey be holdin' us down. The man keeping his foot on de black folk. Like that. She was always baitin' on Cable 'bout that shit. It's no wonder he snapped." Dennison touched the side of his nose with one finger. "Boy's got a bit of a temper, right? We all saw that, the time he took down the three retards in... what the fuck town was that? Jackson? Jacksonville? Jackstown? Guys with cream pies, and he fuckin' levels 'em. Don't let that movie-star face fool you, honey. Texas Ranger Cable has a temper on him."

"Video shows you getting off on the fourteenth floor, about the time of the murder."

"I already explained that to Woods. I went straight to my room. Didn't see nothin'." Dennison craned his head around. "Where's that damn waitress?"

"Went right to bed, huh?"

"Exactly. Slept like a baby. Never had a problem fallin' asleep; I think it's 'cause of my clear conscience."

"A political consultant with a conscience," Rita said. "Go figure."

Sam

DARLA WAS HOME WHEN my brother and I made it back from seeing Damian Ford. The adrenaline high from confronting both the Nazgul and his boss had drained away, and my feet were dragging as I followed Matt in through the kitchen door. We found Darla browning some ground beef in a skillet; the smell triggered instant hunger pangs. She looked up and blew a strand of hair off her face.

"Sam, it's been too long." We hugged, and I felt better, just like that. Darla had that way with people. People liked her automatically—they couldn't help it—and Darla liked them right back. She held me at arm's length and looked me up and down. "And look how skinny you are."

"Or maybe you just got bigger in comparison. Look at you! Are you carrying a football team in there?"

"Hah! No shit. It feels like it." She grimaced and held a hand to her stomach. "Oh. And somebody just kicked a field goal."

Pregnant women made me uncomfortable. I never knew what to do with them. But not Darla. I was always at ease around her. Maybe being an uncle had something to do with it. We made small talk for a bit, but she could tell I was anxious to get back to searching Fortney's email.

"Gimme the keys to your Taurus," Matt said. "We'll go fetch it here and bring you your stuff. You need anything while we're out?"

"A speed reader. Fortney wrote or received about a hundred emails a day. I'm still working through February."

Darla gave me a sympathetic look. "Find anything yet?"

I frowned and shook my head.

"Don't worry, Sam." She smiled and patted my shoulder. "You'll get the son of a bitch. You're too damn stubborn not to."

"C'mon, darlin'," Matt said. "Let's go get Sam's stuff, pick up some KFC on the way back. Save that beef for tomorrow."

"Oh, honey, you do know how to sweet talk a girl, don't ya? Let me change shoes, and I'm all yours."

In the spare room, I fired up the computer and booted the email program. Matt and Darla's voices echoed through the house as they got ready to leave. Happy. Enjoying each other, the way a married couple should. The garage door rumbled open, and I didn't hear them anymore. Maybe someday I would find my own Darla. Tall, blond, blue-eyed, and built like Wonder Woman—that was the kind of girl I wanted to hook up with.

If I didn't find out who killed April Maree Fortney, my dream date would likely be Bubba in Cell Block Nine of the Huntsville Unit of the Texas Department of Corrections.

I opened the next email in line, from DaShondra to Fortney, titled: "Hernandez v Able Remodeling, Continuance Request."

Chapter 17

"*The Lord does not look at the things people look at. People look at the outward appearance, but the Lord looks at the heart.*"
— First Samuel 16:7b

Rita

"Here's a question for you." Rita tasted her martini and positioned the glass on the table in front of her. The alcohol infused her nerves with enough calm to keep her hands steady. "Why did April Fortney have a bodyguard at all? Doesn't the Secret Service do that?"

Trey Dennison had a fresh beer and a plate of hot wings in front of him. His fingers were stained orange. He swirled a wing in ranch dressing and conveyed it to his mouth, dripping a trail of white dots across his plate.

"For presidential candidates, yeah." Dennison sucked his orange-stained fingers and wiped them on a greasy napkin. "Everybody else hires their own security. Fortney was threatened by some whack jobs early on, on account of her being black and all." The campaign manager shrugged. "It wasn't much, but we made a big deal out of it; get some free publicity, you know? End of the day, we leaned on the governor, who gave up a Ranger."

"And you got Cable."

"And we got Cable." Dennison attacked another wing. "We got a lot of mileage out of it," he said while chewing, "on TV a couple of months back. Surprised you didn't see it."

"I don't watch much TV."

"April liked it at first, having a big white boy around to take a bullet for her. She started needling him right away, too. Like I said, it's no surprise he snapped."

Rita let a dribble of her drink pass her lips, enjoying the burn of the liquor on her tongue. She'd skipped lunch, and if she gave in to the desire to suck the glass dry, they would have to carry her out of the bar. She studied Dennison systematically demolishing the plate of wings.

"So what's next for you? Now that you're out of a job."

"Me?" Dennison pointed at himself with a bare chicken bone. "I'll go clean up the office, you know? There's still a butt-load of paperwork to do—get everybody paid, close up the real estate, refund the donations that haven't been spent. Like that. Then I'm on to my next gig." Dennison grinned. "Politics never sleeps, baby."

"Who gets the leftover money?"

The campaign manager wiped his hands. "Back to the donors or to whoever takes over for Fortney. Not my call. Look, I gotta take a piss, all right? Are we done here?"

"Yeah, we're done," Rita said. "But leave word where I can find you. You have my card."

"Count on it, sister." Dennison clapped her on the shoulder and waddled toward the restroom sign. Rita grimaced and blotted her shoulder with a clean napkin. Orange wing sauce on her Michael Kors jacket—that right there was a hate crime.

Sam

AFTER DARLA AND MATT came home from picking up my car, we dug into buckets of chicken, mashed potatoes, and coleslaw around the kitchen table. Shiner Bock beer for me and Matt, a ginger ale for Darla. After dinner, I helped by doing the dishes, which amounted to throwing away all the paper sacks and boxes.

"People go nuts over this race issue," my brother said in response to his wife's comment about the racial tension surrounding Fortney's death. "There's no bulletproof position you can take. I don't care what color you are. There's too much history to overcome. Whites hating blacks, blacks hating Mexicans, Mexicans hating Chinese, Arabs hating every-fucking-body."

"Don't forget the Jews," Darla said, her eyes still closed.

"Yeah, Arabs hate them, too."

"I hear you." I leaned back and rubbed my eyes. "I can't remember Mom or Dad telling even a Polish joke, can you? It wasn't their way. But you remember the two of us, today. Comparing that bartender to a demon from Lord of Rings. Cracking jokes."

"C'mon, dude. That wasn't even close to racist."

"Not by intent, maybe."

"Damn, Peanut. You ain't nowhere near a racist." Matt reached over and rubbed Darla's tummy. "Though I have a confession. If this little tyke turns out to be a girl, and in seventeen years, she comes home with her prom date... and he's black..." Matt sighed. "I hate to admit it, but I'm not gonna feel right about that. I don't like it when I see it now. Interracial couples."

"Because of the kids?"

"No, the kids are pretty much accepted nowadays. I just don't like it. Something inside is turned off by it. I try not to let it affect me, but who knows how much really comes out in how I act?"

"Honey, I know you," Darla said. "If this little girl comes home with anyone who's not a eunuch or Jesus Christ himself, you're gonna have a problem."

"True," Matt admitted with a nod. "Although Jesus better have her home by ten, or there'll be hell to pay."

"What if her prom date is another girl?" she suggested.

My brother groaned and cradled his head in his hands.

Sam

THE CLOCK IN THE CORNER of the computer screen read 11:20 pm. I stared at a bright computer monitor and read email until my eyes felt like bleeding. Darla and Matt had long since gone to bed, and the house was quiet. I took a break to scan some of the news sites and see what was going on in the world. CNN was reporting about me.

"The husband of the late Senate candidate April Fortney, Jawn Fortney, will be holding a rally in Dallas this Thursday to drum up support for his bid to replace his deceased wife on the November ballot.

"Texas election law allows the state's Democrat Party leadership to nominate a replacement candidate when a nominated candidate withdraws or passes away before the general election.

"The rally, to be held at the Cotton Bowl, in Dallas's Fair Park, will be open to the public. Former Presidential candidate Jeremiah Thompson has agreed to appear in a show of support, and the Reverend Cliff Morton is said to be considering an appearance, as well.

"Mr. Fortney has been highly critical of the San Antonio Police Department's handling of the investigation into his wife's murder..."

I clicked over to Fox News and watched a video of a popular radio and TV commentator.

"The rush to judgment here is just incredible. Nobody knows what happened in that motel room. Nobody knows anything. Why is everybody set to crucify this Texas Ranger when the facts haven't even been established?"

"I'm with you, buddy," I muttered. "You're a great American."

Click. Yahoo headline: "Was Race an Issue in the Death of April Fortney?"

I didn't bother following the link to the article. Instead, I went to the Dallas Morning News site. The lead story? April Maree Fortney's last days. I shut down the browser and fought the urge to throw the monitor across the room. After that, I tried my luck at Fortney's calendar by making a list of all the people she'd met with in the past few months. It was a long list. I sighed and stretched, shaking out my hand to relieve the kinks.

I had summarized my notes from earlier and organized the names into columns: Friends, Donors, Politicians, Judicial Matters—though I used the technical term "Judge Stuff"—and Hate Mail. Very few blank pages remained on the legal pad. My head swam with names, dates, and possible connections, but nobody leaped off the page and said, "I killed her! Come arrest me!"

The air conditioner kicked on, and cool air blew from the vent. Tomorrow, I would have to start making sense of all the data. Maybe take down some of the pictures here in the spare room and build a case board on one wall. Darla would skin me alive if I put thumbtack holes in her walls, so I needed some tape. And some string to draw connections. Or buy a big whiteboard and dry erase markers—

A bullet cracked through the left-hand window. It smacked into the opposite wall. A dozen more shots shattered the window, smashing out the glass. I dove for the floor.

Hammer blows of automatic weapons-fire battered the brick wall between the two front windows, then the shooter reached the second window, to my right. The window blew out in a cascade of glass, and more rounds pelted the wall. A fine dusting of white powder drifted through the room as the slugs punched holes in the sheetrock. The shooter rattled off what sounded like a thirty-round mag on full rock and roll, peppering the front of the house from left to right. Tires squealed, and a vehicle accelerated with a roar.

I low-crawled into the hall until I was clear of the room. Going out the front would have been suicide, so I ran for the back door. I paused in the kitchen. The attackers might be trying to drive me into a trap by shooting up the front of the house while a shooter hid in the back.

Time for Plan B. The garage had a door leading to the side yard. If I slipped out that way, maybe I could avoid getting shot to hell. My .45 was in my hand. I didn't remember drawing it. Adrenaline sang in my bloodstream. My vision tunneled down, and I tasted copper on the back of my tongue.

The gunfire had ceased by the time I slammed through the kitchen and into the garage. Cars, lawn tools, and other junk filled the garage. It was as dark as six feet up a dead man's ass. I banged into unseen objects on my way around the front of the cars. The clatter of objects falling off shelves and smacking off the concrete floor sounded like a bull in a cymbal factory.

"Well, *that* was stealthy," I growled.

A chain hook and a deadbolt secured the small door on the side of the garage. I slid the chain back and turned the deadbolt. The door opened outward. I rotated the knob and eased the door open with maximum gentleness, wide enough to peer through the crack. A sidewalk ran alongside the outer garage wall. To my left, the street. To my right, a chain-link fence and gate leading to the backyard. Dogs were going insane around the neighborhood. In minutes, neighbors would be poking their heads out, potentially exposed to stray bullets. Seconds ticked away while I eyeballed the slice of open space through the door. Nothing moved.

"Screw this," I muttered, gritted my teeth, and pushed through the door, low and fast, sweeping my blind spot behind me before moving toward the street.

Nothing out front. Nothing out back. A trace of burned rubber and gun smoke drifted in the air, settling to the ground. A breeze ruffled my shirt. I peered over the top of my Kimber's night sights, tracking left to right and back left, peering into every shadow and gap, looking for a hidden shooter. I checked my blindside periodically in case a trigger-happy killer was sneaking over the fence. But the shooters were gone.

"Sam! Sam!" Matt was yelling from inside the house. He sounded scared. I realized with a chill: his and Darla's bedroom was on the front of the house.

"Out here," I sang out, taking a chance I was really alone. Nobody fired at my voice, so I slipped back to the garage and maneuvered through the clutter. I kicked something in the dark, and it rattled across the floor.

"Sam?" Matt called from deep in the house, somewhere down the main hall. His voice had taken on a note of fear that I'd never heard from my big brother. Ever. "C'mere, man, I need your help."

I found Matt in his bedroom. He had a wad of towels pressed to Darla's head. Blood stained the pillow and the sheets around where she lay. My insides turned hollow, and I lost the ability to speak or move. Curtains drifted in the breeze from the shot-out window.

Matt's eyes were haunted and glassy. "Sam, I need to keep pressure here. Call it in. Call 9-1-1."

Under the towel, Darla was pale. Not moving.

Chapter 18

"*The fundamental cause of the trouble is that in the modern world, the stupid are cocksure while the intelligent are full of doubts.*" — Bertrand Russell

Sam

"Get off me, jackass." Darla's voice, weak and scratchy, buzzed through me like an electric current. Matt looked even stupider than I felt, pressing a towel to her head, his mouth hanging open.

I froze with my index finger poised over the cordless phone. "You're all right?"

"No. This ox is crushing me," she mumbled, pushing away Matt's hand.

"Damn, Darla," Matt said. "You're bleeding like a stuck hog."

"No pig jokes, got it?" Darla sounded more coherent.

"Sorry." He looked at me and mouthed, *What do I do now?*

I shrugged and finished dialing 9-1-1. My finger only trembled a little.

"Honey," Darla said, as if coaxing a child to eat his green beans. "Just ease up a bit there, would you please? You're gonna give me a concussion, you keep on like that."

"Oh. Sorry. That better?"

Matt pulled the towel back from the wound on Darla's forehead, and I leaned over for a closer look. A deep cut about an inch above her eyebrows welled thick red blood until Matt pressed the towel back down. Gently this time.

"Nine-one-one. What's your emergency?" The dispatcher's voice in my ear caught me by surprise.

"Uh, drive-by shooting at..." I struggled for a second to remember Matt's address then rattled it off. "One victim, female, with a head wound. Be advised the victim is eight months pregnant."

"And nine kinds of pissed," Darla growled.

Sam

"THE DOC SAID IT'S A scalp wound from flying glass," Matt told me. We stood in the emergency room waiting area of the Dallas Regional Medical Center. Matt had ridden in the ambulance with Darla when they transported her. I'd stayed behind to deal with the responding officers. After they took a report, I'd used Matt's truck—with an escort by the Mesquite PD—and drove to the hospital. The Sheriff's Department had stationed an officer at the house.

"They think she passed out when she tried to get up too fast."

The hospital doors whooshed open, and a Mesquite patrol officer came in, radio squawking. The guy was the tallest, skinniest cop I'd ever seen. The Ichabod Crane of cops. He leaned his chin into the microphone on his shoulder. "Ten-four," he said then turned the volume down.

"Hey, Matt," he said. On a basketball team, Matt and I could play forward, and this guy would be our center. His plastic nametag read Hutchinson.

"You have to be Matt's brother," Hutchinson said, shaking my hand.

"Guilty."

"That's what the TV people say about you."

Ouch.

"What's up, Carl?" Matt's eyes were two red marbles in dark sockets. I glanced at my watch: 1:32 a.m. The only other people in the waiting room were a family of six Hispanics with a croupy child.

The poor kid wheezed into another coughing fit while three other kids in mismatched clothing played in a corner.

"Good news, man. We caught the guys that hit your house. Dog walker saw the drive-by and called it in. Make, model, and license. Dallas PD spotted the car on I-30, inbound to Dallas. They tried to rabbit, but about a thousand cops came down on 'em like a ton of bricks."

"So who was it?" Matt and I spoke in stereo.

"Couple of homies." Hutchinson took out a can of Skoal and tamped it against his palm. A tobacco craving hit my lip so hard, I nearly snatched the can away. My hand twitched, and I put it in my pocket. He pinched a two-finger dip and slid it into his mouth. My eyes followed the can all the way back into his pocket. I swallowed and dug out my chewing gum.

"One's named Theodore Jefferson Wilson. He was the shooter. Biggest sumbitch you ever seen, too. He had to have two mommas, birth a boy that size."

Matt and I exchanged a look. "TJ," I said. The bartender from Skinny Dippers. "Was the other guy named Ford?"

Hutchinson nodded with his lips scrunched up and looked for a place to spit. He settled on a trash can by the door.

Did I look that disgusting when I spit? Good thing I don't chew tobacco anymore.

"Where are they now?" Matt stood taller and seemed more alive. "I'd like to have a chat with 'em."

"Can't," Hutchinson said, not without sympathy. "They're in Sterret. You try to see them ol' boys, and fourteen video cameras will capture every moment."

"Heh. Don't you know, it's us sheriff's deputies that run the jail," Matt said.

I put a hand on my brother's shoulder. "Man, I'm sorry. This is my fault. I hadn't a gone after those guys, this wouldn't have happened."

Matt swatted me in the belly with a gentle backhand. "Don't be a dumbass. This is their fault, not yours. Look at it this way: D-Max overreacted and tried taking you out. Maybe he'll confess to Fortney's murder, and all your problems are solved."

"Yeah. And maybe the Maserati Fairy will come tonight and leave me a present in the driveway."

"Shit, boy." Matt wrapped an arm around my neck in a rough hug. "This is Texas. We only got Pickup Truck Fairies here. It's open season year-round on them foreign fairies."

Sam

WEDNESDAY MORNING, just before eight thirty, the ringtone of my borrowed cell woke me after two hours of sleep.

"Yah," I mumbled.

"Sam? It's me. Dusty."

"Yeah, go ahead." I rubbed my eyes and sat up on the sofa in Matt's living room, wearing nothing but my boxers and a stupid expression.

"You sleepin' in this mornin'? For a guy under the gun, you don't seem to have no sense of urgentness."

"Late night." I told him about the shooting. "Matt's still at the hospital with Darla. They wanted to keep her overnight for observation, since she passed out and all."

"Man, you for sure got a black cloud followin' your ass, don't you?"

I grunted.

"You got a computer? I got a couple of pictures I want to send you."

"Uh, yeah. Wait a minute."

"Give me your email address and call me back when you get it."

After giving him the address, I disconnected.

Shards of broken glass glittered on the floor of the spare room. Warm air billowed the torn curtains. I peeked outside. The sheriff's deputy stationed in front of the house sat in his car, sipping coffee. The thought of coffee triggered a powerful need on the back of my tongue. I turned on the PC, thankful it had escaped unharmed, and wandered into the kitchen to find the coffee-making stuff. When the Mr. Coffee started trickling, I went back to the computer and checked on its boot up.

Multitasking, they call it.

I sat in front of the PC and navigated into my Gmail account. Dusty's pictures were there, two JPEGs, which I saved onto the hard disk before opening them. When I saw them, I frowned and had to go back to the kitchen for my phone.

"Boots," Dusty said when he answered.

"I've seen these guys," I told him.

"Who are they?"

"I can't remember their names, but they showed up at campaign headquarters a while back. Came in with somebody else who took a meeting with Fortney."

"Well, you ain't the only one can't remember their names. Nobody can tell us who they are."

The pictures were still shots from a ceiling-mounted CCTV camera surveillance recording. Two white guys, maybe late thirties or early forties, with dark hair, wearing casual clothes. Unremarkable as hotel wallpaper. They were getting off an elevator at the San Antonio Hyatt. The time stamp said 23:42, April 7.

Dusty said, "They got off the elevator on the fourteenth floor about ten minutes after you did. Problem is, they didn't have a room on that floor. Hell, we can't find where they had a room anywhere in the hotel."

"So where'd they come from?" I said it more to myself than anything, but Dusty answered.

"Damn good question, *compadre.* Dennison don't know 'em. That Martin woman says she don't know 'em, though she looks like she wouldn't piss on a man if his pants was afire. And you don't know 'em?"

"I remember seeing them come around the campaign headquarters, but that's about all."

"What about when you went to your room? Anything coming back to you?"

"No, nothing. I think maybe I get a flicker now and again, but it could be just wishful thinking. How long were our mystery men on the fourteenth floor?"

"The camera gets 'em back on the elevator at fourteen minutes after midnight."

Thirty minutes, give or take. Long enough? "Okay," I said. "This is good. At least it's a lead, something to go on."

"Pretty slim, but we're on it."

"I'll run these by the campaign HQ here in Dallas, see if anybody knows these ol' boys."

There was a pause while I listened to Dusty think.

"You sure you want to do that, Sam? Why don't you let one of us handle it?"

"I need to move on this thing, Dusty. I can't just sit around and wait for it to come to me."

"Bad idea, hoss. You go in there and start stompin' around, the captain'll rip your gonads off with a pair of Channellocks."

"Yeah..." Sweat prickled my skin from the warmth of the room. It was a muggy spring day, and the air conditioner couldn't keep up with the broken windows. "You may be right. Anything on Damian Ford?"

"His story checks out. He was there, all right. Five minutes, tops. Not enough time to do the deed and set up the scene."

"Damn. I really wanted it to be him."

"Would've made all our lives easier, for sure."

"Thanks, buddy." I ended the call and stared at the phone in my hand.

I still had one Fortney resource I could count on. DaShondra. She'd helped me once. Would she do it again?

Sam

"YEAH, I SEEN THEM BEFORE," DaShondra said, studying the printouts.

I took another sip of ultra-sweet tea and worked at keeping the grimace off my face. Baby wound around my ankles and left long strands of yellow hair on my jeans. I put my hand down, and he butted his head into it. The cat weighed twenty pounds, at least.

"Where?" I asked. "Where did you see them?"

"They came in with a man to see April, time to time." DaShondra pushed back in her recliner and shot the footrest out with a ratcheting noise. The gray tabby, Brutus, jumped up on the arm of the chair and humped his back up for a rub. DaShondra wore a print housedress with a pair of pink fuzzy slippers, tattered and gray around the edges. "This man come in one day, had these two with him."

"How long ago was this, D?"

DaShondra tipped her head back and looked at a spot on the ceiling. "Oh, let me think, now."

The TV was on but muted. On *The Price is Right,* people jumped up and down and yelled without sound. Baby left me and found a spot of sunlight on the carpet, where he rolled up and transformed into a pillow-sized fuzzball.

"The last time was right after you came on. It must've been January?" She made it sound more of a question than a statement. "I remember it being cold outside. Mr. Hull, he brought these two with him."

"Hull?"

She nodded. "They all went in April's office, right past my desk, and closed the door. Didn't say anything to me, you know?"

"Who's Mr. Hull?"

DaShondra shook her head. "No idea. I never did know. April made those appointments herself. Told me it was nothin' to worry about." Brutus purred in her lap, closing his eyes in ecstasy while DaShondra rubbed his head. "They only came in once in a while, you know? Wasn't like all regular. Truth be told, they pretty much stopped coming round, about a month or so ago."

"Huh." I nodded again. So two mystery men show up with a guy named Hull and waltz in to see Fortney. Later, they appear on a security tape in the Hyatt, on the fourteenth floor, with no reason to be there, the night she was murdered.

"Did April seem happy to see this Mr. Hull?"

"I don't really think so, but I paid it no mind, really." DaShondra reached for her tea glass, ice clinking. A drop of condensation fell on Brutus, and he jumped out of the chair, looking offended. "Oh, I'm sorry, little man," DaShondra cooed at the tabby, who ignored her while he cleaned his side. "You want some more tea, Sam?"

"No, thank you, D. I'll be fine."

"What'd you ask me again?"

"Was April happy to see Hull? How'd she act?"

"Now that I think about it, when they last come in, back in January?"

"Uh-huh."

"Well, after Mr. Hull left, she shut the door and didn't come out all day. Didn't take calls. I don't think she said two words to me that day."

"You remember seeing these guys that last night in San Antonio? At the Hyatt?"

DaShondra shook her head. "Nah, not a bit, Sam. I'm sorry. I was so tired that night, the Lord Christ his own self could've walked right by, and I wouldn't've known it."

"They fill out any paperwork? Anything that would list their real names?"

"Nah, nothing like that." DaShondra focused on the ceiling again and shook her head. "I can't think of a thing."

"What can you tell me about Damian Ford?"

DaShondra's eyes shifted to the carpet, and for the first time since I'd known her, she lied to me. "I don't know that name." She picked at some cat fur in her lap, pinched it up, and let it fall to the floor. "I can't tell you nothin' about that."

"I talked to Ford, D. I know he was having an affair with her."

The big woman's eyes welled up, and her lip trembled. She sighed long enough, I thought she might deflate right then and there.

"It wasn't no *affair*," she said after a time. The last word, she spat out like it tasted bad. The rest poured out of DaShondra in a bitter stream. "He'd call up when he wanted some, you know? And she'd drop what she was doing and go meet him. Get all dressed up in Victoria's Secrets and stuff. April, she'd have a look in her eye, like the cat ate the canary. I don't know what she saw in him, but he say, 'Jump,' and she say, 'Frog.'"

"Did her husband know?"

She shrugged. "Who knows what he knew? They were fighting all the time. Could be about that. Maybe he didn't like being second there, too."

"Seems to me he's taking her death pretty much to heart."

She made a push-away gesture with both hands and snorted. "Forgive me, Lord, I don't believe that for a second. I don't believe there was any love left in that marriage."

"Did you know Ford was going to see April in San Antonio?"

"Nah, I didn't know about that." This time, I got the impression she was telling the truth.

"Well, it was worth a shot." I dusted the cat fur off my pants and stood up to go.

DaShondra levered herself out of her recliner with a grunt. "You think they killed her, Sam? Hull and them?"

"I don't know, darlin'. Something I aim to find out."

She held up the prints of the unknown men from the hotel security camera. "You mind I keep these pictures? Maybe I'll remember something if I keep seeing they faces."

"No problem," I told her.

DaShondra hugged me and said, "You find 'em, Sam. If they did that to my April, you find 'em, and Lord help me if I don't mind if they resist arrest, you know?"

"Me neither, D. Me neither."

Sam

GRAY CLOUDS BLANKETED the sky, and the thick humidity made it hard to breathe. Starting the engine to get the A/C blowing, I poked at the radio in Matt's prized Mustang GT-350, looking for a news and weather station. Maybe the forecast would be for a nice cool spell. I got the news before the weather came on.

JC Fortney was giving a speech somewhere, and I came in on the middle of the sound bite.

"*—and that's why I seek to replace my wife on the November ballot. The people of color in the State of Texas have had enough good ol' boy justice, and our voice will not be silenced.*"

The silky baritone of the station's news jockey came on: "*And that from Jawn Calvin Fortney, husband of the late Senate candidate April Fortney, allegedly murdered in San Antonio—*"

"No, dipshit," I said. "She was for real murdered. It was already ruled a homicide. 'Allegedly' would apply to me."

"*—and now that the Senate Minority Leader has endorsed Mr. Fortney's candidacy, it seems all but a foregone conclusion that the State Democratic Party will appoint him as a replacement for his wife's nomination.*"

"No way," I said and jabbed the off button and rubbed my itchy, tired eyes.

Once, when I was ten, a storm came up on the farm while Mom and Dad were in town. Luke was off seeing a girl. Little John and Matt were playing Stratego and threatened me with dismemberment if I bothered them again. On my own, with nothing better to do, I thought it'd be fun to watch the storm from the roof of the barn. The *tin* roof of the barn. In a lightning-filled thunderstorm.

I reached the loft and shimmied out onto the ledge in front. Wind gusted and tried to tear me off. Heart pounding, I edged my way along the front of the barn, a dozen feet or more above the yard, then climbed the steep slope in one rush. I made it to the peak, straddling it. I would never forget the smell of rain and the tingle of ozone in the air. It looked like God was putting on a show, just for me, accompanied by wind and fireworks and fat, heavy raindrops

The folks came home about the time the worst of the rain hit. I waved to them like a maniac, happy and grinning about being out in the rain, on the barn roof. The water sheeted down in an almost solid mass. Lightning stabbed the ground, and thunder shook the air. It was all very fierce and exciting... until Dad spotted me. He bellowed at me, "You get your stupid ass down off the roof! What's wrong with you, boy? Do you want to get killed by lightning?" His voice was loud enough to overcome thunder, rain, wind, and probably God himself.

After my whipping, he said, "Son, there's times a really stupid idea seems like a good 'un at first. You gotta examine that there idea from all sides and figger out the consequences afore you go and commit to it."

Sitting in Matt's GT-350, feeling the engine idle in a direct connection between my butt and my testosterone output, I had an idea I was pretty sure was stupid. I examined the idea from all sides and couldn't find a way it didn't seem dumb. *Too bad I never did learn to come in out of the rain.*

Chapter 19

"*Politics have no relation to morals.*" — Niccolo Machiavelli

Rita

Rita Goldman punched out a number on her office phone and pinched the handset with a shoulder when it started ringing. It was the middle of the day, and a combination of too much coffee and the lunchtime hungries was making her edgy. She wiggled the mouse wheel up and down, making her screen jump, while she waited. The LexisNexis article on the monitor twitched, blurring the headline. *Injunction Against Millennium Metals Fails.*

"FBI, Martinez. Can I help you?"

"Marty, it's me, Goldman."

"Me Goldman? Don't know her. I know a *Rita* Goldman. Kind of a spiteful little shrew of a woman. Nice shoes, though."

"Funny guy. Listen to me. Do you still work Public Corruption there in Dallas?"

"A full-time job, baby."

"You ever sniff anything about Judge April Fortney?"

"Ah, the woman killed by that deputy sheriff, right?"

"Texas Ranger," Rita corrected. "But yeah, that one."

"Nothing. She was squeaky clean, far as I could tell. Nobody ever filed a complaint, and I never heard a peep on the grapevine."

"What about this Millennium Metals deal? Did that seem strange to you?"

"Millennium...? Remind me, what was Millennium Metals?"

"A metal recovery and recycling plant in South Dallas. Judge Fortney ruled against the Citizens for a Clean City when they filed for an injunction to get Millennium Metals to cease operation. The plant was getting a lot of bad press for dumping toxic crap into the air and water."

Martinez's shrug was almost audible. "So what?"

"One, the evidence against Millennium is... substantial. Two, Judge Fortney ruled against Millennium four years ago when a similar injunction was filed. And three, the Clean City people signed a petition of three hundred names, all constituents and potential voters of Mrs. Fortney, against the plant's continued operation. And finally, in her record, I can't find a thing showing a similar ruling. All her campaign literature makes a big deal out of her being an environmental crusader, you know? It seems weird she'd flip." Rita ladled on her Bronx accent for effect. "And I'm not a lawyah, but the injunction looks irawn-clad. Ya know what I'm sayin'?"

"Well," Martinez said with a yawn, "nothing tripped a flag here. Nobody ratted her out. If she received something to favor the company, it never came across my desk. Which says not a lot. I only see about one percent of the graft in my jurisdiction, and I've got two full-time jobs keeping up with *that.*"

Rita snorted. "Job security, right?"

"Hah-hah! Touché, Goldman. Later."

Rita dropped the handset back in the cradle. Her office chair creaked—it had a tiny squeak that needed oiling, and one day, she would blast the whole thing with WD-40—and clasped her hands behind her head. Whitlach would be pissed if he knew she was still digging into Fortney's past. Both of the Fortneys. She'd ordered up a number of records on the judge and her husband.

Why? she asked herself again. *Why can't I get on the program with everybody else?* Was it the cowboy's blue eyes and broad shoulders? She didn't think so. He-men hulks and cowboys of all stripes were definitely not her type. It wasn't her ovarian tubes tying her in knots. No, something didn't smell right about the pat case handed to everybody on this one. So while everybody else focused on Ranger Cable, pursuing other angles seemed appropriate. And besides, what else would she be doing? Looking over Detective Woods's shoulder?

Bleh.

That Fortney had pulled herself away from a life of prostitution, put herself through law school, and basically turned her life around... It showed a lot of guts. Rita admired guts. Somebody needed to pay for taking away Fortney's life—the right somebody. If a ghost from her past—or her present—had reached out and taken her down, the only way for Rita to find that evil spirit would be through a forensic dive into the couple's finances.

Rita clicked her screen over to Fortney's financial documents. She keyed in the first search term—"Millennium Metals"—and looked for a hit.

Nothing.

Not that it would ever be that easy.

So who owns Millennium Metals? Rita quirked her lips, frowning. She navigated to the Dallas County Clerk's office to search business name filings. If somebody at Millennium had paid the judge for quashing that injunction, maybe they'd donated to her campaign under a personal name. *Does Millennium Metals have anything—anything at all—to do with why Judge Fortney wound up dead in a hotel room?* Rita shrugged to herself. *Who knows? But it's weird.*

In her mom's voice, she said, "And if there's one thing I hate, it's weird."

Sam

I TOOK THE BECKLEY exit off I-45, not far from the Dallas Zoo, and rumbled north toward Jefferson Avenue. The contrast between DaShondra's middle-class suburban neighborhood and Jefferson Avenue was dramatic. Auto shops and *taquerías*, coin laundries and *supermercados* lined the street. Every third business was closed. Even the churches had eight-foot-tall iron fences. Dogs ran feral, and rheumy-eyed cats slunk between buildings. My Special Ops brother, Luke, had operated in and around Mosul, Iraq, in the last two years before he died. He sent me some pictures once, to give me an idea of the conditions there. The place was paradise compared to Jefferson Avenue.

The Mustang seemed sad to leave the freeway, and its throaty purr begged me to hit the accelerator, but I held it back. Getting pulled over for hot-rodding would be severely sucktastic.

I stopped for a red light at Jefferson and Tyler. A midnight-blue Chevy Impala with narrow tires banded around huge rims idled up beside me. Thumping bass from the car's stereo system buzzed my windows and sent homicidal twitches from my spine to my brain stem. The Impala's window tinting was dark enough to use for a welding helmet. It did nothing to dampen the sound waves pulsing from the inside.

How could somebody enjoy listening to a booming arrhythmic noise? And why do I feel guilty for assuming a black person is driving the car? Profiling? Or a logical deduction based on past experience? Nevertheless, in the duration of the red light, I played a mental fantasy where I jumped out and shot the Impala's speakers, swapped mags, and shot them some more. I doused the car in gas and set it on fire. I shoved it, *Thelma and Louise*-style, off a cliff and watched it go *thump-thump-thump-splat*.

The light changed, and I hit the gas too hard. The tires squalled, and the rear end tried to fishtail. To get away from the guy in the Impala, who had to be laughing at me, I turned right at the next light and rounded the block.

JC Fortney kept a business office in the back room of one of his dealerships, Rocket Motors, from which he ran his automotive empire. Except for rare occasions, I'd never known him to be anywhere else. For the four months I'd traveled with April Fortney, three times she'd had a dinner or lunch where she wanted her husband present. Each time, we stopped at Rocket Motors to pick him up. Once, we had to wait while he changed into a tux in the office bathroom. The place always reminded me of the Island of Misfit Cars.

The sun burned away the clouds. Stunning, bright beams reflected from chrome and glass. Cars sported slogans in yellow shoe polish, things like "Zero Down" or "Lo Miles." In similar bold letters, the office glass read *Habla Español* on one window, No Bad Credit on the other. When I cut into the lot and parked the Mustang in an open spot near the door, a skinny kid in a white shirt and narrow tie hurried to greet me. Maybe he thought I wanted to trade the GT for a 1999 Toyota Celica—"Gas Saver!"—parked next to me. When I flashed my star, the kid made a U-turn and found something interesting to do on the other side of the lot.

The air conditioning inside the Rocket Motors office was stuck on frigid. It was so cold, my breath should have fogged. Glass-walled cubicles took up the majority of floor space beyond the foyer. In one cube, a Hispanic couple hunched forward on their chairs and listened to a pitch in liquid Spanish from a sharp-dressed Latino male. Two more tie-wearers shot the bull in another cube, tilted back in identical poses, hands clasped behind their heads. I waved them down when they saw me and started to move.

A single central hall led through the middle of the cube-maze to a T-junction. JC's office was to the left, the last office on the left. I heard him before I saw him.

"I don't care what that pencil-dicked son of a bitch said!" JC's baritone rolled down the hall with the force of a tent preacher. He had a clarity and tone that made people want to stop and listen, just for the melody.

"No," he said as I reached the T-junction, "there's only one word needs to form on that man's lips. That word is yes. Got that? Good, you call him and tell him I said that. Tell him he doesn't want me for an enemy. Tell him—" He noticed me standing in the doorway. "I'll call you back," he said and hung up.

I nodded my chin at the phone. "Somebody else you want to burn in effigy?"

To my right, Fortney's pal Martine Boudreaux brooded in the corner. At six-four, with no place left on his body to add muscle, Martine brooded well. He could be a professional brooder. I'd asked once what he did, and JC had told me, "He does stuff for me."

"The fuck are you doin' here?" Martine demanded.

"Martine, old buddy. Long time, no see. Let's do lunch sometime. Have your people call mine."

"You think you a funny, mothafuckah?"

"No, but at least I ain't JC Fortney's dick-holder."

Martine took a second to process what I'd said. He shoved out of his chair, smoke drifting from his nostrils.

"Martine!" JC's heavy voice boomed off the walls. "Sit the fuck down."

The big man sank back into his chair, and I relaxed my fists. A little.

JC studied me with a pair of the lightest green eyes I'd ever seen in a face as dark as his. Tight rows of braided hair dangled around his collar. A black suit, maroon shirt, and solid-black tie gave him a gangster look. "Sam Cable. Of all the people in the world, I did not expect to see you."

"Two things I wanted to get cleared up, JC. One, I did not kill your wife. Two, stop stirring people up. It's not doing anybody any good."

The leather creaked when JC leaned back in his chair. A clock on the desk ticked away seven seconds before he responded.

"That's where you're wrong, Sam Cable. Have you seen the latest polls? I'm a dead heat with the strongest Republican, and it's still seven months till the election. The primaries are just a few days away, and the GOP will put up their usual carbon-copy candidate to run against me. You seen their slate of candidates? As to the other thing..." Leaning forward, Fortney opened a brown box on his desk, took out a cigar, and started the ritual of lighting it while he spoke.

"As to you killing my wife," he said, firing the tip of the cigar with a miniature torch. "You speak as though"—*puff-puff*—"as though you think I give a shit."

"You don't care who killed your wife?"

"No, not that. I just don't give a shit about"—he made air quotes, the cigar making jiggly white smoke trails—"your confession of innocence."

"It's not a confession; it's a statement of fact."

JC waved his hand in the air like a priest giving benediction, cutting through a layer of cigar smoke. "You don't need to convince me, Sam Cable. It's a jury you need to convince."

"Did you know she was having an affair?"

JC's green eyes narrowed, but he didn't speak.

"Did you know she used to dance at strip clubs?" I continued.

Behind the mask JC wore, a rapid calculation took place. Knowing JC, he was running two differential equations at once, factoring in all the consequences before speaking. He was smarter than me in that regard.

"Just like white folk everywhere, Martine," he said with a grin, while keeping his eyes on mine. "The nigger done good, got above her station, so the man, he got to tear her down. Call her a whore and shit."

Martine laughed. "Amen to that."

I placed both fists on the desk and leaned over. Low and quiet, I said, "So that's how you want to play it? Throw the race card down early and often, is that it?" I needed to shake him up. He was too composed, too calculating. What would rattle loose if he got mad? I took a deep breath and added, "Remember this: I never called her a whore. I just said she worked at strip clubs. How did you know she turned tricks? Were you a client?"

The amusement drained from JC's face like I'd opened a tap. "I think you need to leave, Texas Ranger Sam Cable, afore we embarrass you by throwing you out."

"Why'd you kill her, JC?"

"Fuck you, Cable."

"Was it because you found out she was a teenage hooker? Or was it because you caught her screwing her pimp?"

Martine popped out of his chair and slugged me a good lick in the kidney. The sucker punch sent a shockwave through my back and damn near paralyzed me for life.

I spun with the grace of a zombie and managed to get both arms up. I blocked an overhand right, followed by a jackhammer left cross. Zings of pain radiated down my back and turned my legs to jelly. Martine pummeled me. My arms and ribs took a raw-meat pounding. The only thing holding me up was my butt propped on JC's desk.

Martine zipped his right fist in low and hard, a hook to the side of my body, with no finesse but lots of power. When he did, he left his face wide open. I moved with the shot, took it in the short ribs, jabbed with my left. Three sharp, quick blows to the nose flattened it like a dropped tomato. A good smack in the nose hurts like hell, makes a man's eyes water and backs him right the hell up. Martine reeled and tried to cover, which was when I found enough strength in my legs to plant a side kick into his shin. It cracked like a green stick.

Martine shrieked and went to one knee. "Ow, shit, mothafuck-ah! That fuckin' hurts."

"I sure hope so." It came out more of a gasp than a sentence. I sucked in a lungful of air and looked Martine in the eye. "You get up off this floor... and I'll put you down for good. You hear me?"

He must have believed me, because he nodded and settled to the floor, glaring poison, rocking back and forth with his leg pulled up against his body.

I looked back at the man behind the desk. "This ain't over, bro. It's gonna come out, what she was, what she used to do. It's gotten too big now."

JC stared at me as if I'd crapped on his carpet. He didn't say anything.

I shoved Martine aside and walked away, making two right turns and hitting the glass doors. The heat outside felt like a mother's embrace, and I welcomed it. My back ached, and I had a strong need to take a leak. In the morning, my arms would be a pretty shade of yellow and purple. I winced when I got into the car and twisted my ribs. My whole left side felt like it had been hit by a cannonball. Buckling the seat belt was real fun.

"So, Sam," I said to the rearview mirror. "What did we just accomplish?"

The answer: A whole bunch of nothing.

Speaking of April Fortney to her husband in the way I had was not my best moment, but stirring the pot was never pretty. My goal had been to look Fortney in the eye when I told him about his wife. The results were inconclusive, partly because his attack dog had jumped me at the critical moment. By the time Martine went down, whatever natural reaction Fortney might have had was gone, replaced by his used-car-dealer mask.

So now what?

The San Antonio PD wanted me in jail. Damian Ford wanted me dead. A person or persons unknown wanted me hanged for murder. And now, I had stirred up JC Fortney and his pet mouth breather. Even my own mother was pissed at me.

I put on my sunglasses and fired up the Mustang. "Not a bad week's work, you ask me."

Chapter 20

"*It always seemed to me that a man who would betray the trust of his fellow citizens is the lowest of all.*" — Louis L'Amour, *Lando*

Sam

I found a Chili's Bar & Grill in Mesquite and asked for a booth near the window. A chubby waiter in a red shirt and black jeans brought me iced tea, took my order, and left. My stomach growled, and I tried to placate it with tea.

I laid out the photos of Tom and Dick, mystery men from the planet Who-The-Hell-Are-You. I had noticed these guys at the Fortney campaign HQ. It was a passing look, kind of an eye-lock followed by a polite nod, then I moved on to something else. Wished now I'd paid more attention. Tom was a white male, approximately six feet, dark hair buzzed short. The man called Dick was blond-haired, blue-eyed. A real Iowa Cornhusker type with that Midwestern look of open-faced, happy-to-meet-you cheeriness about him. Both were well-built, athletic-looking men in their mid- to late twenties. They wouldn't look out of place on a professional sports team...or in uniform, come to think about it. Ex-soldiers? Mercenaries? According to DaShondra, these two guys came into the campaign headquarters in early January, following another guy who looked to be the boss. They dropped by from time to time and did nothing while the boss visited with April Fortney. Nobody knew who they were, except presumably Fortney herself. Then they show up in the Hyatt the night Fortney is killed. Suspicious, but meaningless without knowing who they were. Maybe I could find Moriah again and ask *her*. "Better yet," I muttered, "have Dusty talk to her."

If April was into something juicy, chances were Moriah had a hand under the bowl to catch any drips.

"Sir?"

The waiter stood there with my hamburger and a confused look. A college-aged guy with black hair and a moon face. He reminded me of that kid in the Harry Potter movie, the one who played Harry's mean cousin. His nametag said Tyler.

"Nothing, sorry. Here, let me move these and you can set that here."

"Are you a cop?" Tyler asked, looking at the badge on my chest.

"Texas Ranger. And before you ask, no, I don't play baseball."

His brow furrowed. I'd confused the poor kid.

"Texas Department of Public Safety," I clarified. "State Troopers."

"Oh," he said. He made no move to leave. "Are these bad guys?"

"I don't know about that." I sounded more abrupt than I intended, so I softened up. "Could be a couple of Imperial Storm Troopers disguised as accountants."

"What?"

"Nothing." I shook my head. So much for trying to relate to the next generation. The scent of fresh cooked beef and hot fries made my mouth water. "Don't mind me."

Tyler squeezed out a waiter's professional smile and escaped to the kitchen.

I dove into the hamburger.

Next on the agenda: find out who Tom and Dick were in real life, and who they worked for. *For whom they worked*, Agent Goldman's grammar-cop voice rattled in my head. What if Moriah doesn't talk to Dusty? Or lies and says she doesn't know these guys? I snagged a pinch of fries and popped them into the ketchup, then my mouth.

Have to cross that bridge after I burn it.

Tyler, the waiter, whizzed by my table, using the *no-look* technique to ignore me in case I wanted something. I think they teach that at waiter school. My borrowed phone buzzed and chattered alongside my plate. It was Matt.

"How's Darla?" I asked.

"She has a splittin' headache, which she can't take nothing for, on account of the baby. So right now, she's meaner than a skilletful of rattlesnakes," Matt said. "Thanks for askin'. Now listen up. D-Max and TJ made bail and bonded out."

"What? When?" I put down my handful of burger.

"An hour ago. My buddies working the jail said a big money attorney showed up in court, argued down the bail and got 'em released on fifty grand each."

"And they paid that?"

"Lawyer brought in a cashier's check an hour after the bond was set, got 'em both kicked out."

"Where'd two lowlifes like that get a hundred K?"

"No idea. And how'd they get a lawyer like Henry Simpson Blake? That's the question."

"Who's he?" I asked.

"Blake's one of the top criminal defense attorneys in the city. He don't work for shitass little strip club owners. If you're the richest man alive and you get thrown in jail for showin' your pee-pee at the playground, then Blake *might* take your case. Assuming you delivered a Brink's truck full of cash to his office as a retainer."

"So, yeah," I said. "I guess that *is* a good question." I thought about that for a bit. No revelation hit me. Where would Damian Maxwell Ford have come up with the juice to hire a top gun attorney?

"Hey, Matt?" I said. Better get it over with. "Something else."

"Hmm?"

"I went to see JC Fortney in his office today."

There was a silence on the line. The kind of silence between the final tick of the timer and the bomb's explosion.

"You. Did. What?" Matt's voice was deadly low. He sounded about the same as when I told him I'd blown up his G.I. Joe action figure with a firecracker. "Tell me you did not do that."

"Yeah, I did. I wanted to shake him up. I also needed to look him in the eye when I asked him if he'd killed his wife."

"Jesus, Sam." Matt sighed. "Just like always. You go straight at something until it breaks. Or until it breaks you."

"You know what they say: No stoppin' a man who knows he's right and keeps a-comin'."

"Louis L'Amour."

"Remember how we read all his books as kids?"

"Yeah, but some of us didn't take 'em as the gospel truth. So what happened? Did he confess?"

"No such luck, but hey, I want you to do something for me."

"Tell me." It said a lot about him that Matt didn't hesitate. He was still ready to help, no matter that I'd nearly gotten his pregnant wife killed.

"Run Martine Boudreaux through the system, find out what you can about him. He's been JC's pit bull for years. Does his dirty work."

"Good idea," he said. He even sounded like he meant it. "Take me about ten minutes. I'll call you back."

I shouldn't be hungry, given that the two guys who'd shot at me and my family were out of jail and on the loose, but somehow, heartburn or not, my stomach didn't get the message. I finished my lunch, down to the last crispy, burnt French fry. My watch said it was twenty minutes away from two in the afternoon. Plenty of time to make it back across town and see if D-Max was back in his office at Skinny Dippers. I wanted to find out how he managed to get Henry Simpson Blake, Esquire, to come bail his scum-sucking ass out of jail. That connection was too glaringly out of place to ignore.

I didn't tell Matt where I was going. He'd want to go with me. One, he was in deep enough already, and two, I didn't want him to have to lie later if he witnessed anything he might have to testify about.

Tyler brought me the bill—somehow they can always tell when you're done, but not when you want something—and I paid it. Even left him a decent tip. As I got up to leave, Tyler gave me the waiter smile again.

"Have a nice day," he said.

"That'll depend on the cooperation of others, Tyler."

Rita

RITA GOLDMAN TRACKED down the head of Citizens for a Clean City, Reese Anderson, at his job with the U. S. Post Office Bulk Mail Facility in Dallas. She called the main switchboard and poked numbers to navigate the automated system until she could get to an operator, who transferred her to Anderson's extension. Where she left a voicemail. Hanging up, she gathered her things to leave for lunch. Two steps away from her cube, her phone rang, and surprise, surprise, it was Reese Anderson, calling back.

"That was fast," she said.

"Not ever' day you get a call from the FBI," Reese told her. He had a scratchy, deep voice, with overtones of molasses and corn whiskey and all the things she associated with the South. "What can I do for you?"

"Talk to me about the Millennium Metals case, Mr. Anderson." Rita sat back at her chair and grabbed a pen from the keeper, pulled a pad close. "What happened there?"

"Heh." Reese sighed. "Where to start, that's the question."

"Give me the thirty-thousand-foot view first."

"Millennium Metals is an ecological disaster. They dump chemicals, lead, all kind of poisons...acid and whatnot, into the sewer and into the ground. The whole place is soaked with toxic waste, Agent Goldman. It was closed for years until some new fellers bought it cheap and opened for business last year or so."

"So then what happened?" Rita asked when Anderson paused.

"A few of us livin' in the neighborhood got together and started protesting. Went to the City Council. Went to the EPA. Nothing much seemed to happen, so we formed up a Political Action Committee and hired us a lawyer. Actually, Hiram took on the case for a dollar, as his momma lives two blocks from the plant."

"And this attorney filed the injunction?"

"That's right. Went to court in front of Judge Fortney. God rest her soul. We all figured we had it in the bag. I mean Judge Fortney, she come from that part of town. Still lives not too far away, and she been politicking with the same people wanted the plant closed. Hell, she knows half of 'em on a first-name basis."

"But she ruled against you. That surprise you?"

"Sure did. Surprised the bejeesus out of me. All of us."

"She ever say why?"

"No, she clammed up tight. Wouldn't say 'boo' to nobody. Just went and hid back in her chambers and kept everybody away, you know what I'm saying?"

"So you never did find out why she ruled the way she did?"

"Never. That manager of Millennium Metals, he just sat there with his big-time lawyer, like a cat that ate a cream-filled canary. Never wanted to smack a brother in the face as much as I did him."

"Who was this?" Rita asked, scrawling notes. "This manager?"

"Little two-bit piece a sh—crap named Damian Ford. Calls himself D-Max."

Sam

BY TWO P.M. THE SUN had burned holes in the cloud cover and shot beams of light straight to the ground. The Mustang's heavy engine rumbled happily as I zipped along an almost traffic-free Interstate 30 toward downtown Dallas. I drove on autopilot, the hamster wheels in my head spinning with more questions than answers. How could a man like Damian Ford leverage a high-roller attorney like this Blake guy? It's not like Blake would leave his card tacked up on the bulletin board down at the jail. That type of lawyer only takes clients by referral. Or, they do it pro bono, for the publicity. But Ford was no Rodney King, or OJ Simpson. His trial would barely raise a blip on page twelve of the paper.

Simple answer: Ford was doin' the nasty with an influential judge. Maybe he came into contact with Blake through April Fortney. No, that made no sense. Fortney and Ford kept their thing a secret; it's not like they'd go to cocktail parties together. I could picture April Fortney going through the reception line: "Hi, I'm Judge April Fortney, and this is my former pimp and current lover, D-Max. Say hi to the Congressman, D-Max."

I snorted. Unlikely.

"Dang," I swore as my cell phone buzzed in my front pocket. I had to do a gymnastic contortion to dig it out before it quit buzzing.

"Hey," Matt said when I answered. "You're gonna love this."

"Talk to me."

"You asked about Martine?"

"Duh."

"Well, I ran him like you said. He's one of those folks came from New Orleans after Katrina. Moved here and never left. Well, apparently down in the Big Easy, Martine got himself into some trouble with the law."

"Stop teasing me," I said. "Spit it out."

"Mr. Martine Boudreaux was arrested in 1999 for sexual assault, and again in 2002 for the same crime."

"Okay," I said, drawing it out. "And so?"

"Well, I dug a little further, which is why it took me so long. The victim in each case claimed Boudreaux drugged them while at a club, took them back to their place, stole all their money and then raped them."

"Date rape? As in using a date rape drug?"

"Exactly."

"Incredible. What kind?"

"GHB."

I realized I'd taken my foot off the gas and had drifted down to under fifty. I goosed it up to freeway speed before I responded.

"GHB? I showed marginally high for GHB on my blood work."

"I know. Ain't that interesting?"

So now I had two stops to make. One, I had to get the answer to Damian's connection to Blake, whether he wanted to give it up or not, then I needed to go see Martine and find out if he was still playing around with GHB.

"Thanks, Matt. I gotta run something down. Go take care of Darla, and I'll call you when I get somewhere with this."

"Don't do anything stupid."

"Who? Me?"

"I mean it, Peanut. You don't always gotta take something head-on. Sometimes discretion is the better part of not getting your ass kicked."

"Give Darla my love," I said, and turned off the phone.

Chapter 21

"*Hell, I'll kill a man in a fair fight or if I think he's gonna start a fair fight or if he bothers me or if there's a woman or if I'm gettin paid—mostly only when I'm gettin paid.*" – Jayne, *Serenity*

Tony & Danny

After ditching the black Nissan, the driver with the South Boston accent and his partner went to the short-term rental apartment they shared. The driver, Tony Abbado, stubbed out his cigarette in the glass ashtray on the kitchen counter. He smirked. Not a kitchen counter, a breakfast nook. A stubby counter stuck out from the wall separating the kitchen from the living room, and they called it a "breakfast nook." The apartment lady had new names for things he'd been around his whole life. "Faux" this and "faux" that, instead of what it was—cheap junk, badly installed.

Abbado tipped a splash of Bushmills into his coffee cup, topped it off with Folgers from the coffeemaker, thankful he could at least get decent coffee as opposed to the imported shit from frou-frou uptown coffee shops. His cell phone lit with an incoming call, and Abbado picked it up from the marble—*faux* marble—countertop and thumbed it on. He listened more than spoke then said, "You got it," and hung up. He got off the stool and found his partner, Danny Boylan, in the back bedroom, sacked out on top of an unmade bed.

Danny wore his work clothes, a T-shirt and jeans. He had white tube socks bunched on his feet.

"Rise an' shine, buddy." Abbado kicked the edge of the bed.

"Whah?"

"Time to earn the daily."

Boylan sat up and yawned. "What's the word?" He fumbled with black dress shoes, pulling them on after tugging up his white socks.

"Our little buddy, Dee Maximum Idjit, has done stuck his dick in it."

Boylan cocked an eyebrow and ran a hand through his wheat-colored hair.

"He did a drive-by." Abbado mimed shooting a machine gun. "Ack-ack-ack. Tried to take out the cowboy."

"What a fucking idiot." Boylan shook his head and tied his shoes. "Why?"

"Who knows what goes through that guy's mind? Anyway, boss says cut our losses, get rid of the little shit."

"It's what I've been sayin' all along, isn't it? He's the only thing tying us to the judge. Get rid of him, problem solved. Just like that." Boylan snapped his fingers.

"Yeah, you're management material, you are. Tuck your shirt in."

Abbado went to take a leak in the faux toilet. He flushed, washed his hands, and grimaced at the bags under his eyes. With dark hair, dark eyes, and a name like Tony Abbado, he was taken for Italian more often than a descendant of the Emerald Isle. Earning respect in the Irish mob was hard enough, but looking like a wop made that hill twice as hard to climb.

He shrugged. Didn't matter. The problem was staying ahead of this little game here in this hot-as-a-shithouse state. Win this one, and they all got to go back to Boston, fat and happy.

He called out, "Hey. You ready?"

Boylan, as big and pale-faced as a rugby player, lumbered down the hall, tucking a pistol in his waistband. "Let's do it."

"Yeah," Tony said. "Let's."

Sam

THE NEW BARTENDER AT Skinny Dippers was a scrawny woman who looked as though she'd worked her way through an entire biker gang, one Harley at a time. She wore cut-off jeans old enough to have been hand sewn by Levi Strauss and a plaid lumberjack shirt over a tank top. On stage, a platinum blonde danced to the beat of a rap tune in a hooker-style schoolgirl uniform skirt that came to ass-cheek level, a garter and glitter. She pranced up to a glassy-eyed customer with a dollar bill in his hand and wiggled her boobs.

"What'll you have?" the bartender yelled over the beat of the music when I leaned on the bar.

"D-Max."

She glanced at my badge and shrugged. "Ain't here."

"Mind if I go look?"

"Knock yourself out."

The office door was unlocked, and my detective skills told me right away the room was empty. And it had been cleaned up. No notes lying out saying, "Here's how I framed the big, dumb cop."

Back at the bar, Biker Chick finished popping little straws into the drinks on a tray for a waitress then looked at me. I tried to melt her with my charm, using my second-to-highest wattage smile. I had to be careful; the highest setting might incinerate her on the spot.

"Any idea where he is?"

"Nope."

"Where's he hang when he's not here?"

My charm penetrated, at least a little. She gave me the names and addresses of two other clubs that Ford owned and said that was all she knew. I dropped a ten on the bar and left.

Rita

RITA GOLDMAN TRACED the ownership of Millennium Metals back to the investment firm of Garrett & Hull. The firm owned—in whole or part—everything from night clubs to metal recyclers and laundries to biotech firms.

"These guys have their fingers in so many pies, they could open a bakery."

She keyed a search on the partners, Michael Hull and Theodore No-Middle-Name Garrett. "Let's see what kind of pie—"

Her desk phone rang. Whitlach.

"My office. Now."

Dial tone.

"Rude fucker," Rita muttered.

Whitlach started in on her before she closed the office door all the way behind her. "I just got through talking to Detective Woods of the SAPD. You know what she tells me? She tells me she hasn't seen you all week. How can you be a liaison, Goldman, when you don't liaise with anybody? Huh? Can you tell me that?"

Rita took a seat in the right-hand visitor chair, crossed her legs, and cleared her throat. "I'm pursuing my own leads."

Whitlach sighed as though his teenager had just admitted to wrecking the car for the third time. He stared at her for a long time then pursed his lips. "All right, Goldman. You're a smart woman. IQ in the one-fifty range, right?"

Rita hesitated. Nodded.

"That's what I thought. Aced the tests at Quantico. Top of your class. Bright shining star and all that." Whitlach pinched his nose and squinted as if he had a headache. "So maybe I'm misreading something here."

"Sir?"

"Lay it out for me." He spread his hands across the desk in a magician's gesture. "Show me what you got. Tell me why you think this guy didn't do it."

Rita shifted in her seat, crossing her legs in the other direction. "I never said—"

"Don't crawfish on me now, Agent. Run it down for me. Use small words."

"Okay." Rita took a deep breath. "Okay, all I'm saying, there's some anomalies with this case. First, the 9-1-1 call comes in six hours late. Suspicious, but okay, so what? Don't mean a thing by itself. Then the PD finds Ranger Cable in the room with the vic. If he killed her, why'd he hang around six hours? Slightly elevated GHB." Rita waggled her hand. "Could be traces of a drug, could be nothing, right? Racist material in his stuff, when the guy has zero history of racist anything—"

"That you know about."

"That I know about," she conceded. "But really convenient to show up now. And what's the story here? I mean, so try to make sense of this. He hates blacks, right? That's what the pamphlets suggest. So he killed her because she was ragging on him? But he was in bed with her, naked, suggesting they had sex—although, I might add, the coroner found no traces of intercourse, consensual or otherwise. So did he kill her in a lover's quarrel, or on account of her being black and all? One or the other works, but not both. And neither one works too great, if you know what I'm saying?"

Whitlach said, "Could be he's one of those guys, he's drawn to sex with black women. He doesn't like that part of his character, and so the hatred comes over him when they're about to bump bellies. Or he comes on to her, and she says no."

Rita nodded. "But everybody says they hated each other. People on the campaign said they stayed as far apart from each other as they could. Barely spoke. The sex scenario would work better if they, you know, were clicking even a little bit, right? And not for nothing, but the guy's a freaking Boy Scout. I mean, you should see this guy. He makes... he makes Superman look like a homeless guy."

Whitlach picked up a pen from his desk set and twirled it around his fingers. Once, twice, a half-dozen times. "As much as I hate to add to this little fantasy, somebody tried to whack your Boy Scout in Dallas. Drive-by shooting. Stupid, bush-league stuff."

"What? When?"

"Yesterday. I just heard it from Woods. You would know it, too, by the way, if you were liaising like you were supposed to."

"They catch the guys?"

"Yep." Whitlach consulted his computer screen. "A mutt named TJ Wilson did the shooting. The car was driven by Damian Ford."

Rita blinked. "Say that name again."

Sam

TWO HOURS AND TWO STRIP joints later, Ford remained among the missing. The two other clubs, Goldfingers and Twisters, were even more run-down and smelly than Skinny Dippers. I had some hope for Goldfingers, given the name matched one of my favorite Bond movies, with Honor Blackman in the role of Pussy Galore. Sadly, I met disappointment when I found Goldfingers was in an advanced stage of decomposition, lying dead in the middle of a moldering strip of empty buildings, directly on the flight path for Love Field's north-south approach. Blue-and-orange Southwest Airlines jets screamed overhead every five or ten minutes, their landing gear almost brushing the roof of the club. I did not find Pussy Galore. Well, I did, but not the Honor Blackman kind. And no Ford.

The other club, Twisters, an all-nude place in Arlington, reeked of moldy carpet, sweat, and something I didn't want to think about.

The guy at the door wanted a twenty-dollar cover until he saw my badge, then he stepped aside and bowed me in like I was royalty. The woman on stage leaned back and spread her thighs, moving to the beat of an old disco song—almost. She was naked except for a garter stuffed with bills. She was also at least five months pregnant. I found no one who knew the whereabouts of Damian Ford. Leaving the place felt like escaping.

The Mustang's leather seat had gotten hot while the car sat in the sun. I cranked the starter and turned the A/C on max, wincing from the soreness in my back. A whiff of my own body made my nose hairs curl. I'd been wearing the same camel sport coat for a week, and it needed cleaning. My new white button-down shirt, fresh from the JC Penney Big & Tall shop, could use a wash, too. At least the blue jeans could last a few more days.

I'd woken up next to a dead body Sunday morning. *Hard to believe it's only Wednesday afternoon. Time flies when you're about to be arrested for murder. Is this how people feel when they see me in their rearview mirror?*

"At least I didn't do it," I said to myself. It didn't make me feel any better. Come to think of it, that was what everybody I'd ever arrested said, too. I rubbed gritty eyes and fished sunglasses out of my pocket to counter the glare from the road. Interstate 30 ran straight through downtown and out to Mesquite, where Matt lived. It also ran close to Rocket Motors so I could make a quick jog over there and see if Martine had a pocketful of syringes filled with GHB.

Going back to Matt's after nearly getting Darla killed felt wrong. The only reason I wanted to go back there at all was that I needed to borrow his computer to finish looking at Fortney's email. After that, I thought it would be best if I moved to a motel.

My cell phone buzzed. Speaking of the devil, Matt's name showed in the caller ID. He said, "Meet me at Pappa Jack's. Friend of mine I want you to meet. He knows something about D-Max."

"Where?"

"I told you. Pappa Jack's."

"Which is where?"

Matt gave me directions, and I closed the connection. Now I had a new stop to make.

"So what's it going to be? Martine, email, or Pappa Jack's, which sounds like a place that might have beer."

No contest. I shifted into first, popped the clutch and headed to Pappa's.

Chapter 22

"*You can't teach an old dogma new tricks.*" – Dorothy Parker

Sam

Pappa Jack's turned out to be a bar in a trendy neighborhood east of downtown Dallas called Deep Ellum. In this case, *trendy* was a synonym for *decrepit*. Bars and galleries with cool names abutted empty warehouses and abandoned offices. The city had installed some modern art statuary, and murals covered the sides of buildings. Inside Pappa Jack's, Matt occupied one side of a booth, wearing civvies, while a large black man in a business suit filled the opposite seat. The man had seen a few miles of bad road in his day.

"Delman Taylor." His voice rumbled from the depths of a huge chest. He crushed my hand in a powerful shake.

"Sam Cable," I told him and took a seat next to Matt, who scooted over to give me room. I flexed my hand under the table.

"What have you been up to, little brother?"

"Looking for Ford. Without success. I can't even find TJ. Big as he is, you'd think he'd stand out."

"They running?"

"No, I think they're close by."

"How do you know?"

"Same way I know my keys are still in the house when I can't find them in the morning. They have to be around here somewhere."

"We'll find 'em," Matt told me with a shoulder pat. "But next time, don't go off like that without me." He gestured at the man across the table. "Delman's lived in Dallas since people came here in covered wagons. He's been on the planning commission, the school board, and the city council. There's not a thing about South Dallas he doesn't know."

"Okay?" I looked from Delman to Matt, eyebrow raised.

"He knows April Fortney," Matt said. "She came from South Dallas and launched her political career from there. Come to think of it, Damian Ford did, too. Grow up in South Dallas, I mean, not launch his political career. D-Max is too dumb to be a politician."

"Don't say that," Delman rumbled. He sounded like he could start an avalanche with a deep breath. "There's plenty of dumb politicians in this world. And Damian's not as dumb as he lets on."

"You could be right." I grinned. "But I got the impression Ford thinks an election is something caused by a lap dance."

Delman laughed, causing several heads to turn and look for the earthquake. The waitress—a goth girl with a pincushion face and a tattoo climbing up her neck—came by, and I ordered a Newcastle Brown. Matt asked for a Coors Light, and Taylor said he wanted another mojito.

"Mojito?" I asked. "Seriously?"

"No one laughed at me yet," he said with a shark grin. As if.

"By way of background," Delman said, "let me start by saying: everything with April Fortney's politics is a black-and-white issue."

"Meaning?" I asked.

"Everything is about whites and blacks. In her world, the whites got it and the blacks don't. Anything gets done in this town north of I-30, it's another example of our people getting the shaft. And her opinion is not unfounded, I might add. Our constituent base has a right to be suspicious."

Our drinks came, and Taylor paused to sip his mojito and smack his lips in pleasure. He had a walnut complexion, both in color and texture, with dark-brown eyes and close-cropped hair. His red tie hung loose around an unbuttoned collar. The man could easily hold a basketball in each hand and have room left over for a couple of ten-nis balls.

"And how does this relate to her murder?" I said.

Delman squinted and took another sip of mojito. "The way Matt explained to me, and assuming you were framed as you say, this setup looks very professionally done. Was not a spur of the moment thing, correct?" He acknowledged my nod with one of his own. "Which means two things, to my mind. One, it's about money. Or call it power, which equates to the same thing, often as not. Two, the per-petrator knows exactly what buttons to push to bring maximum heat. Hold on a sec. Let me explain."

Delman sat forward, elbows on the table and hands interlocked. "The first part is easy. Money and power. April Fortney represented an obstacle or threat to somebody, either denying them what they wanted—money, power—or providing those things by her death."

"Revenge," Matt said. "Jealousy. Don't forget those. Maybe she was killed by someone with a motive like that."

"Ah, but see"—Delman held up a cigar-sized finger—"look at the setup here. This wasn't just about getting Mrs. Fortney out of the way. This was tagging our boy here with the deed. That leads to the second part of the equation: pushing buttons. Now, let us suppose for the sake of supposing, that Mrs. Fortney was the intended victim and not young Ranger Cable."

He gestured at me. "You, sir, were white icing on the cake, as it were. Racially motivated murder. A hate crime. Suddenly, all the at-tention, all the hoopla-doo, is focused there, with Black Lives Mat-ter getting more ammunition, and all the media people falling over themselves to pander to my people. And thus, our murderer has suc-cessfully diverted attention by lighting a bonfire, while quietly sneak-ing away"—Delman walked his fingers along the table—"allowing the trail to go cold in the meantime."

"How could he know that would work?"

"How could it not work?" Delman spread his hands wide. *Look around*, his gesture said. "Name me a high-profile crime involving either a white victim and a black perpetrator, or the reverse, where the event has not polarized the community and stirred a hornet's nest of anger. Going back to Rodney King, OJ Simpson, and Trayvon Martin, all the way to today's issues in Chicago and Ferguson."

Delman vacuumed up the last of his drink and waved his empty glass at the Pincushion.

"So, I say again," he continued. "How could it not play out in a similar fashion when a blond-haired, blue-eyed son of the South is found next to a dead woman of color? The Loud People have already chosen sides, and they are setting the narrative."

I drew a deep breath. "So you think somebody wanted her out of the way and planned a shitstorm to cover his tracks."

Delman nodded, and Matt said, "Makes sense to me. No way a scrub like Damian Ford concocted all this."

"No," the councilman conceded. "I don't see Mr. Ford in that role, either. More intelligent than he appears, but not so much as to be capable of this kind of strategic thinking. Ah, thanks," he added when the waitress appeared with his drink.

Pincushion finished picking up the empty glasses and pointed at my bottle. "Another?"

"Huh?" I glanced down and was surprised to see I held an empty. "Sure. Matt?"

"No, not me. I'm at my limit. So, Delman, what about the husband? JC Fortney? How does taking his wife's place fit into this? Wouldn't that constitute motive?"

"I don't think it does, Matthew, except to say that I wouldn't put it past Jawn Fortney to do in his wife if it gained him a dollar more than it cost. He has never been a crusader for 'the people.'" He put air quotes around it. "Nor has he expressed more than the usual suspicion and distaste for the way the white establishment runs this city."

I opened my mouth to speak, but Delman stopped me with a raised palm. "I know it's better today than yesterday, and better this year than last year, and this decade and so on; you don't have to tell me that. I get it. I've seen the change in my lifetime." Delman's voice began to rise in pitch and intensity. "But I also know I can't drive through Highland Park without attracting police attention. In my lifetime, I have been segregated, *de*segregated, bussed, disrespected, *sus*pected, detained, and questioned, all due to the color of my skin."

I sipped the new beer that Pincushion brought. "Actually, I was going to ask how well you knew the Fortneys, personally."

Delman leaned back and blinked. He glanced around, as if becoming aware that his oratory had risen in volume enough to turn some heads. "Ah. My apologies." He chuckled and said in a softer voice, "I sound like Abraham Lincoln and Dr. King, all rolled into one. I do get carried away at times, listening to myself. I've known JC since he sold cars for Baker Automotive on Illinois, over in Oak Cliff. I met April not long after she ventured into politics. We were never directly opposed, but we bumped shoulders quite a bit."

"Any hints of a... shady past where she was concerned?"

"No, none that comes to mind." Delman swirled his straw and sipped about half the glass in one take. "JC, on the other hand... well, let me say that there's a reason the used-car salesman stereotype exists. He's sneaky, but to go to these lengths?" He pursed his lips and wagged his head. "I don't think so. I think the person, or persons, who framed you already know the dynamics of racial tension of which I spoke. Tapping into those dynamics was easy enough. All they needed was a person of a Caucasian persuasion handy, and *voila*. Problem solved. Which means that Fortney got cross-wise with somebody over money. In Dallas politics, that means a white somebody."

I leaned back in the booth and drained my second beer, which had disappeared as fast as the first. Good thing I'd eaten a late lunch.

"So here's what Delman and I were thinking, before you came in," Matt said. "The two white guys at the hotel, what'd you call 'em?"

"Tom and Dick."

"Tom and Dick are hired guns, right? According to the security footage, they get off the elevator ten minutes before you do. In the meantime, Fortney's getting ready to meet Mr. Damian Ford, former pimp and lover. She's pulling on her naughty stockings and high heels, right?"

I nodded and rolled my hand for him to continue.

"So when she gets a knock on the door, she's thinking, 'Oh my, he's early,' but she's not suspecting a hit squad. She opens the door, and Tom and Dick jump her. Ack! She's dead." Matt made a very helpful pantomime of someone hanging from a noose. "So then they wait for you to come along to help complete the scene."

Delman said, "Or you surprised them as they came out of Fortney's room."

"Or that," Matt said. He tilted his head back and drained the last drops in his Coors Lite bottle. "That's it for me. I have to drive home, and if I get popped for DUI, it won't be pretty around my house."

"How's Darla?"

"Staying with her mom, thank God."

"Good." I contemplated my empty bottle. "I'd better rein it in, too."

"Pussies." Delman rocked the house with another laugh. He caught Pincushion's eye and pointed to his empty glass.

"'I got the motive, which is money, and the body, which is dead.' *In the Heat of the Night*. Good movie."

"Appropriate, too," Delman said.

After the waitress delivered the drink, I said, "So who paid for Tom and Dick, our mystery assassins, to bring such sunshine to my day?"

Delman pointed his index finger at me as if aiming a gun. "You find that out, Mr. Cable, and I do believe you will have solved the crime."

"Gee, Delman. Thanks," I said with a lopsided grin. "I never would have thought of that."

The councilman's laugh vibrated the glasses on the table.

Chapter 23

"*Commissioner Kenneth Mayfield, who is white, said it seemed that central collections 'has become a black hole' because paperwork reportedly has become lost in the office. Commissioner John Wiley Price, who is black, interrupted him with a loud 'Excuse me!' He then corrected his colleague, saying the office has become a 'white hole.' That prompted Judge Thomas Jones, who is black, to demand an apology from Mayfield for his racially insensitive analogy.*" — *Dallas Morning News*, July 7, 2008

Sam

After a spaghetti dinner, I went back to Matt's computer and read more of April Fortney's emails. I searched for D-Max, Damian, Ford, TJ, and all the combinations of names that might be even vaguely associated with her past. Nothing hit. A lead weight settled around my shoulders, and my eyes drifted to the door every few minutes. My intuition was telling me to hit the door, keep running, and not look back. I shook off the thought like a wet dog shaking off water and switched gears.

I needed to write a statement. Seventy-two hours was the deadline for statements from officers when they were involved in a death, and I'd pushed past that by a little. I buckled down and typed my narrative on Fortney's death, all six pages of it, from the moment I left the bar in the Hyatt lobby to the arrival of Quintana and Valdez, the two SAPD cops. After spell-checking, I emailed it to Captain Marshall; he could send it on to whoever needed it. Internal Affairs, my attorney, Detective Woods, and the marching band of Texas Tech University for all I cared.

A tension knot twisted the middle of my back. I stretched, and things popped. Quitting for the night seemed like a good idea. Between writing the narrative and reading emails, I'd been in front of the computer about four hours without a break. My vision blurred at odd moments, and I had to keep refocusing on the text.

"Okay, Sam, one more folder."

Judge Fortney had created umpteen dozen folders and subfolders for storing emails. She was also an email hoarder. She saved everything from important communications to obligatory thank-yous. Some folders were nearly empty, whereas others were jam-packed with long email chains of court cases, budgets, dockets, campaign strategy, and recipe exchanges with her friends. I had been opening each one and methodically working my way down. My next folder was labeled Miscellaneous Legal Drafts.

"Riveting stuff, I'm sure." I clicked the first email in the folder, titled US vs ICU. When I opened it, the email looked like pornospam. I double-blinked and leaned closer to the monitor. The email was addressed to Judge April Fortney with her correct address. Several photos were pasted into the body. Each one revealed an explicit view of April Maree Fortney engaged in a sexual act with Damian Maxwell Ford. And they were from different places, different bedrooms.

"Matt, come here!"

My brother shoved into the room and followed my pointing finger.

"Holy shit," he said.

In the first picture, the judge directly faced the camera and was easily identifiable, in spite of the very, very... intense... look on her face. The remaining four pictures were variations on the theme. Ford and Fortney were engaged in carnal knowledge. It appeared consensual and mutually participatory. And mutually enjoyable.

"Holy shit," Matt repeated.

"Great insight. Do you think she's aware of the camera?"

Matt shook his head. "No, I don't. But ain't it interesting how she has her face pointed in the right direction every time."

"Almost like it was planned, huh?"

"Blackmail?"

I frowned and went back to picking at the email. "It looks like it came through a remailer. One of those server things that disguise your email."

"Server things? I thought that was a waiter."

"And to believe you managed to procreate," I mumbled.

"Any message in the email?"

"No, I've scrolled all over it, can't find a thing."

"Do a search," Matt said. "Look for that sender in her email."

"Now who's a techno-genius?"

"Apologies, Mr. Jobs. Please continue."

A search turned up nothing. No more messages from the sender, and using keywords from the subject line did nothing, either. After twenty minutes of clicking and tapping, all I had was the one email.

"Better let Dusty know," Matt said. "DPS propeller-heads can crack her computer, find out what else is on it."

"Good idea. At least it'll be a place for him to start. You catch the title? US vs ICU?"

Matt's eyes narrowed. "It's weird, huh?"

"No, don't you get it? Us versus I See You. Or maybe United States versus I See You. Either way, it's sending some kind of message."

"Stupid message." My brother flopped into a chair and stretched his legs, yawning like a grizzly bear. "So if Fortney was being blackmailed, Ford must've been in on it."

"Yeah, looks like it. How else could they get the camera set up in just the right spot in the room, every single time."

"Amen, brother. But why would Ford need dirty pics of Fortney getting naked and doin' the nasty? He had enough dirt on her already, knowing she used to be a dancer and a prostitute. Did he need photographic proof for something bigger than a checkered past?"

"If so, why kill her?" I argued. "Why kill a woman you're blackmailing? She's paying you with money or sex, so why stop the gravy train?"

"You're forgetting, bro, about Tom and Dick. They had time to do the deed, not Ford. Near as we can tell, he didn't do it. And Ford wouldn't show up in a place where he was about to have somebody killed; I give him more credit than that."

Palm, meet forehead. "Too tired. I should have remembered that."

"Why don't you call Dusty?" Matt said, slapping his thighs and leveraging out of the chair. "Make a copy of everything, the email and whatnot, and hit it again in the morning."

"Good idea."

"Of course it is." Filling the doorway, Matt paused with one hand on the jamb. "Speaks wisdom, your brother does. He is one with the Force."

"One with the farce, you mean." I reached for my cell to punch up Dusty's number. Matt's chuckle echoed down the hall as he walked away. I got Dusty on the first try, and after he finished cussing me for calling so late, I described the email and how I found it.

"Well, ain't that somethin' else," Dusty said. "Good job, Sam. I'll tell the geeks doin' the computer stuff to find that email, see if they can tell where it came from. Hey, listen..."

"What?" I shifted the phone to my other ear and propped my sock feet on the desk. Matt's computer went to screen saver, thankfully blocking out the images of April Fortney.

"Your ol' boys Tom and Dick ain't as smart as they think they are."

"How so?"

"They parked their car a few blocks away from the Hyatt, but a street cam got 'em anyway. Better yet, guess what?"

"Dusty, if I beat the crap out of you, you'll be nothing but a husk. Stop teasing."

"Hah! Don't be a hater, Sam. Listen. We not only got Tom and Dick, we got the license number of their car."

I sat up straight, and my feet thumped to the floor. Sweat popped out on my forehead. "You better not be shittin' me, Dusty."

"I shitteth thee not." Dusty sounded as pleased as a Baptist who'd bus toured heaven and got a T-shirt signed by Saint John himself.

"Who's it belong to?"

"It's a pool car for a company outta Dallas called Garrett & Hull."

Garrett & Hull... Something jumped up in the back of my mind and started doing handsprings, but when I tried to latch on, it ran away.

"Mean anything?" Dusty asked.

I paused. "Not sure. My brain's turned to pudding."

"Cow pudding, you mean. Kent's chasing the lead, trying to find out who these guys are. He's working on getting a warrant to impound the car and search the business, but I don't think a judge's gonna sign paper without a little more PC."

"Probable cause! They..." I paused and reset. "It's gotta be more than coincidence that these two guys are there at the time of the murder."

"I agree, ol' buddy, but right now, all they are is 'persons of interest.' Without more direct evidence, a judge ain't signing a warrant for a multi-million-dollar business what pays its taxes and does good work in the community."

"So Barrett & Hall is legit?"

"Garrett & Hull." Dusty coughed, taking the phone away from his mouth. "Damn, I got to quit smokin.'"

"No sympathy from me. I quit dippin', and it hasn't bothered me one bit."

"Course not. You be the legendary Sam Cable, man of steel, head of bone."

"Anything else?"

"Only other 'nomaly we found at the hotel, there's two guys checked in using a fake ID at six p.m., got one room together. They didn't leave till in the morning. Could be gay, though they don't look the type."

"What type's that?"

"Well, y'know... *gay.*"

"Were they on the fourteenth floor?"

"Nope. Sixteen. Though they could've used the fire stairs. No camera there. The credit card they used was a prepaid Visa; no way to trace it. The room's been cleaned and reused and cleaned again. Trace evidence is gone. So, it could mean something, but probably don't. I'll shoot you the pictures when I get back to my computer in the morning."

"All right, brother. Keep me posted."

I dropped the phone on the desk and thought about April Fortney. A lot of hookers started out loving their pimps. It was how some of those guys turned their girls out on the street, used the woman's love against them so they would do the pimp's bidding and... *entertain* strange men in smelly motels. But to stay involved, long after she quit the life? Was it possible she still loved the guy?

How did April get involved with D-Max in the first place? Does that even matter? And how did she get out of the life? To get away from strip clubs and prostitution to put herself through law school must have taken a wagonload of guts. I had to hand it to her; she'd really come a long way. For the first time, I looked at April Fortney like I'd never looked at her before. Without her mask on, a new April Fortney showed up to claim my attention. A person.

I'd joined the Texas Department of Public Safety for a reason. Everyone who applied to the Rangers had to be a state trooper for ten years first. Captain Marshall had pulled some strings—he'd watched out for me, even then—and I'd made it on the first try. The Ranger badge meant a lot to me. By the time I was twelve, the flames of justice had burned bright, fueled by countless good-guy-versus-bad-guy movies, Louis L'Amour, Mickey Spillane books, and Spider-Man comics. That flame had ashed over somewhere along the way, as it tended to do when one grew up. But the embers were there. And whoever had killed April Fortney had thrown a bucket of gasoline into the fireplace.

The weight of this thing hung over me, from the astonishing amount of shame I felt—knowing I wasn't guilty—to the guilt over not having protected her when it counted. I may not have been guilty of her murder, but I was damn sure responsible for not saving her life. I failed April Fortney. The phrase I'd used with Matt earlier, borrowed from L'Amour, came back to me. "Ain't no stoppin' a man who's in the right and keeps a'coming."

"So stop feeling sorry for yourself," I said to myself, "and go find a killer."

Chapter 24

"Justice cannot be for one side alone, but must be for both." – Eleanor Roosevelt

Rita

The burble of activity in the Dallas field office of the FBI played like elevator music, half-heard, completely insignificant. Phones trilled, and people laughed. Voices rumbled in the background. Men and women in business suits passed the open door of her borrowed office with folders or open laptops, though Rita couldn't describe a single one of them. The stacks of numbers ordered in rows and columns on her monitor held far more interest.

Rita never understood why people hated paperwork. There was a sense of completeness and satisfaction in building a prison of documentation around a suspect. Indexed and labeled exhibits. Color-coded spreadsheets. Files collated, tabbed, and cross-referenced. Clear, concise reports with all the blanks filled in correctly. If all the facts of a case could be straightened out, laid end to end, and packaged into a compelling monologue of a story, then there would be no choice left but to convict. Order created from the chaos of crime. Rigidity molded around a fluid situation. Paperwork rocked.

Before finding the connection between Damian Ford and Millennium Metals, she had been halfway through an analysis of Fortney's campaign finances. When that connection came up, she put the campaign finance analysis on a back burner and grabbed a commuter flight to Dallas. She leaned on Agent Martinez to give her a hand with running down the connection. Rita went to visit Garrett while Martinez tracked down Hull.

Wasted effort, as it turned out.

Then she was back to the incomplete financial analysis. Halfway done was all the way unfinished as far as she was concerned. The last piece of the puzzle, she found in her email inbox. The bank had forwarded the Fortney campaign bank statements, which meant they'd bent over backward to comply with the subpoena. *When was the last time a bank cut loose their records in a matter of days?*

"Nev-*ah*!" Rita sang in a mocking voice. They obviously didn't want the bad press of standing in the way of an investigation of this magnitude.

Speaking of fast turnarounds...

Rita dialed Detective Woods's cell.

"Hey, Bernia, it's Goldman. You left me a voicemail about the DNA results from the scarf coming in?"

"Yes, ahem, I have those here."

"Fuck me. Five days? Who gets DNA done in five days?"

"The SAPD lab does when the mayor and chief of police both get calls from the governor, two senators, and—I think but can't confirm—the President of the United States. All of them want this matter, ah, 'cleared up expeditiously,' is the way it was put to me."

"So what was the expeditious result?"

"The, ah, the sample came back, ah—" She coughed. "Excuse me. A complete match for Samuel Duncan Cable."

"So that's it then." Rita made it a statement.

"It would seem so."

"You think he did it?"

Woods *ahem*-ed. Rita waited her out, letting the silence build. "I think, Agent Goldman, that we have a very solid case at this point."

"That's not what I asked. I asked: do you think he did it?"

"As I said," Woods told her after more raspy throat noises, "I think we have a very solid case. I will be presenting these findings to a grand jury very shortly, I'm sure."

"Well. Okay, then." Rita pursed her lips. She'd run out of things to say and told Woods to keep her in the loop. An instant before hanging up, she remembered what she wanted to tell the San Antonio detective. "Hey, Bernia? Hey, you still there?"

"Yes?"

"Not for nothing, but you should try some Claritin or something."

"I have. Extra strength. And allergy shots twice a month." She barked another cough. "It doesn't seem to help."

"Well... Good luck, then."

"You, too."

Rita tapped her head with the phone handset long after punching the disconnect. *Continue digging into the campaign or give up?* If Cable was indicted, his career was as good as finished, no matter the final verdict. Cops rarely recovered from that kind of mark in their jacket. And there remained the strong possibility of something far worse. Conviction. Conviction and prison time. Potentially the death penalty.

The DNA evidence was compelling. Cable's blood was on the murder weapon. He'd been in her room with no alibi as to when he'd gotten there. He and the victim had bad feelings, publicly acknowledged. Looking at it, the narrative almost held together, but below the surface, cracks appeared. Like Damian Ford and Millennium Metals.

Rita tested her gut and found she wasn't buying into the narrative. Something else was happening here, more complex than a lover's quarrel or a race crime. And it looked like it was up to her to find out what that something was.

"You're gonna thank me later, cowboy," she muttered. "Don't fuckin' disappoint me and be the goddamned killer."

Sam

I SPENT THE NIGHT WRESTLING with the bed more than sleeping in it. About two o'clock in the morning, the Memory Fairy visited and left behind a surprise—I recalled where I'd heard the name Hull. DaShondra had mentioned it in one of our conversations. He was the guy who'd been to see April Fortney with the two mutts, Tom and Dick.

I tossed and turned a long time, trying to put the pieces together, but there were too many gaps. At four o'clock, I surrendered. I showered, made a pot of coffee, and ate breakfast. Then I turned on the computer and went to work.

I had to make some assumptions. Whoever owned and ran Garrett & Hull, or whoever managed it, had the juice to plant two hitters under my nose, close enough for me to smell their aftershave. Based on the length of time these guys had stayed around, they weren't contractors, either. Tom and Dick had to be long-term employees of Garrett & Hull, and their visit to the Hyatt was no coincidence, especially considering Hull had something going on with the judge. *How does blackmail play into it, though? Ford was there that night, too, so what was he up to? And—the big question—why would Ford or Tom and Dick want her dead?*

The Garrett & Hull website was very barebones, only one page, with a contact link that took me to a generic webmaster email address. A short statement and biographies on the home page gave me a cursory overview. With an office in North Dallas, near the Galleria Mall, Garrett & Hull apparently invested in "speculative and high-risk" venture capital projects. The principals were listed as Theo Garrett and Michael C. Hull. The bio for Garrett—no picture—said he graduated from Vanderbilt with a BA in Business, worked for a Who's Who of Wall Street firms before founding the investment company with his long-time pal, Mike Hull. Hull's bio—also no picture—said about the same thing, except instead of a history of Wall

Street employment, Mikey's resume just said, "Mike Hull has over twenty years' experience in the C-suite. He brings a wealth of knowledge..." Blah, blah, blah. Nothing concrete. No listing of their current "high-risk" ventures. Website-in-a-Box-type stuff.

Other business sites, like Manta and Hoover's, had even less information. The same contact info as the Garrett & Hull website was all I could find. And diddly-squat came back on searches for both Garrett and Hull by themselves. No address, no phone, no mention in the papers, no awards, nothing. Not altogether strange. A lot of people didn't make the web—although with two high-rollers like these, I'd expected more.

My cell rang.

"Hey, podnah," Dusty said. "Garrett & Hull is owned by Theodore Steven Garrett and Michael Charles Hull."

"Tell me something I don't know."

"Okay, smartass. Do you want to know where they live?"

"Now that would be welcome news. Fire away."

Sam

THEO GARRETT'S HOUSE was closest. I jumped into the Mustang at 10:20 and roared out of the drive. In minutes, I had the muscle car cooking along Interstate 635, which looped around the north side of town. I wasn't on the road ten minutes when I passed a Western-wear store, and my head reminded me my hat was in San Antonio evidence. I maneuvered to the next exit and doubled back to the store. The interior smelled of tanned leather, boot polish, and blue-dyed cotton. Jeans, jeans, and more jeans filled cubbies along the walls, and more clothes hung on the racks in between. On one side, rows of boots aimed their pointy toes at the customers. And at the back... *Hats.*

A cream-colored Resistol summer-weight straw hat called my name. A Palo Duro. It had a thin leather band and a slightly turned-down brim.

From behind me, the female clerk said, "You look just like Nick Nolte in that Ranger movie."

I grinned at her reflection in the mirror. "Only taller, and more handsome."

"Oh, no doubt. Took the words right out of my mouth. Come sit here and let me see that. Something looks... off."

She sat me down in front of her and spent a long time adjusting the fit. The buttons on her Western shirt were the snap kind, and the button under the most strain was at my eye level. Her name tag read "Mindy." I verified it several times.

"You need one size bigger, I think," Mindy said at last.

"Hmm? Okay."

I wore the hat out of the store, and it wasn't until I was back on the road that I saw the handwritten phone number on the receipt. Mindy had spelled her name with a heart over the letter *I*.

Theo Garrett lived in a gated community off Keller Springs Road in North Dallas. The guard shack at the entry was bigger than my apartment in Longview. I flashed my badge at the guard and drove in like I knew where I was going. The Mustang bulled along twisty streets lined with trees and well-tended foliage. And money. The houses varied in size from gigantic to obscene. Sprinklers chopped across golfing-green yards, and there were no Playskool toys anywhere in sight.

Garrett lived in a McMansion the size of a football stadium, only a little more dramatic. With an impressive façade of stone and timber stuck on a plain brick two-story house, the place put me in mind of a love child begotten by Frankenstein's castle and a prison. I gunned the Mustang into the circular driveway in front of the house and cut the engine.

Rolling down the window, I listened for a minute. Blissful peace saturated the air. In fact, the neighborhood could have been a cemetery. A lawn mower buzzed, and some birds tweeted, but that was it. No laughter, no shouting, no kids playing stickball or throwing a football in the front yards. Granted, it was a weekday, and most kids would be in school. But still.

The Garrett house appeared rich and well-appointed from a distance, but on closer inspection, small weeds poked through cracks in the drive, and the bushes around the house were untrimmed, the leaves starting to turn brown.

I got out of the car and put on my new hat, which already fit as though I'd worn it forever. Mindy of the Hearted *I* was a good hat fitter.

The front door had a sun-beaten look. The oak, or mahogany or whatever, was splintered and needing refinishing. I pushed the faded, cracked doorbell. It didn't ring, so I used my cop-knock on the door, banging hard with the meaty side of my fist. I paused to pick a splinter out and knocked again.

Steps rapped from inside—a woman in heels, by the sound—and the door opened. A dark-faced Hispanic woman, about five foot two, with black hair, chubby cheeks, and a maid's cap poked her head out. When she saw my badge, she froze in place and looked at me without speaking. At that moment, I didn't think she was capable of speech.

"*Señor* Garrett." My voice made her jump. "*Por favor.*"

She overcame her panic enough to say, "N-No here." The poor woman looked like I was about to drag her off to prison or rape her. Or both.

"Where is he? *Dónde está?*"

A pause and a watery blink. "Hospital."

"Which hospital?"

I had exceeded either her English skills or her tolerance of being near policemen, because she held up one finger and leaned back into the house long enough to call out, "*Señora*!" With that, the woman made another wait-a-minute gesture and closed the door in my face.

I shifted and waited. A mockingbird flitted across the lawn, banking into the trees, showing the white racing stripes on his wings. A bead of sweat trickled down my neck, and my shirt stuck to my back. When I reached for the door to knock again, it opened in advance of my fist, causing the old woman on the other side to flinch back in surprise.

"Sorry, ma'am, didn't mean to startle you."

"Who are you? What do you want?" The gray-haired crone spit the words at me like bullets. The crabby woman may have topped five feet once upon a time, when she was still eating small children, but age, osteoporosis, or maybe a broom crash had twisted and bent her until she had to look at me with her head cocked to the side. She wore flip-flops and a shapeless house dress that was faded worse than my grandma's dishrags. She leaned on an aluminum cane.

"Texas Rangers, ma'am." I tipped my hat. "I'm looking for Theodore Garrett."

"He's not here," she snapped. "He's in the hospital. Got the cancer."

"I'm sorry to hear that, ma'am. Can you tell me which hospital?"

"Why do you want to know?"

I blocked the sun from where I stood, leaving her in shade, but she had to squint and hold up one hand. "Just following up on a routine matter. Nothing important."

"First the goddamn FBI, and now the Texas fucking Rangers. All y'all after somethin', but you won't say what."

"Excuse me? FBI?"

She looked at me as if I'd just peed on her porch. "Are you deaf, boy? The Federal Bumbling Idiots already been here once. I sent 'em down to Presbyterian where my son's dying, so they can ask their goddamn questions."

"Presbyterian Hospital?" I asked.

"That's what I said, wasn't it? Now get out of here so I can close the door. You're letting all the air conditioning out."

I tipped my hat again and backed away, reaching for my car keys. "Yes, ma'am. Sorry to have troubled you."

"Wait just a minute," she commanded.

I stopped, and she squinted at me, going so far as to step across the threshold for a better look. I stepped back. If she pulled out a dead chicken, I wanted a good running start.

"I know you," she said. "You're that fellow I saw on the news, killed that colored woman."

"Excuse me? No, ma'am, I didn't kill her at all."

"It's okay with me if you did." Her mouth pulled into a rictus that I recognized as a smile. Oversized white dentures wobbled when she spoke. "Uppity bitch, stirring up all those people down there."

"What people?"

"The goddamn colored people." She made it sound blindingly obvious. "They get to yelling and marching, and the next thing you know, they break loose and start killing each other. They got no control, those people. They just live off welfare and breed kids and do dope."

The old woman had to stop to draw breath, so I said thank you and escaped to my car before she could give me more of her thoughts on black culture. By the time I pulled out of the drive, the front door was closed, and the old lady was nowhere in sight.

Chapter 25

"In this day and age, what the fuck is this world coming to? I can't believe this, prejudice against—a Jew broad—prejudice against Italians." — Tommy DeVito, *Goodfellas*

Sam

I hate hospitals. I always got lost in them. They designed hospitals so that once people come in, they can never leave. Their way of making sure the bill gets paid. I checked at the information desk—once I found it—then had to stop three different people in scrubs for directions before I found the right room.

Theo Garrett looked older than his mother. A wasted skeleton in a bed surrounded by modern medical equipment, Garrett could have passed for dead if it weren't for the beep of his heart monitor and the hiss-click of the oxygen machine. His waxy skin gleamed under the fluorescent lights, and his pallor revealed an interstate map of veins under his skin.

Criminal mastermind? Mafia hit man? In his condition, he couldn't whack a dead fly with a broom.

"How long's he been like this?" I asked the nurse who followed me in.

"Two months or somet'ing like that." A black man in his twenties, the nurse wore blue scrubs and white shoes. His name tag identified him as Joseph, and he had a mild Haitian accent.

"Two months? In a hospital bed? He's not getting any better, is he?"

Joseph shrugged and looked genuinely sad. "No, sah. We make him comfortable, you know?"

I nodded. The bills for a private room and full-time hospital care had to be outrageous. I asked Joseph who paid for the room, and he held up his palms.

"Check wit' Patient Billing."

I patted Joseph on the shoulder and left the room. The door thumped shut, cutting off the noise from the machines that kept Theo Garrett in a state of zombie-life. I sighed. "Another suspect eliminated."

"Sah?" Joseph asked.

"Nothing, sorry. Just thinking out loud." I stopped at the nurse's station and said, "Tell me something, Joseph."

"Yes?"

"How do I get out of here?"

Sam

THE MAIN OFFICE OF Garrett & Hull was next on my list. It was located in a granite-and-glass high-rise at the junction of the North Dallas Tollway and I-635, just to the west of the Galleria Mall. The building's lone security officer paid no attention as I scanned the listings to find the right floor. I hit the elevator button and rode up to the fourteenth floor. The irony of their office occupying the same floor as Fortney's Hyatt hotel room did not escape me. The offices were closed, its doors locked, and the lights—what I could see through the frosted glass side-panel—were out. I tried the door a second time, just to be sure, and the knob remained locked. I said a word my mother wouldn't have been proud of and dug out the piece of paper with Hull's address.

A sandwich place on the ground floor set me up with a roast beef on wheat with plenty of mayo, tomatoes, lettuce, and American cheese. That and a bottle of water cost me over ten bucks. I fingered my handcuffs and considered arresting the man behind the counter for theft.

The Middle Eastern guy looked at me and said, "Is problem?"

"Problem? No. I'll go get a loan and come back for dinner."

"Closed dinner. No dinner."

"So sad."

I ate in the car, wincing when bits of lettuce, tomato, and mayonnaise dribbled on Matt's leather seats. No doubt I would pay for that someday.

Two toll roads got me to US Highway 75, where I headed north. The toll road bill would end up at Matt's house, not mine. I'd pay for that later, too.

Hull lived on two dozen acres of prairie dotted with oak and surrounded by a three-rail white fence. Afternoon sun gleamed off two roan horses grazing near the gate, tails swishing. The big ranch-style house sat among a stand of heavy shade trees. Built of dun-colored brick with four bland, square windows in front, the house was nothing special to look at. A post stood next to the drive with an intercom and a call button mounted in a weatherproof housing.

I pressed the button and waited, the Mustang's engine rumbling.

"Yes?" the voice answered, tinny and distorted, like at a drive-thru restaurant.

"Two super tacos, to go."

"Excuse me?"

"Texas Rangers to see Michael Hull."

There was a long pause before the buzz sounded and the gate clanked open.

"Please drive to the main house," said the crackly voice.

"And pay at the second window."

My new friend failed to answer, so I rolled up the window and waited for the gate. The drive to the house wasn't long, maybe a hundred yards of crushed gravel that ended at a paved driveway. Partially screened from the road by trees, the apron was big enough for a basketball court. The gravel drive pointed directly toward an unattached three-car garage.

A young man, college age or a little older, tossed a basketball at a hoop installed over the garage door. He wore a muscle shirt, shorts, and flip-flops and looked as if he majored in football and did pushups with his face. He had a flat-top haircut, a square chin, and a broad nose with a permanent mark where the helmet used to hit it.

"Help you?" he asked when I got out of the car.

"Looking for Michael Hull."

"Got a warrant?"

"Not here to arrest him," I said with my hands out, palms down. "Just want to ask him some questions."

"Then you can get back in your car and drive away," the kid said. He stood tall enough to stare me in the eye and had that look of pig-headed stupid-mean that comes to some boys early and never leaves. The man had that look. The look that says, "I wanna see if I can kick your butt." I'd seen that look many, many times, beginning in grade school. Without saying a word, the challenge rolled off this character like the smell of battery acid, strong and pungent. I flexed my hands and thought about it. Would dumping a can of kick-ass all over this kid's head be worth it?

Cicadas sang in the grass, providing a background hum.

"Look, son. My cowboy fu is strong today. Step aside, or I'll beat you so bad, you'll be picking teeth out of your turds for months."

The guy's face went red and twisted into all kinds of ugly. He sucked in a breath, a sure sign his next move would be violent.

A voice from the home's front door called out, "Hey, Trevor, what's wrong with you? Huh? I pressed the buzzer to let the guy in; don't give him a hard time."

A stocky guy in gray suit pants and a salmon button-down shirt stood there with a glass of something amber over rocks. Average height with Sans-A-Belt slacks working hard to hold his belly in, the new guy had a ruddy face and a head of thick sandy hair.

I took a guess. "Mr. Hull?"

"Yeah, that's me. Who're you?"

"Cable, Texas Ranger." I studied Trevor and saw he wasn't going to do anything after all. I brushed past him and showed Hull my wallet ID. "Like to ask you a few questions, if I may."

"I don't have a clue where my ex-wife is buried—uh, I mean, where she's livin' today." Hull laughed hard, deep from his belly. "Come on in, Ranger Cable." He had a Zig Ziglar kind of charm and a thousand-watt smile. And the sincerity of a televangelist. Hull waved me through the door and patted my back when I passed him. "Don't mind Trevor. He likes to think he's watching out for me. Let's get out of the heat, huh?"

Heat was right. The day had started warm and humid then turned hot and humid. Stepping inside the house chilled my skin, and I nearly shivered from the cold air. Hull must have kept his thermostat set at sixty-eight degrees.

"Geothermal heat pump," Hull said when I commented on the chill. "I got a bunch of tubes and shit buried in the yard. Transfers heat more efficiently. I can run my AC as low as I want and still not pay as much as you do for electricity."

A brick fireplace big enough to cook a water buffalo dominated the living area. Golden wood paneling covered the walls, and a creamy, thick carpet lay on the floor. With furniture, the room would have been beautiful; without it, Hull appeared to be camping out in his own house. He had three folding canvas camp chairs and a card table arranged around the fireplace.

"Sorry for the accommodations, Ranger." Hull rattled the ice in his glass and took a sip. "I'm doing some remodeling, and all the furniture is in storage."

"What kind of remodeling?"

"Oh, you know." Hull shrugged. "The usual."

"Ah."

"Please." Hull waved the glass in his hand. Ice tinkled. "Have a seat."

I frowned at the camp chair. "No. Thanks. I think I'll stand."

"Drink?"

"No, thanks."

Trevor came in and took up a position by the front door, giving me a mean look. I tried not to wet myself.

"Hey, Trevor," I said. "Why don't you move over there, where I can see you? I get twitchy with muscle heads standing behind me."

Trevor glared, but Hull made a motion with his head, and the big man moved to the other side of the room. Hull refilled his glass from a bottle of Maker's Mark on the card table. He didn't bother with ice.

"So." Hull moved over to stand with one hand on the mantel. "What can I do for you?"

"How long has your partner had cancer?"

Hull looked at the carpet, and his face took on the look of a mourner at a funeral. "Sad thing. Sad day. Ted was diagnosed with stage-four breast cancer in the January before last. Can you imagine that? A guy with breast cancer? I thought only women got that."

"Me, too," I said. "So tell me about Garrett & Hull."

He took me through the history of the firm, which was about as uninformative as the website.

"Mr. Hull—"

"Mike. Call me Mike."

"Mike," I said. "Did the FBI come to see you and Garrett about anything?"

Hull shrugged. "Yeah, they came." He poured a little more bourbon in his glass. "Or I should say 'he came.' There was just the one, a guy named Martinez."

"What did he want?"

Hull frowned. "Asked a lot of questions about one of our invest-ments." He sipped his drink. "We own an interest in a metal recycler in South Dallas. The judge... hey, hold the phone. I remember where I saw you before. The same judge who ruled in our favor was the one got killed, down in Austin—"

"San Antonio."

"That's right, San Antonio." He pointed at me, the Maker's Mark slopping over his finger. "Aren't you the guy that killed her? I saw your picture on the news. Man, you got some balls."

"No, I didn't kill her."

"Damn, boy, that's still something, though. Am I right?"

Hull had a lilt to his speech I couldn't immediately place. It had a cadence similar to Agent Goldman's, but not the same. "Where're you from, originally?"

"Boston," he said, pronouncing it more like *Bahsten*. "Before that, my people came on a slow boat from Ireland, potato dirt on their shoes."

I pulled the pictures of Tom and Dick from my sport coat. "Rec-ognize them?"

Hull put his glass on the mantel and took the photos. He raised both eyebrows and stuck his lip out while he studied the photos. I kept my trap shut while I waited. After a long minute, Hull said, "Yeah, I know 'em. Tony Abbado and Danny Boylan."

"Tony and Danny? You're kidding me." *So much more original than Tom and Dick.*

"No, they used to work for me."

"Used to?"

"Yeah, I cut 'em loose about a month ago."

"What did they do for you?"

"Same as him, there." Hull pointed with his glass-carrying hand at Trevor and sloshed more whiskey out. He sucked it off the back of his hand. "Man in my position, an investor, you know? We make enemies at times. Helps to have somebody around to... smooth out the edges."

I looked at the muscled statue by the door. "That what you are, Trevor? A smoother of rough edges?"

The blond kid sneered and said nothing.

I went back to Hull. "They're driving a car registered to Garrett & Hull."

"Are they now?" He cocked his eyebrows, doing a fair job of acting surprised. He squinted back and forth at the two photos, as if examining them for flaws. "Which car?"

"Toyota Camry."

"Ah." Hull's blue eyes fixed on mine, and he grinned his toothy grin. "I forgot about that."

I raised my eyebrows in question.

"I sold Tony that car six months ago."

"And you didn't transfer the title?"

Hull shook his head. *So sad.* "It was a cash sale. He gave me the money; I gave him the title."

"Of course. Full names and employment applications?"

Hull did his best to look crushed, but I sensed a twinkle of a smile in those wide blue eyes. He wagged his head in exaggerated sadness. "I don't have that stuff. Theo kept up with the accounting, and when he went down with the cancer, all that stuff is locked in his brain."

"You kept records? I-9s, that type of thing?"

"Theo did. No telling where they are now."

"You know the IRS will get all over you if you don't report their income. Forms like 1099s or whatever."

"I understand, Ranger. I'm hoping Theo comes out of it enough to tell me what he did with that stuff."

"You ever visit the judge?"

"Yeah, I went to see her. We had a case pending in front of the judge. I wanted to see, would any, uh, consideration be given to a, um, campaign contributor." He gave an exaggerated wink. "All politicians are for sale, Cable. It's just a matter of finding the right price. Turns out, the judge ruled in our favor, anyway. Didn't have to pay nothing."

"Why do you suppose that was?"

Hull cocked an eyebrow, tipped back his glass, and drained it. "We must've had a good case, I guess."

I tried a few more questions, but I was beat, and I knew it. I'd played my ace and gotten whipped. I should have seen it coming. I'd expected Hull to deny knowing the two goons from the Hyatt, but he'd played it smarter than that, probably guessing we'd already made the connection. Hull answered every other question with that same look of open-faced honesty that was as genuine as a plastic peanut.

"Well, Mike, I'm sorry to have bothered you."

"No bother at all, Ranger." He beamed sunshine and rainbows at me. "No bother at all."

I escaped, trying hard not to see Trevor's smirk.

Chapter 26

“*I'm a very important person on my planet. Like a queen, a goddess even. There are those who worship me.*” — Laurel Weaver, *Men in Black*

Sam

I pulled in to a gas station to feed the Mustang and dug Agent Goldman's card from my wallet. I dialed her cell while I waited for the pump to finish draining my bank account.

"Goldman here."

"Goldman, Cable. Why are you chasing down Garrett & Hull? What do you have on them?"

"Cable? Sam Cable? Why are you calling me about this? You're supposed to be suspended."

"I'm fixin' to be suspended by a rope if I can't figure out who did this. I heard that two guys who worked for Hull were in the Hyatt the night Fortney was murdered."

She drew in a sharp breath, and I waited.

"We should talk," she said. It sounded like *tawk*.

"Okay. Where and when?"

"You know where the Dallas field office is?"

"In general. I can find it," I told her. "Give me an hour. No, wait. Make it two."

"Two hours." She hung up.

I fired up the Mustang and rocketed south on US 75. Two hours gave me enough cushion, given traffic and distance, to make one stop along the way. It was time to pay another visit to my good pal Moriah Martin.

Moriah stayed close to her roots in the southwest quadrant of Dallas and about as far from Hull's place as Jupiter's moons. She lived in a post-war bungalow in a small pocket of well-tended homes, the neighborhood under siege by ratty apartments and Laundromats. A white house with aluminum siding and yellow window trim, Moriah's place had a neatly kept lawn and flowerbeds of orange geraniums. The driveway was empty. No garage, only a carport. I suspected she wasn't home, but I knocked anyway. The wooden screen door vibrated in the frame from my pounding. No response. I opened the screen and tried the inner door with the same lack of results.

To be thorough, because I'm a stubborn mule, I went around to the chain-link gate and let myself into the backyard. I knocked on the back door. The shades were drawn, and peeking through the gaps didn't earn me anything but eyestrain. With my luck, the neighbors would be calling the cops soon to report a Peeping Tom. No one answered the back door, either.

I had another forty minutes before I needed to leave to see Goldman. I went back to the car, rolled down the windows, and waited. The day had clouded over again; the weather idiot said there was a forty percent chance of rain. Not a breath of wind stirred, and the heat in the car went from uncomfortable to swampy. Sweat soaked my shirt. A dog barked from somewhere close by. Another answered.

My cell phone buzzed, and I snagged it off the passenger seat. Captain Marshall's number popped up on the display.

"You sittin' down, boy?" were his first words.

"This can't be good."

"San Antonio PD's draftin' a warrant for your arrest."

The words hit me in the guts. I said a whole bunch of things that never made it off my tongue.

"Captain, I—"

"The DNA on the stocking came back. They rushed it through, and it's yours."

"Shit."

"Yeah, shit is right. I don't know what to say."

"How long do I have?"

"Be here in San Antonio, seven a.m., Monday morning." He sighed. "I'll take you in myself, quiet like. I already worked a deal with them."

"What about Dusty and Kent?"

"They ain't found nothin', except the car them ol' boys used. Kent's in Dallas now, going to find the owner, these Garrett people."

"Don't bother." I explained to the captain what I'd been up to and what I'd found. I expected an explosion, but his response was pretty mild.

"Well, somehow that don't surprise me."

"I think Hull's crooked as a snake on a staircase."

"Could be. I'll have Kent keep an eye on him."

"You think we have enough for a search warrant? For Garrett & Hull."

"Maybe," he said. "But we got till Monday to make sure. The trail's cold here in San Antonio. We're comin' up to Dallas, see what this Maria person can tell us."

"Moriah."

"That's what I said. Now shut up and listen. You stay away from that woman. You taint this investigation, and it's gonna be your ass that burns for it. Let us handle it. Understand?"

I mumbled an affirmative.

"What was that you said?"

"Yes," I told him and punched the end button like I wanted to break it. Sometimes, I missed being able to slam down a phone.

If Moriah had any knowledge of Tom and Dick—Tony Abbado and Danny Boylan, I meant—then wouldn't she be a potential threat to them? Wouldn't they want to shut her up? Or did she have no connection at all? If she knew anything incriminating, Abbado and Boylan would find her and kill her.

I shifted in the car seat, unsticking my shirt from the leather upholstery. I sucked up my pride and called Marshall back.

"Look," I said. "I don't want to leave Moriah twisting in the wind." I relayed my concerns in a few short sentences.

"We'll get somebody on her. Wait there till I can send over one of the boys, in case she shows up."

"You need to send somebody by the campaign office, too."

"Thank you, Ranger Cable, for that law enforcement tip of the day. Now. Let me go do my job."

"Yessir."

An hour later, Bob Koontz—known to some wiseasses in the office as Cunts—showed up in a tan Jeep Cherokee. Six feet of solid steel, Koontz had a dry sense of humor and a ready smile. He could also shoot the testicle hair off a gnat with any kind of long gun ever made. That was why I made a point of pronouncing his name correctly.

I gave him the rundown on the situation.

"I got it, hoss," he drawled. "Now saddle up and get outta here. You're blockin' my view."

"Bite me."

"You wish."

I fired up the Mustang and barked the tires when I pulled out. Twenty minutes after six on Thursday night. Three days, more or less, to solve this thing and find out who set me up. And then prove it.

Piece of cake.

Sam

THE FBI HOME BASE IN Dallas included a complex of three buildings that covered as much ground as the old Texas Stadium had. Strong chain-link fences surrounded the property, along with retractable bollards to prevent car bombers from crashing into the building. They even had their own street: Justice Way. Yes, the Federal Bureau of Investigation possessed a teeny smidgen of self-importance.

Goldman met me in the lobby. Lean and muscular in her slacks and cream-colored blouse, with a Sig Sauer high on her right hip, she reminded me of Linda Fiorentino in *Vision Quest*. Maybe not the looks, but the attitude.

Her voice, however, was pure Fran Drescher. "Oh my Gawd. I forgot how tall you were. What do they feed you boys down on the farm?"

"Bite-size Yankees."

"I hope you like 'em kosher."

She waited while I signed in and got a visitor badge, then she led the way through a bureaucratic labyrinth of corridors and cubes. I followed Goldman into a tiny office in a carbon-copy hallway with a number on the door instead of a name.

"Welcome to my borrowed closet." She waved me to a seat, circled the desk, and slumped into the swivel chair.

"Seems I've been following the FBI around all day," I told her. "First to see the wicked witch of North Dallas"—I ticked off a finger at a time—"then to visit the guy in the hospital, Garrett, and finally, I showed up at Hull's house, up in McKinney, right after Agent Martinez."

She exaggerated a shiver. "I hate hospitals." The FBI agent tipped back in her chair and laced her hands behind her head. "So, explain to me: what have you been up to, tramping all over my investigation with your pointy-toed boots?"

I dropped my hat in the chair next to me, got comfortable, and told her my story. It took me about five minutes to cover everything from the last time I'd spoken to her up to seeing Hull. Goldman gave me her entire attention, pinning me with dark eyes and asking an occasional pertinent question. When I finished, the FBI elf jumped to her feet and bounded to the whiteboard on the wall, grabbing a marker. She wrote *Fortney* in the center.

"Okay, so pay attention here," she said. "We got our victim, the judge. Over here, on this side, we got her current lover and co-star of some naughty pictures." She scribbled *Ford* to the left of *Fortney*. "Who runs Millennium Metals—"

"What?" I jerked out of the chair, my mouth dropping open. "Ford runs Millennium Metals?"

"Oh, you didn't know that? I guess the FBI's good for something, huh? Pay attention here—this is important. Millennium Metals is linked to... Garret... and Hull." She wrote the names and drew connecting lines on the board. "Now Hull, along with two thugs, Boylan and Abbado, visit Fortney during her campaign, and, incidentally, win a judgment—"

"Injunction."

"Injunction, right, against a whole lotta voters in Fortney's district." Goldman stepped back from the board, which resembled a schematic for a garage-built teleportation device. "What would a reasonable person suspect, given those circumstances?"

"Garrett & Hull, or Hull alone, is using the blackmail pictures to get what he wants."

"Exactly! You're not as dumb as you look."

"Gee. Thanks."

"You're welcome."

"So why kill her?" I reached for a can of tobacco then remembered I'd quit. "They got what they wanted—the injunction. What could they gain by killing her?"

Goldman shrugged. "Keep her quiet? Maybe she got an attack of conscience. Who knows? My warrant for Garrett & Hull's financials went through this morning. Let's see what we can dig up."

"That was fast."

"I know, right? Judges don't like other judges getting killed. It sets a bad precedent. Pun intended."

Goldman sat back at her desk, capturing her mouse, and clicked and tapped with hummingbird speed. An intense woman, she exuded a steely competence and a cybernetic intelligence. Somehow my ears had grown accustomed to her voice, and I could listen without wanting to shoot my brains out. Like anything else, either adapt or die.

"What are you doing, by the way?" I sat down and tipped my chair back, balancing it on two legs.

"Financial stuff. You wouldn't understand."

"Show me the money! *Jerry Maguire*."

"What's with you and the movie stuff? Jeez, get a man's hobby, would ya?" The clicking and tapping continued for a long time.

I watched for a while. Six minutes. That was how long I could watch someone else type. Pictures on the wall captured my attention. One showed the New York skyline on the day after 9/11, smoke pall hanging over the city. Another was of firefighters coated with gray dust, tears cutting muddy tracks down their cheeks. I put my head back and closed my eyes. Goldman's fingers flying across the keyboard created a lulling rhythm in the background. *Tappity-tap-click-click-tappity-tap-click-click*. Like a train flying across the continent on steel rails...

I rode west on the Dreamland Express until Special Agent Bronx Voice snapped me out of my doze.

"Yeah. See."

I jolted and opened my eyes. "See what?"

Goldman leaned back and put her hands behind her head. A smile curled the edges of her full lips. When she stretched, her blouse tented over small breast-like mounds. I've seen bug bites that caused more swelling, but on her, the gesture looked sexy. She continued speaking, rocking in her chair. "I knew there had to be money somewhere in this deal. On paper, Michael C. Hull is over his head and sinking fast."

"What about Garrett?"

"That's part of the reason Hull's under water. Garrett's money is tied up because he never signed a power of attorney before his cancer took him under. Hull mentions that in a loan document where he applied for interim financing for Millennium."

"What about the company's other investments?"

Goldman turned her palms up, focused her eyes on the screen. "High-risk stuff. They had money in two biotechs, one electronics widget maker, a security company and—count 'em, three software start-ups. All collapsed one by one over the past two years. All but Millennium."

"That's great stuff, Goldman."

"Lucky for you I'm the best forensic accountant in the Bureau."

"Humble much?"

"Humble's for monks."

"No wonder the guy's living in an empty house." I stood up and paced the small room. Two steps one way, two steps back. "He probably sold all his furniture to pay his bills."

"That, or he's bailing out. Stashed his money offshore and getting out while the getting's good."

"Damian Ford," I said, "was bailed out of jail by a high-rolling attorney. Something Blake, the name escapes me right now."

"Henry Simpson Blake?"

"That's the guy. If Ford was in bed with Garrett & Hull, then that explains how he got such a big-shot lawyer to come get him."

"You should be a fucking detective or something. Sherlock Holmes of the Range." Her sarcasm seemed to be a reflex response; she seemed unaware she was obnoxious. The roller wheel on her mouse *scritched* as she went down page after page, never looking up. Then... "Oh. My. Gawd."

"What?"

"You want a connection? How's this for a connection?" She spun the monitor around and tipped back, looking as pleased as a banker with a new mortgage. I put both hands on the desk and leaned close to read the document on the screen. The light scent of Agent Goldman's perfume tickled my nose. Spicy, with a hint of flowers.

"What am I looking at?" I asked.

"A field surveillance report on Timothy Murphy from our Boston office. Murphy's a made guy with the Boston mob. I dumped everything with a keyword search on Michael Hull and found this."

"'Subject Murphy met with Noonan, Gary Thomas, and Hull, Michael Charles... unable to record conversation... suspected money laundering...' So who's this guy Murphy?"

"Irish mafia. Reportedly part of the Winter Hill boys."

"Irish mob? Hull's part of the Irish mob?"

"Could be."

"What about Tony Abbado and Danny Boylan?"

"Way ahead of you." *Click-click-click, tappity-tap-tap.* The light from the monitor reflected tiny blue dots against the darkness of her pupils. "Nothing on Boylan, or rather, too much on Boylan. You know how many Daniel Boylans there are in NCIC? Megacrap. The list goes on for-*evah*. Abbado, not so much." She spoke without looking up, more to herself than to me. "Anthony A. Abbado, DUI; Anthony J. Abbado, theft, theft, possession with intent to sell; Anthony M. Abbado, racketeering—"

"Try him. Anthony M."

"Sure." *Click-click*. She spun the monitor to me. "Take a look. This is the guy from the Hyatt, correct?"

"That's him." The mug shot showed the dark-haired man from the surveillance recording of the Hyatt's fourteenth floor. Thick brow ridge, rocky cheekbones, and a fighter's nose.

Goldman turned the monitor back and scanned pages at light speed. "Ah hah! Known associates, Daniel F. Boylan, Irish OC connections, yadda-yadda-yadda, Irish mob this, Irish mob that. Lemme look here a sec…" *Click-click*. "Yep. There he is!"

This mug shot pictured a fresh-faced farm boy type, wheat-colored hair, blocky head and barrel neck. Identical to the one captured on surveillance recordings from the Hyatt, shoulder to shoulder with Tony Abbado.

"So two guys working for the mobster Hull show up on the fourteenth floor the night I get framed for a murder. The murder of a woman being blackmailed—"

"We assume."

"—by Hull. That can't be coincidence."

"It's… interesting."

"Interesting? Is that all you've got? C'mon, we have to tell Woods. Maybe get her to drop that warrant."

"No, cowboy, *I* will talk to Woods." The undersized agent bolted up from her chair, all energy and passion. "You've done enough fucking around this case. We'll be lucky a judge doesn't throw out any evidence on Hull as tainted. By you, you big dumb hick." Goldman stalked around the desk and faced off against me, invading my personal space.

"Are you trying to be scary?" I asked. "It's not working."

"Go home, John Wayne—"

"Nick Nolte, you mean."

"—before I arrest you for obstruction. All we have so far is a bunch of coincidences. We think"—she started ticking off points with her fingers—"Ford and Hull were blackmailing Fortney; we think they had a reason to kill her; we think Hull's boys were there on his orders the night of her murder… We *think* all this stuff, but we can prove none of it. Any of it."

"But—"

"No, shut up and listen to me. You need to go home. Eat some bacon and beans. Watch *Bonanza* reruns. Let me take this from here and build a case."

Her tough-as-nails act was pretty cute. I grinned and raised an eyebrow. "Admit it, Goldman. You're starting to like me."

She sighed. "Not even a little bit."

Sam

"SO TOM AND DICK BELONG to this guy Hull?" Matt asked.

"Tony Abbado and Danny Boylan. Yeah."

We sat on cushioned patio recliners on my brother's backyard cedar deck, serenaded by night bugs. Another weather front generated a rain-cooled breeze, and the temperature had dropped below seventy. Lighting flashed to the north, followed much later by the rumble of thunder. Both of us were stripped to running shorts and muscle tees. After I got back from seeing Goldman, I managed, for the first time in over a week, to get in a run. Knocking the rust off and moving my body had been hard at first, and I knew I would be sore in the morning, but for the moment, my muscles were happy, relaxed, and pleasantly tired.

My lip itched for a dip of Skoal.

"Yeah, Matt, I do. This is how it plays to me." I sipped a Shiner Bock, and condensation dripped on my bare leg. "He gets the pictures with Ford's help and emails them to Fortney, says to her, 'Pay up or else.' Hull wants Fortney to kill the injunction. His guys, Tony and Danny, are there to..."

"Encourage her?"

"Yeah," I said. "Maybe that, or just to keep an eye on things. Anyway, Fortney decides her integrity is worth more than her reputation or she makes a threat or whatever."

"She pisses them off."

"Exactly. They have to get rid of her."

"So they show up in San Antonio, and *skkkiickk!*" Matt made a strangled noise and held a hand up to his neck.

"Sure, they kill her, jab me with the date rape drug, and throw me under the bus."

"Lotsa guesswork, Peanut."

"No shit. But it feels right."

"Why you?"

"Who knows?"

"What about the empty house?" Matt leaned forward in his chair. "You think Hull's fixin' to run?"

"Maybe. Or running low on funds."

A fat raindrop smacked me in the head. Two more slapped the deck.

"Time to go in." I levered myself out of the lawn chair.

Matt beat me to the kitchen door and held it open. "Get some sleep. Maybe the FBI will have it all wrapped up by the time you wake up."

"Maybe." I paused at the threshold. The first wave of heavy rain blew in sideways. A strong gust cut across the patio and tipped the chair I'd been sitting in. It rattled across the deck. "But I think I'll get back to Fortney's emails, just in case."

I didn't move. I stood in the doorway and let the rain-wet gusts chill my skin. Funny that Captain Marshall never threatened me with the consequences if I took off and headed for the Caribbean on a boat. Either he believed I would never run, or he wanted me to make a break for it. I said that aloud to Matt.

"Does it matter that he said anything or not?" he said.

"No, not really."

"Would you have run?"

"No."

"You've never run from anything in your life."

"Too pigheaded, I guess."

"I agree." He punched me on the shoulder and went to bed.

Chapter 27

"*Wickedness is hurting people on purpose.*" — John D. Mac-
Donald, *Nightmare in Pink*

Tony & Danny

"Hey, boss?"

"Jesus, Tony, you know what time it is?"

"Early bird gets the worm." Abbado chuckled. "Or in this case,
the Ford."

"You found him?"

"Yep. Shacked up with one of his hookers. The other one, too.
Big boy got frisky, and we had to put him down. Wanted to know
what we should do with Ford."

"Hmm. You remember the judge's cunt friend? Maria Martin?
Moira? Something like that. You think you could track her down?"

"Sure. Piece o' cake."

"If Fortney ever stopped sudden, she'd be shitting the other one
for a week. It's been itchin' me that she might know something she
shouldn't, understand? Take Ford there. Make it look like they did
each other."

"Heh. I like that. Okay, Mike, easy peasy. Consider it done."

Rita

STALLED IN RUSH-HOUR traffic early on Friday morning, Rita
tapped her hands on the steering wheel in time to *Footloose,* the
fourth cut on her '80s mix CD. One of her '80s mix CDs. Ahead of

her, a conga line of cars alternately bunched and expanded. Per usual, she was stuck behind a panel truck farting noxious blue smoke.

She prioritized her to-do list. *First, find the connection—if it existed—between the nude photos of Fortney and her decision involving Millennium Metals. Where to look? Email? Other electronic documents? Maybe call the techie guy in charge of the forensic workup on Fortney's computer, see what he could pull from her PC.*

Second, find the two mutts, Abbado and Boylan. Maybe they could be pressured to turn on their boss. "Fat chance," she muttered. "A couple of mob boys? They'd rather die first."

Three, find Damian Ford. Start with his financials, see what he owned, maybe—

Her cell rang, and she groaned when she saw the display. Cable. Reluctantly, she tapped her Bluetooth earpiece. "What?"

"Moriah Martin came home late last night."

It took her a second to catch up to what he said. "And?"

"If anybody knows what April Fortney was doing with the Millennium deal, it'll be her. Plus, I'll bet you goldfish to gold nuggets that she knows the real score with Damian."

Rita's jaw clenched. Cable's Texas twang set her teeth on edge and gave her an involuntary eyelid twitch. "Where are you?"

"Thirty minutes away, minimum. With traffic, more like forty."

"All right, you sit tight. Don't do a thing. I'll go talk to her right now."

"Got a pen? I'll give you the address."

"No, I'm driving."

"I'll text it to you then. See you there." And he hung up.

Rita found a gap to her right and sliced over two lanes at once, catching the exit from the highway. She shot down the ramp, blipped through a light as it turned yellow, and whipped into the parking lot of a 7-Eleven convenience store. She thumbed through email on her phone while she waited for the text to come through. When it did,

Rita plugged the address into her navigation app and found she was less than ten minutes away. Time enough for a coffee and a Danish from the 7-Eleven before she had to worry about Cable showing up and sticking his enormous clodhopper boots in the middle of everything.

No way did she believe the cowboy would sit and wait for her to do the interview with Martin. He would be right there, with his goddamn giant shoulders and his blue eyes. He would be pissed when she cut him out of the interview. Well, too bad, so sad. Rita would put him in handcuffs and leave him locked him in the car while she spoke to Martin, if that was what it took. She might even crack a window so the PETA people wouldn't get upset over keeping a dumb animal locked in a hot car.

The guy's taller than the Chrysler Building, it's not like I can karate chop him into submission. What if he doesn't want to be handcuffed?

"Easy," she said aloud. "I'll shoot him."

Sam

"ALL RIGHT, BOY, LISTEN good," Captain Marshall told me over the phone. "Dusty is on the way to Moriah Martin's house. Prolly an hour out."

"I'm on my way there, too."

"You sit your ass in the car and don't do nothing till Dusty gets there, you *comprende*?"

"Can't, boss. I got an FBI agent, has an interest in the case and wants to do the interview. I'm just following FBI direction."

"The FBI?" Marshall shouted in my ear. "The Fuckin' Bunch of Idiots? Aw, shit, boy. Now look what you done."

"Couldn't be helped, boss." I hung up before he could say anything else.

The muscle car kicked me in the ass when I hammered the accelerator. I wanted to beat everybody to Martin's place and get in there first, before everybody got in my way. Ask forgiveness, not permission. I'd lied to Goldman when I said thirty minutes. I was past the halfway point and gunning the Mustang through gaps in traffic that left a lot of mad people behind me. I swerved around a slow-moving beer truck and hit the overpass to I-35 South at 90 miles per hour. The car had a lively and rugged feel and seemed happy to give me all the speed I wanted. There was a ton of pedal left under my foot.

At 7:15 on the dot, I made the turn onto Moriah's street and rolled up behind the unmarked Dallas Police vehicle parked on the curb. It had to be Koontz's replacement. Blue Malibu with no hubcaps, cop lights on the rear deck, and a guy sitting in the driver's seat. About as unobtrusive as a tuba at a funeral.

I climbed out of the Mustang and put on my hat but left my sport coat on the hook in back. A boat could float on the humidity in the air.

"Hey! Dallas Police." It's not wise to come up on a lawman's blind side without announcing yourself. "Texas Rangers here. You good?"

No answer. The guy didn't move, and something tickled inside my belly. I unsnapped the hold-down on my Kimber and approached the car, one hand on my gun butt.

Another car pulled up behind mine. Goldman. I ignored her scowl and turned back to the cruiser.

"Hey! Yo! You awake?" I rapped a knuckle on the side of the car. No response, and the cop's head didn't even twitch. "Shit, if you're asleep, I'll kill you myself." I stepped up for a closer look. The officer in the car was in plain clothes. He had sandy-brown hair and a pale face. Both eyes were closed, and he slumped to the right, against the doorframe.

"Is he dead?" Goldman asked.

I reached into the car, and a waft of air tickled the finger I held under his nose. "No, he's still breathing."

I swept the area, checking for threats, but the street was empty. No traffic, nobody out mowing, nobody sitting on their front porch. Not even a lemonade stand.

"Hey." I shook the cop's shoulder, and his head rolled. "Whoa. What do we have here?"

"What?" Goldman came around for a look.

A goose-egg lump bulged over his ear, crusted blood at the top, in a livid shade of purple.

"Aw, shit. Call for backup!" I yanked the Kimber free and ran for Moriah's door.

My boots thudded across the pavement. I leaped the curb and hit the grass, running for the yellow-trimmed door. I had to pause on the porch to yank the screen open, then my size-thirteen boot slammed into the hollow-core door by the lockset. The lock splintered, and the door blew back and banged against a wall to the right. Two heavy thuds, like a pair of encyclopedias being dropped, came from somewhere in the house. Gunshots.

I went in low, to the left. My three-dot sights tracked across the living room. Sofa, chairs, bookcases, small entertainment center. Farther back, dining area with glass table and modern chairs. To the right, a hallway. Farther back on the same wall, opening off the dining room, probably kitchen. Nothing else.

"Texas Rangers!" I yelled. "Police!"

I slipped left, varying my aim between the hallway and kitchen. Motion at the kitchen doorway. Two shots flared out, blowing the stuffing from the chair next to me. I rolled behind the arm of the sofa and snapped a shot that missed.

Another shooter popped out of the hallway and triggered three rounds that smacked the drywall over my head. He ducked back before I could shift my sights.

I was not in a good place. The sofa wouldn't stop an angry fly, let alone a bullet, and it wouldn't hide anyone bigger than Goldman. I felt like a cartoon bear hiding behind a pine tree. Nothing else in the living room offered any better cover. The coffee table was glass, and the entertainment center was smaller than the sofa. The guy in the kitchen stuck an arm out and popped off a wild shot that punched into some books on the coffee table. I fired and missed. Too slow. He'd already ducked back.

Whack-a-Mole. With guns.

The kitchen shooter poked his head out again and banged away. Chips flew from the hardwood floor, and the coffee table exploded in a cascade of glass. Sofa cushions jumped as he tried to walk a line of bullets into me.

I lined up my sights and squeezed off one round, splintering the doorframe next to the gunman's face. The heavy bullet clipped through the molding and caught the shooter in the left eye. The gunman's head snapped back, and he collapsed in a boneless tumble. Red splattered the wall behind him. As he fell, I got a better look at his face. Danny Boylan.

A crash from one of the back rooms, down the hallway on my right. Shattering glass.

Goldman called out from the front porch, "Cable, where are you?"

"One shooter down!" I barked. "At least one more in the house. Go around the side. Cover the rear."

I shuffled down the hall, my pistol sweeping right as I passed a bathroom, did a quick check to make sure nobody was hiding in the shower, and moved on. The hall dead-ended in a T-junction. The noise came from the back, to the left, so I went that way, hard and fast. My boots thundered on the hardwood floor, and I hit the door like an avalanche, punching through it and rolling in. A bedroom. A window on the back wall was broken out. A gust of warm air stirred the curtains. Motion caught my eye—a figure running across the backyard. I rolled across the bed and went to the window, lining my sights up with a guy motoring across the lawn toward the alley.

"Abbado! Freeze!"

The gunman made no sign that he heard me. He vaulted the chain-link fence and hit the alley running, heading toward a foam-green Taurus parked in the weedy alley.

I levered my body through a window designed for midget people. Glass scraped my back, and I felt a cold sting, followed by a warm wetness.

Goldman appeared to my left, clanging through the gate, slapping it back out of the way. She held her weapon in a two-handed grip and swept it toward Abbado in the alley.

"Don't shoot him!" I yelled. "I need him alive!"

By the time I made the back fence, Abbado was piling into the front seat. Brake lights flared as I cleared the fence. The engine stuttered and fired up, but not quickly enough. I put a bullet through his wing mirror as a warning shot, but he tried it anyway, gunning the car. His front wheels spun for traction in the muck of the alley. I stepped right to get an angle and blew out the front driver's-side tire. The car slewed sideways. At that range, I could've picked off individual lug nuts if I wanted. I popped the rear driver's-side tire, as well.

Abbado rolled out of the car while it was still moving, using the momentum to bring himself up to one knee. He moved fast. Faster than I believed possible. He braced his gun hand and whirled toward me. The barrel of his weapon swiveled, a micro-instant from lining up.

Firing once, I blew out his left shoulder. He grunted and slammed into the Taurus, the force of the heavy bullet pile-driving him backward. The stubborn bastard cracked off a shot that zinged past my ear, close enough for me to feel the pressure wave.

"Goddamn it, stop!"

His second shot blew up a chunk of muddy ground at my feet. Abbado squinted and fixed his eyes on mine. There was no quit in them. His gun rose.

The three-dot sight on my .45 lined up under Abbado's heart, and I triggered three shots that punched him in the chest, one after the other.

His eyes rolled up, and he flopped forward. Brown water splashed when he face-planted into a puddle, and trashy muck swirled around his head. No bubbles rose to the surface.

"That was for April Fortney, you son of a bitch."

Chapter 28

"*Follow the money.*" — Investigator's maxim
Sam

Special Agent Goldman met me at the back fence. Mud splattered the legs of her pantsuit and caked her shoes. She carried her weapon two-handed, held low. Somewhere along the way, the silver clasp had lost the battle, and her black hair flounced behind her. Her face had lost color, and her eyes were two sizes too large.

"What happened to 'don't shoot him'?" She pointed to Abbado sprawled in the alley.

"He changed my mind." I hefted one boot onto the top bar of the fence and clambered over with less skill than I'd used getting over it the first time.

Goldman lifted a muddy foot for inspection. I ignored her shaky voice and trembling hands when she said, "Cable, if these shoes are goddamned ruined, I'm sending you the bill."

"Sure. I'll buy you two pair."

She snorted. "You don't make enough money, cowboy. The house? Is it clear?"

"Good question."

The back door was locked, and I really didn't want to try climbing back in the window. The cuts on my back burned, and the shakes were coming on. I had to concentrate to swap the Kimber's spent magazine for a fresh one.

We trudged through damp black soil spotted with Saint Augustine and dandelions. Stepping stones were placed along the side of the house. A chorus of dogs barked, and people started gathering on their front porches or peering from open windows. Moriah Martin's front door still hung open. I pushed ahead of Goldman and entered first.

"Fuck a duck," Goldman said when she saw Boylan slumped to the floor. "How many did you shoot?"

"All of them, I hope."

I led the way down the hall, checking the bathroom again, and turned right at the juncture, toward the front of the house. At the end of another short hall, a door stood half open. A pair of legs on the floor said at least one person was down.

"Texas Rangers!"

"FBI!" Goldman barked from behind me.

Easing forward, I nudged the door open with the barrel of my gun. I flattened myself against the wall and looked one way, then did the opposite wall for good measure. All my precautions were needless. Moriah Martin lay sprawled on her queen-sized bed, staining a yellow bedspread with the blood from two chest wounds. At the foot of the bed, Damian Maxwell Ford stirred and groaned. A strip of flesh lay open on the side of his head where a bullet had grazed his skull. Mr. Ford was lucky to be alive.

I checked Moriah for a pulse. Her wrist was cool under my fingers. She was gone.

"He's coming around, looks like," Goldman said of Ford.

I drew up a small chair from the vanity and sat in front of Ford. I toed the man until he started to snort and blink. Sirens wailed, and brakes screeched out front, which seemed to energize Ford. Bleary eyes popped open and focused on me for the first time.

"Damian Maxwell Ford? Can you understand me?"

"Yeah, bitch," he mumbled. "I hear you."

"Looks like your buddies turned on you, D-Max. You're lucky I showed up when I did. The whole Irish mob appears to be after your ass."

"Means shit to me," he muttered, throwing me a mean look.

"So, wise guy," Goldman said. "You know the drill. You got one shot here. Do the right thing and tell us about Michael Hull and April Fortney, and I see what I can do to get you into WitSec."

"You gonna make me disappear?" Ford sneered. "Who you, anyway? A Keebler elf?"

"A Keebler elf with the FBI, dipshit." Goldman pulled her credentials and showed him the fancy printing on her ID. "You ready to talk? Or should we lock you up where Hull's boys are sure to find you?"

Ford cursed, frowned, and snorted up a gob of spit, which he deposited on the floor next to him. All the air seemed to go out of him. "Yeah," he murmured in a sigh. "Let me see the deal."

I looked at Goldman and smiled for the first time in a week.

Sam

FROM THE TIME WE PROCESSED Damian Ford into jail until the time we got the last *t* crossed and *i* dotted on the paperwork, I sweated about a gallon of blood. Every tick of the clock gave Hull an extra second to get away. After booking, we had to find Ford an attorney, which meant a public defender. I doubted Henry Simpson Blake would represent his former client without Michael Hull's money paving the way.

The defense attorney conferred with his client while we huddled with an assistant district attorney. A pretty blonde with silky hair and green eyes, the ADA looked as if the hardest thing she ever did was pick out a dress for the cotillion. Looks could be deceiving. Turned out she had a razor-sharp IQ and a feral hunger for bad guys and public defenders. Even Goldman was impressed.

Two hours after booking, the two attorneys met in mortal combat and hammered out a deal. Ford would plead guilty to conspiracy, blackmail, and—for the attack on Darla Cable—assault with a deadly weapon. Eighteen months state jail time, two days off for every day of good behavior, in exchange for complete and full testimony against Michael Hull and any accomplices for any acts of blackmail, the murder of Moriah Martin, and any other violations of law they may have committed. That included jaywalking, spitting on the sidewalk, traffic violations, or tearing off mattress tags. Amen.

Dusty Boots arrived at showtime, clapped me on the back, and entered the interrogation room with Rita Goldman. I got to watch the interrogation on a monitor tied to a CCTV camera—two-way glass was out these days—while the mismatched pair took Ford through his story.

"Talk to me, Damian," Goldman said. "First off, I know about the lead smelter and Garrett & Hull blackmailing April Fortney with some naughty pictures. What I don't get is why you guys killed her? She stopped the injunction. She did what you wanted."

"Hey, first off," Ford said. "That blackmail stuff, that was Hull, okay? I had no part o' that."

"No, but you helped set her up for it."

"He made me do that," he said.

"Who?"

"You know. Hull."

"Tell me the story, start to finish."

And he did. The way Damian told it, he and Hull had been hooked up for a long time. Hull blew into town about ten years ago with a briefcase full of cash. "He some kinda Irish mafia or somethin', y'know?"

Hull knew all the right people and plugged himself into the strip club business. He not only invested his money in Skinny Dippers but also helped Ford open two more clubs. In exchange, Ford laundered money for Hull's partners back east. Then Hull branched out on his own, teaming up with a Dallas money guy, Theo Garrett. Ford didn't know whether Garrett was connected back east or not. They started taking on investors, delivering some really big returns, which attracted even more investors. They paid the original investors with money from new investors and so on.

"You mean a Ponzi scheme?" Goldman asked.

"Don't know about no fuckin' Ponzi."

"Never mind, keep going."

Then the economy tanked, and Garrett got sick. Hull decided to cash out and get the hell out of town. Go back to Boston a big man, with a pocketful of cash.

"At least, that's what he told me. But he say to me: 'Damian, I gots one more deal we can do. Makes us both rich.'"

"And that was?"

Millennium Metals. The idea all along was to build the company up, inflate the balance sheet, and sell it off to some fool before the EPA arrived and shut it down. Everything went according to plan until the Citizens for a Clean City came along. The injunction pending in Judge Fortney's court would kill the sale. So Ford and Hull blackmailed Fortney to rule against the CCC. And it worked.

"So what happened?"

"Nothin' happened. Ever'thing went juss how Hull wanted."

"So why'd y'all kill her?" Dusty asked. "Fortney, I mean."

"I done told y'all, I didn't kill her. Hull didn't either, far as I know."

"So who did?"

Ford shrugged. "Hell if I know. Hull, he told me, he thought the big muthafucker done it."

"Ranger Samuel Cable?"

"That's him. Saltine cracker, through and through."

I shifted in my seat. We were so close. All Ford had to do was throw Hull under the bus for murdering Fortney. Why wasn't he? I wanted to reach through the monitor and bang Ford against the wall until he made a silhouette in the sheetrock.

"He has these two guys he keeps around," Ford said. "They do most of Hull's business—"

"What are their names?"

"Some white-bread names, y'know? Extras from *The Brady Bunch*. Danny and Tony. They came around April, time to time, just to remind her, y'know, of what would happen if she got cold feet."

Goldman switched gears. "So how did you know Moriah? Why were you at her house?"

Dusty and Goldman went at Ford for another hour, during which he laid out enough dirt to hang Michael Hull for bribery, money laundering, extortion, blackmail, fraud, and a number of other charges. But not murder. He wouldn't budge on that.

Goldman met me in the hallway when they came to take Ford back to detention. "He says Hull didn't do it."

"I heard. It just doesn't make sense. We have his goons showing up at the hotel the night of the murder. Fortney could take him down if she decided to come clean. He *had* to cut ties with her, to feel safe."

Goldman shrugged and opened her mouth to say something just as the deputies escorted Ford from the interrogation room in his freshly pressed orange jumpsuit.

"Hey, Big Tex," Ford said with a chuckle. "I be out before you." He laughed as they led him away.

Sam

WE SAT AROUND A TABLE in the conference room we'd commandeered at the county jail while Goldman hammered out the warrant, typing a bajillion words per minute. Captain Marshall stomped in about halfway through the process. He proceeded to glare bullets at me while I gave him the short version of Ford's story. His expression eased when I got to the part about Ford implicating Hull in a blackmail plot and the Millennium Metals scheme.

I finished by saying, "Kent and Dusty went to keep an eye on Hull while we got the paperwork done."

"It ain't enough of a statement to get you off, boy," Marshall said, "but it may be enough to get the grand jury and the SAPD to slow down a mite in their hell-bent rush to hang you. As far as I'm concerned, you're off suspension as of now." He gestured to the speakerphone on the desk. "Get Kent on that thing."

When I reached Ranger Kent Fulkerson, Marshall asked, "What's the chickenshit bastard doin' now?"

"Things are stirring, looks like," Kent said. His voice came in crackly and fuzzy. "Two Suburbans pulled into the property, and five guys got out and went in the house. That was about an hour ago. Since then, we've seen a lot of movement. Looks like they're loading up the Suburbans and getting ready to boogie."

"We can't hardly hear you, Kent. That your phone?"

"Goddamn front's moving in. Lightning's playing hell."

"All right," Marshall said. "It's up to you and Dusty to hold the fort. Don't let them ol' boys leave until we get there. Block the road with your vehicle and shoot anybody that tries to get past you."

"Roger that."

Marshall punched the off button. "Where's that paperwork?"

"Here," Goldman handed the captain a sheaf of pages, hot off the printer.

"I'll go find a judge," Marshall said. "You get up there and back up Dusty and Kent. Don't let that ol' boy get away."

"Not a chance in hell," I said.

Chapter 29

"*Sound the horn and call the cry,*
How many of them can we make die!" — Heather Alexander, "March of Cambreadth"

Sam

At 6:21 p.m. the weather report indicated a severe thunderstorm warning for Collin, Denton, and Dallas counties. The radio fuzzed with interference from lightning strikes, and the sky to the north promised nothing but heartache and turmoil. I drove while Goldman rode shotgun and complained. About everything.

My cell rang as I bucked through traffic, gunning and braking in hard spurts. I answered without checking the display. "Cable."

"What's up, Peanut?"

"Makin' progress, Matt. Can't talk now. Going into a meeting. Call you later." I ended the call and turned off the phone.

"Who was that?" Goldman asked.

"My brother. Deputy Sheriff."

"Why didn't ya tell him what's up?" Goldman asked.

"His wife looks about twelve months pregnant. I tell him what's up, he'll want to come. He winds up taking a bullet, Darla would beat me senseless." I glanced at her. "And I'd deserve it."

She nodded. Her hand tapped a steady beat on the armrest, and she swallowed.

"How many field takedowns have you been on?" I asked.

"Including this one and the one this morning? Two."

"Well, don't you get killed. The FBI will throw me in a deep, dark hole in the ground if I get their best forensic accountant killed."

"I'll be pretty pissed, too."

"More than usual?"

Traffic came to a standstill north of Dallas. I jerked and jammed the Mustang into every open slot I could find, trying to gain a few inches here and there. A river of brake lights led north on US 75, headed into a steel-gray wall that flickered with lightning. Whenever I could, I took the shoulder and zipped forward, no doubt pissing off every other driver on the road. On the other side of McKinney, traffic lightened enough that I could let the muscle car roam free. I found out that at one hundred ten miles per hour, the Mustang handled pretty well.

"Slow down, cowboy," Goldman complained. "I'm too pretty to get scraped off the road."

At 6:58 p.m., I took the exit ramp and followed my directions to the county blacktop road between McKinney and Van Alstyne where Hull's place was located. Five miles of farmland later, I pulled off the road next to Kent's Explorer and Dusty's Yukon. The two Rangers had moved their vehicles so they blocked the driveway outside the gate to Hull's property. A drainage ditch ran parallel to the road, so my vehicle canted to the right. I figured it would help Goldman get out of the car.

"What's happenin'?" I said when we gathered.

Kent Erickson stood almost as tall as me and had black hair, dark eyes, and a full mustache. He wore a tan flat-brim hat with a braided leather band and carried a Winchester .30-30 propped on one hip. On the other side, a bone-handled .45 auto stuck out in a cross-draw holster. He turned to the side and spit. "Been getting a mite stirred up over there. I think they know we're here."

"Oh my God," Goldman said, "I'm in cowboy hell."

"Who're you?" Kent asked.

"FBI." The small woman showed her credentials.

"Well," Kent drawled. "You sound like a damn Yankee Screech Owl."

"What do you mean 'stirred up'?" I asked.

"Them ol' boys been running around like ants for the past hour or so, loadin' up them Suburbans. Look to me like they're fixin' to scarper off."

Goldman looked at me with a confused expression. "What the hell did he say?"

"It looks like a risk of imminent flight to me, which would give us grounds to proceed with an arrest prior to the arrival of the warrant. What do you think?"

"Let's get 'er done," Dusty said.

Kent smiled and spat. "We hang around holdin' our dicks—pardon me, ma'am—they could bolt."

"Are you guys insane?" Goldman demanded. She looked more angry than scared. "Call for backup before you try something stupid. Better yet, wait for the warrant team to show up."

"This ain't the Branch Davidian. We don't need an army." Dusty looked at me. "You want somethin' bigger than that Kimber?" He held a modified AR-15, cut down commando-style with an extended magazine. On his hip rode a Wilson Tactical .45 ACP.

"What you got?" I followed Dusty to his toy box in the back of the Yukon. Inside, he kept a Bernelli shotgun, a Remington bolt-action with scope, and a LaRue Tactical chambered in 7.62.

Goldman stalked over and stood next to me. "Oh my God. Boys and their toys."

"Rangers go a long way from home base and into some pretty rugged country," I said. "We tend to keep a small arsenal of guns close to hand." I looked at Dusty. "Gimme the LaRue."

"Good choice, my friend."

I checked the magazine, chamber, and safety then took a second thirty-round mag, which I crammed in my back pocket. Dusty's spare tactical vest was a tight fit, but I squeezed out enough Velcro to hold it together. Goldman had brought her own.

"We need all this, we're in trouble," I said.

"I'd rather have it..." Dusty said.

"And not need it. I know."

We gathered at the gate. I nodded at Kent, who'd retrieved an ax from his toolbox after putting on his own body armor. Kent handed me his rifle and jumped the rail fence next to the gate's control box. With a grunt, the dark-haired Ranger slammed the ax through the conduit carrying power to the mag-lock. With a tiny pop and a spray of sparks, the lock lost power and released. Dusty pulled against the weight of the chain-drive mechanism. Kent joined him, and the gate squealed open far enough to admit us in single file.

"You boys ready?" Kent asked. "And you, ma'am?"

Agent Goldman's eyes were bright. "Insane. Plain fuckin' crazy. All right, I'm in."

We spread out across the gravel drive and walked four abreast toward the house. Lightning flickering against the backdrop of a darkening sky. Goldman picked her way along the gravel drive, cursing the muck on her shoes, the Texas weather, all mule-headed, backward-ass cowboys in general, and me in particular. She tried walking beside the drive and had to keep on her toes to avoid her mid-sized heels sticking in the mud. As a result, she fell behind the group.

When she was far enough back that she couldn't overhear us, Kent spit a stream and leaned close to me. "Hey. the Fed's kinda cute. You oughta tap that."

I grimaced. "Not my type. I like 'em tall, blond, and dumb."

"You mean, like you?" He laughed, and so did Dusty.

Goldman kicked off her shoes and caught up in her bare feet, wincing as things jabbed her soles. The conversation dried up after that, and all we could hear was the crunching of our boots on gravel and the pesky chirping of Goldman's curses as she worked to keep up.

At twenty yards, one of the men carrying a box from the house noticed us and shouted a warning to his pals. Men with guns disgorged from the house and fanned across the drive, taking up blocking positions. In less than a dozen heartbeats, six men faced us—four with tactical weapons and two with pistols. They had the look of soldiers recruited from the IRA—short-cropped hair, trim and fit bodies, and neutral expressions. It could have been a parade ground, as far as they were concerned, and this just another formation drill.

The meathead I'd met the first time I was there anchored the middle. I pointed at him. "Trevor, you and your boys stand down."

On my right, Kent spat and cocked his Winchester. "We're here for Michael Hull. The rest of you need to grab your gear and head for the hills, before you piss me off."

Agent Goldman wobbled up next to Dusty, on my left. "And if you think these guys are trouble, you should see what the federal government can do to ya. Agent Goldman, FBI."

A couple of the men across from us shifted and exchanged glances.

I snicked the safety off the LaRue carbine and settled my feet into a shooter's stance. I took a deep breath and let it out.

"Well, hello, boys!" Michael Hull stood in the open doorway of the house, dressed for the golf course in tan pants and a cherry polo shirt. "What can I do for the mighty Texas Rangers?"

"Michael Charles Hull," I yelled, "you are under arrest for fraud and blackmail. Call your boys off. Now."

"No, sir, I don't think I will." Hull carried a highball glass in his left hand. The right hand was tucked in his pocket. He took a pull off his drink, and the clink of ice carried across the open space. "I pay these fellows good money to protect me, so I think I'll let them earn their keep."

"You boys really wanna die for this scumbag?" I addressed the lineup, meeting the eye of each man in turn. I sensed a lack of enthusiasm from several of the gunmen, but no one dropped out of line. I fixed my eyes on Trevor, standing directly in front of me. He grinned and squeezed the handgrip of his HK91 assault rifle, a manic expression on his face.

"You know," I told him, "you can get out of this without dying. There's still time to deal."

"He's lying to you, boy," Hull called out. "Can't trust the Rangers. You know that."

"You know I'm right, don't you?" I said. "You know the drill. Testify and you get a deal. Y'all know what's gonna happen if you don't. We start shooting, and some of y'all are gonna die. Fire on law enforcement officers, and even if you live, you'll get the needle when they catch you." I pinned Trevor with my stare and let the barrel of my rifle drift so the muzzle pointed at his crotch. "Put your gun down, Trevor, or I shoot you in the balls." I panned my stare to the next guy, who held a semi-auto pistol dangling at his side. "Next, I shoot you through the heart before you can twitch."

To the redhead across from Goldman, I said, "Agent Goldman's an FBI-trained shooter, boy. She'll put a bullet between your eyes in the time it takes you to blink."

"And you other boys," Dusty said, "are just as dead. So what's it gonna be? It's fixin' to rain, and I hate gettin' wet." Thunder rolled, punctuating his sentence.

A tense count of five passed with nobody moving. Hull stood in the doorway, silent, his look turning feral and a sly grin crimping his lips. *Breathe*, I said to myself. *Remember to breathe.* The mercenaries' body language showed they really weren't ready to die for the cause. One more nudge, and they'd back down.

Flash-crack!

The surprise bang of a nearby lightning strike jolted everyone. One instant we were a still-life picture of a modern OK Corral, and in the next, it was a blur of motion and gunfire.

Trevor fired the first shot, and his bullet exploded sod between my feet, showering my pants with mud. I shot Trevor in the crotch. He folded like a card table and collapsed. I pivoted, and the LaRue bucked in my hands. The guy next to Trevor never got his HK into action. Blood puffed from his shirt, and he was catapulted backward by the force of a .308 slug to the chest. A bullet smacked my vest and knocked me on my ass. The vest stopped the bullet, but the mule-kick force of it broke at least one rib and shocked the wind right out of me. Kent was down, not moving, and Dusty was on one knee, firing with robotic precision. Fire, shift, aim, fire. Goldman lay flat on her belly in the grass, popping away with her Sig Sauer. I struggled to catch my breath.

Three of the soldiers were down, and another ran for the house. Somebody yelled at the runner to freeze, and he face-planted in the driveway, arms going over his head. A dark-haired gunman with a thick chin and a hook nose was still in the fight, rounds cracking from his AR-15 like popcorn, all seeming to come directly at me. A bullet burned my cheek, and another took my hat clean off. My *new* hat.

I dove to my right, buying a second and forcing the guy to shift his sights. I rolled into a kneeling position and cracked off four rounds, aiming at center mass, bracketing my shots. One went high right, splintering the guy's shoulder. The next went low left, taking out his leg. The last two hit dead, solid. Perfect. The man looked stunned as the AR clattered to the ground at his feet. He took a long time to fall and *whumped* when he hit the concrete.

I pivoted behind my rifle, looking for more targets, but the fight was over. Hull was gone, having retreated into the house at the first shot.

Dusty struggled to sit up, his face white. I scrambled over, and he waved me away.

"Go see to Kent," he wheezed. "Bullet... hit my vest."

"Yeah, me too," I gasped back.

Goldman beat me to it. "Head wound," she said. "Looks bad, but he's breathing."

"Let's go get Mr. Hull," I told Dusty.

Agent Goldman looked up, pistol dangling from one hand, the slide locked back.

"You okay?" I asked her.

"Oh. My. Gawd." The agent's eyes were like dinner plates.

"Probably ought to reload," I said.

She double-blinked and followed my pointing finger, staring at her gun with a momentary lack of comprehension. Goldman managed to drop the empty mag, but replacing it proved to be beyond her. She shivered so hard, she couldn't get the new magazine in the slot. I took the gun from her and did it myself, deliberately setting the safety before I handed it back.

"You did good," I said.

She nodded and tried to swallow.

"Call for an ambulance?" I said, making it more of a question than an order.

She nodded again and started patting her pockets for a cell phone.

"We better go get that ol' boy in the house afore he gets away," Dusty said. "Whaddya say?"

"Yep. One second, though," I said, holding up a finger. "Let's make sure these boys are secure before we turn our backs."

Trevor lay in the fetal position, both hands cupping his crotch. He moaned and clenched his eyes shut. Sweat glistened on his forehead and matted his hair. I toed him in the leg with the tip of my boot. Dusty kicked his weapon away.

I leaned over him. "Hey. Remember me?"

Trevor cracked one eye open long enough to glare at me. "I think you shot my dick off," he gritted out.

"We'll find it and sew it back on. Don't die on me. I'm gonna want you to testify."

"I ain't sayin' nothin'," Trevor spat.

"Then I'm not looking for your dick. Enjoy prison."

We finished securing the weapons from the other shooters. Two, besides Trevor, were wounded but alive. I jerked my head at Dusty, and we moved to the house. I took up a position to the right of the open door, Dusty to the left. Setting the rifle aside, I pulled my .45. Going into the close confines of a house, the handgun would be less awkward. Easier to maneuver around corners.

"Hull!" I shouted. My sore ribs stabbed me, and I winced. "We're coming in. Best you not be armed when we do, 'cause I'm a mite pissed at you right now."

"Don't shoot." Hull's voice sounded hollow. "I'm done. I'm coming out." He stepped onto the porch with both hands raised. In his right, he still held his highball glass.

I kicked Hull's feet out from under him and took him to the ground, shattering the glass on the drive and spilling liquor. I planted a knee in his back and put the muzzle of my .45 in his ear. "Give me a reason why I shouldn't punch your ticket right here."

Hull had gone red in the face, and he'd scraped his chin on the concrete. He twisted his neck, fixing me with a cocky grin and reddened eyes, a "screw you" expression on his face.

"You're not gonna shoot me." He wheezed a little, having to work at breathing with my two hundred pounds in his back. "You don't got the balls."

My vision narrowed to a red-rimmed tunnel. I wanted to slam his face into the ground again and again. To wipe that smug look off his face. Pay Hull back for April Fortney and Kent Erickson. Make him hurt. Make him bleed. I snagged my hand in Hull's hair and shifted my weight, setting my grip so I could slam his meaty, grinning face into the concrete.

Agent Goldman laid a hand on my arm. "Don't do it," was all she said. Not harsh. Not a command. A request, given as gently as anything I'd heard her say.

The anger drained off and turned to disgust. I let go of Hull's hair and snagged his wrist instead, bringing his right arm back while reaching for the cuffs on my belt.

"Michael C. Hull," I said in a monotone, "you are under the arrest for the murder of April Maree Fortney. In addition, you will be charged with blackmail, fraud, money laundering, and a whole bunch of other shit, all the way down to any outstanding parking violations. You have the right to remain silent..."

Hull started with a chuckle, and by the time I'd finished cuffing him, he'd escalated to full-out laughter. "You really think I did Fortney? You're a dumb mutt, boy, you know it? I never laid a hand on that woman's kinky hair." He laughed and shook his head.

"Take him to the car," I told Dusty. "Before I forget myself and shoot him, after all."

Chapter 30

"Hasta la vista, baby." — The Terminator, *Terminator II*
Rita

Rita stretched to relieve the knot between her shoulder blades. Sometime in the wee hours of Saturday morning, her adrenaline high had drained away, leaving her hollow and shaky. Brittle. Her eyelids drooped, and the conference room table invited her to lay her head down and sleep. Around the table, showing similar signs of fatigue, slumped the Texas contingent of Marshall, Cable, and Boots. *Where the fuck is Little Joe and Hoss?*

"So tell me again..." The voice of Detective Bernia Woods, San Antonio PD, came over the speakerphone. "Abbado and Boylan are tied to Hull, and you're saying they killed Fortney because of the blackmail situation, correct?"

"Correct," Rita said.

Cable leaned forward, forearms blocked on the wood-grain table, scowling at the phone. His eyes, normally bright and smiling, were muddy and red. He sagged in his chair, round-shouldered. Running on fumes. No more gumption in his git-along. Whatever. He looked fucking tired.

Woods continued, "They were the two guys who got back on the elevator at 12:14 in the morning, right?"

"Correct," Rita said again. She glanced at the Ranger captain, Les Marshall, who was letting her do the talking, for once. He nodded at her solemnly, encouraging her with a wink.

"Well, here's the problem," Woods said. "Three calls were placed from Fortney's room phone after that time."

Woods's statement hung there, and Rita could feel the air leaving the room.

"And you're just now telling us?" Rita snapped. "To whom were the calls placed?"

Cable looked at Boots and mouthed, "To whom?" She shot him the bird, and his lips twitched in a near-smile.

"The first at 12:20 to the front desk," Woods stated, "who confirmed Fortney requested a wake-up call."

"And the others?" Rita asked.

"*Ahem.* At 12:36, a call was logged from Fortney's room to Ranger Samuel Cable's cell phone. That call lasted thirty-six seconds. The next call... went to Cable's room."

Rita focused on Cable. "You remember any of this?"

The tall man shook his head. "How long did that call last?"

"Two minutes. No voicemail. It was picked up."

"You're saying Fortney called me *after* Abbado and Boylan showed up, and she spoke to me for two minutes. And also called the desk for a wake-up."

"That is correct."

"There's no mix-up on the time stamp? Sometimes the surveillance system is out of sync with—"

"No, we checked."

"So they couldn't have killed her," Cable said.

Bernia let silence speak for her answer.

"Which means," Rita said, "we're back to square one, despite the blackmail and Hull's resisting arrest, and, and, all the other shit."

Woods's sigh came over the phone very clearly.

"Well," Rita muttered, "that fucking sucks."

Marshall's brows drew together, lightning flashing behind his eyes. *Uh oh, brace for impact.*

"Are you shittin' me?" Marshall barked. "That would have been nice to know before I had a man wounded arresting a goddamn *blackmailer*!"

"It's not my job to call you, Captain, and keep you updated. You were conducting your own investigation, and your men had access to the phone records. Well, they would have, except they left for Dallas before we had them in hand."

"Have you checked Sam's cell phone?"

"We don't have it."

"You don't? Who does?"

"It was never recovered."

"Well, that would have been nice to know, too! Goddamn it, Woods, quit holding back. What else do you know?"

Rita quit listening and focused on Cable, wondering what was going through his mind. *Talk about defeat snatched from the jaws of victory.* They'd fought a miniature battle four hours ago, capturing Hull at great personal and professional effort. For basically nothing more than a financial crime.

"You okay?" she mouthed silently when she caught his eye.

He nodded and gave her a weak half smile. What a contrast from a few hours ago. Facing down the mobsters at Hull's place, Cable had showed no fear, no hesitation, none of the nerves that'd rattled her. During that confrontation, her rational mind had deserted her. It ran away and hid under a dumpster, leaving her with only animal instinct and Bureau training. Like scenes from a John Woo film, flashes of memory replayed in jerky sequence. She was on the ground, a man's shape outlined behind the square block of her sight picture. Her pistol jumped in her hand, recoil shocked her arm, unfelt. The boom of the shot seemed distant. A man, falling, arms akimbo. A taste of pennies in her mouth... an earthy, weedy smell in her nose.

Even now, small tremors tickled her fingers. Her first action, and it had nearly scared the shit right out of her. Nearly literally. Only superb bowel control had saved her *beaucoup* embarrassment. Maybe she wasn't cut out for this line of work, after all.

But Cable. Moses wept. She could picture him standing there like it'd happened two seconds ago. A Marvel Comics action figure. Carbine spouting tongues of flame, his face lit by the muzzle flash—*blam-blam-blam!*—like a blacksmith hammering steel. No hurry, no waste. Pure, controlled violence. A Texas Terminator. Rita blinked back to the present and studied the Ranger. None of that automated destructo-bot remained. Sam Cable appeared all too human, and he was having a shitty day.

"Wait," she snapped. The conversation—argument—going on in the background between Woods and Marshall penetrated her thoughts. The yelling had given way to a more civil discussion. Everybody had decided to get on the same page now that the horse had left the barn. "What was that you said? The husband alibied out?"

"Yes," Woods said. Her voice had taken on a testy, irritated buzz. "He was at a fundraiser in Dallas the night of the murder. Multiple witnesses attested to his presence until well after midnight. Until 12:42, to be exact."

"And Ford?"

"Left the fourteenth floor before the calls in question, as well."

"So who does that leave?"

Dead silence returned to the room. Goldman's eyes flicked to Cable, who shook his head like a wounded bull, back and forth with metronome precision. He pushed away from the table and left the room. The door clicked behind him.

"Wait a minute," Boots drawled. "We're forgetting one set of suspects that we can't account for."

"Who?" Goldman and Woods chorused.

"The two quee—ah, gay fellers. The ones checked in with a fake ID and used prepaid plastic. We still don't know who they are."

"I still say that doesn't matter," Woods explained, as if to a group of children. "People shack up all the time using fake IDs."

"You see them on camera?" Rita's brow furrowed. It was the first she'd heard of two guys with fake IDs in the hotel. *I should've spent more time liaising and less time shooting at people.*

"Sure. Checked in at six p.m., left the next day around ten in the morning."

"Lemme see," she ordered. "You got pictures?"

"Does an alligator shit in the river? Hold on a sec." Boots's voice trailed off as he fiddled with his smartphone. He mumbled, "I sent 'em in an email to Sam... no wait, I forgot to do that... Where the hell? Ah, here."

Boots handed her the phone. On its tiny screen, a still shot from a surveillance camera at the check-in desk showed two white males—late twenties, one bald, the other in a cap with the brim turned backward. The bald one was in front, both arms resting on the counter.

"I don't believe it," Rita breathed, a chill running down her back. "I know these guys."

Sam

SUNDAY MORNING, DARLA made me breakfast when I got up. Matt stayed in bed and attacked a pile of logs with a rusty saw.

Darla sat across from me. "So what now?"

"That's the big question. I have no idea. Seriously, I'm fresh out." I shoveled down eggs and followed them with a goodly slug of coffee. "Sometime *after* Abbado and Boylan left, April Fortney supposedly called me. I don't remember a bit of it. Sometime *after* that, somebody killed her."

"Don't worry, Sam." Darla leaned across the table, which took some doing, considering her pregnancy girth, and gripped my forearm. "Y'all will figure this thing out. No way you're going down for this."

I lifted a shoulder in a half shrug, having a hard time working up any emotion whatsoever. "At least I don't have to report to jail tomorrow. Woods agreed to hold off the arrest until they verified Hull's whereabouts the night of the murder."

She asked, "What does that FBI agent, Goldberg, say?"

"Goldman? She doesn't seem to want to talk. I called her this morning. She told me she was working on something and would call me back if it panned out."

"Sounds to me like she's helping."

"Seems to be. But you can't count on a fed for much. They tend to have their own agenda."

"Did they ever find your cell? Or check your voicemail?"

"I checked my voicemail remotely. Nothing. The phone's off the grid. Not like in the movies. There's no magic chip that lets you pinpoint a phone if it's powered down."

Darla sipped her decaf. Pregnancy had filled out her cheeks and softened her face. Her hair was pulled up into one of those complicated hair knots held by a plastic clip, except for the front, where bangs fell over her forehead. A corner of white bandage peeked from under her hair.

"Thanks, by the way," she said, her attention shifting to the glass patio door. A squirrel bounced along the deck rail outside then sat up with its tiny hands poised. A long-tailed boxer, ready for the bell.

"For what?"

Her glance flickered at me, on and off. "For not calling Matt to come help you take down that gangster."

I chuckled. "No problem. Big doofus would've just gotten in the way."

A smile flicked on and off her lips, and she rested one hand on her swollen tummy.

I drank my coffee and watched the squirrel. *Keep fighting, little buddy.*

Rita

RITA GOLDMAN AND TWO uniformed officers from the Ennis police department crept through a grove of trees behind a rental house where their targets were said to reside. The cops were part of the Ennis SWAT team, all biceps and wire-tight expressions. The occasional muted voice whispered from their tac radio earbuds. Rain dripped steadily through the trees and deadened the remaining sounds. She had not slept in thirty-two hours or had time to change out of her muddy and grass-stained clothes. The once-pristine low-heel pumps on her feet were a total write-off, and her Donna Karan jacket had lost a button. She kept fingering the loose threads where it once was.

After Dusty showed her the pictures of the supposedly gay couple, Rita had charged up on pure excitement while waiting for her laptop to fire up and plug into the network. She hit the criminal databases for aliases and tattoos. Based on her interaction with these two, she was sure they had a record somewhere.

And she was right. Once she had the names, she soon had an address, located in a medium-small town thirty minutes southeast of Dallas. Thirty minutes later, Marshall got off the phone with the Ennis police.

"Confirmed," he said. "The place is occupied, and the plainclothes guy got close enough to spot our boys in the house."

"It's him?" she had asked. Her throat had tightened, and she bounced one knee under the table, hyper as a caffeine junkie. "Snake?"

Marshall's wolfish grin crinkled around his eyes. "Jason Byerly, aka Snake. And his running buddy, Tyler Ritterman."

Snake and Tyler. Two men Rita had last seen sharing a beer with April Fortney's campaign manager, Trey Dennison, in a bar in San Antonio. Two men who also showed up as having checked in to the Hyatt where Fortney was killed. Their rap sheets, when combined, accounted for eighteen separate felonies, from murder—not convicted—to extortion—pled out, limited time served—and numerous assaults—varied adjudications. Misdemeanors, she didn't even bother counting. Intelligence suggested the two men were enforcers for a loose confederation of criminal syndicates operating throughout Texas and the surrounding states.

She laid a hand on the Marshall's arm. "Should we call Sam?"

"Let's go find out how they're mixed up with Mr. Campaign Manager, first. I want to know more in case this turns into another false lead." The Ranger captain headed out the door, pulling everyone else in his wake.

An hour later, Rita found herself among the trees and bugs and probably all the goddamn snakes in Ennis, Texas, with rain soaking her outfit, her gaze fixed on the back of the rental property said to be occupied by the two-man crime wave of Snake and Tyler. No fences surrounded any of the properties in this neighborhood; all the houses backed up to a central wooded area in the middle of the block. Rita and the two SWAT officers had the back door while the entry team took the front. She slapped a mosquito lunching on her neck.

Tell me again how I got stuck back here?

The tac radios crackled with the go order, and her companions, whose names she'd forgotten, surged forward in a two-man bounding overwatch advance. Good technique. Rita let them move ahead without her. She'd had enough of getting shot at for the month, and the only things holding her upright were adrenaline and determination. She had no confidence in her ability to make sound decisions under duress, anyway.

Let the boys handle it.

Just in case, however, her Sig 9mm rested its comforting weight at the apex of her extended arms, muzzle down. Rita paused at the edge of the trees, twenty yards from the rear of the single-story house. Air conditioners stuck out from two of the four windows, and a storm door covered the rear entrance. Rain pattered the grass and *plonked* off the rusty barbeque grill tilted on three of four legs.

"Police! Police!" The shouts from the front of the house carried clearly, followed by the crash of the ram as it hit the door. The windows lit up, then came the muted *whump* of flashbangs. More shouts crowded close behind, muffled from inside the house. Her SWAT escort formed up on either side of the back porch and held position.

The window on the far end, to her left, exploded outward in a shower of glass.

"Look out!" she screamed.

A male, shirtless and barefoot, crashed through it. He hit the ground with a hard thud and rolled through the broken glass. Bald head. Tattooed forearm.

"Byerly! Freeze! You're under arrest!" Her voice sounded shrill, pitched at the edge of human hearing.

In less than a heartbeat, Byerly rolled to his knees. He held a nickel-plated revolver in each hand. She lined up her pistol, but the front sight was dancing so much, she had no confidence in her shot.

The two SWAT officers, surprised and off balance, reacted to the threat with excellent reflexes. They just weren't quite excellent enough. The first officer, with his back to Snake, was slammed forward by the concussion of two heavy rounds striking the rear of his protective vest. The second officer, in a better position, lashed out with a tongue of flame from the muzzle of his tactical weapon, trading fire with the half-naked Byerly, who cracked off two shots so close together, they sounded as one. Both missed at less than a dozen feet.

Rita unstuck her feet from where they were rooted and charged across the open backyard. "Freeze, Byerly!"

The tattooed man cocked and fired each weapon in succession, like a cowboy in an old Western movie. The Ennis SWAT officer jerked back, hit in the body, and his weapon fell to the ground. Byerly, a wild look in his eyes, scrabbled to his feet. Blood streaked his back and sides where the window glass had slashed him.

Rita slid to a stop at five yards, her feet nearly going out from under her. She assumed a shooter's stance, legs braced, gun forward. The thudding of her heart and her harsh breathing came to her from a long way away. Drizzling rain soaked her skin. The rest of the world lost focus as she framed Snake Byerly over her sights. Rita felt like she could count the pores in his skin between one heartbeat and the next.

He froze in mid-step, his eyes narrowed to slits. His knuckles tensed, and the guns flexed in his hands.

"Byerly." Her voice echoed in her head, as though it came from a deep tunnel. Thunder rumbled. "You twitch, and I'll fucking kill you where you stand."

"You don't have the balls, you Jew bitch," he snarled.

"It don't take balls to shoot a fucker like you." The words came out steady. Firm. Deadly. "Just one tiny squeeze."

"Byerly! Freeze!" Cops and feds and Texas Rangers poured from the back door and around the sides of the house, shouting commands. In seconds, a dozen guns were pointed at him. "Get on the ground!"

Snake Byerly let the guns slip from his fingers. He didn't break off his stare until uniformed officers tackled him to the ground.

Rita safed and holstered her weapon. She put her hands in her pockets so no one would see them shake. Her thudding pulse flushed her system with more adrenaline. Sounds were clearer, colors more vibrant. Even the rain felt good. Her pain and doubts sloughed off like dead skin. With a small shock, she realized she felt... great.

I could get used to this.

Chapter 31

"*Our lives begin to end the day we become silent about things that matter.*" — Martin Luther King, Jr.

Sam

By the time Monday morning rolled around, thunderstorms had brewed up from Central Texas, blanketing the area for the third day in a row. Heavy rain pelted the ground, and thunder rumbled. I drained two cups of coffee and made an effort to kick off the blues and get back to work. I called the captain and Goldman, one after the other. I got the captain's voicemail, but Goldman picked up.

"Cable?" Goldman's scratchy voice assaulted me.

"What's up?"

"I think you want to come see this."

"There's a Bogart marathon on TMC today, so this better be good."

"You'll see. Meet me in an hour. My office."

She left me staring at a dead phone.

An hour later, Goldman met me at the front portico. She dove into my passenger seat when I pulled up to the entrance. She finagled her umbrella through the Mustang's door, cursing it the whole way. Goldman wore blue slacks and a white blouse; several gold bands jangled around her left wrist as she fiddled and fussed. My wipers thumped the rain away in sheets while I waited for her to get settled.

"C'mon," Goldman said after buckling her seatbelt. "Let's move it, buddy."

"Where's the fire?"

She grinned, dark eyes flashing and hair whipping. The size of a chipmunk, Goldman had a bird's nest for hair, and a voice that could knock squirrels from the trees, but there was something about her—

"Fortney's Dallas campaign office. You remember where it is?"

"Sure. Why there?"

"You'll see." Her lips compressed in a smug look, but she refused to say anything else.

I shifted into first and popped the clutch.

Fortney campaign headquarters anchored the middle of a strip mall on Second Avenue, not far from Fair Park. To the left, a thrift store sold used clothes, and to the right, a law office promised help with DUIs and workers' comp claims. The rain had passed over the area, washing the streets and filling the gutters. A makeshift memorial had grown on the sidewalk in front of the campaign office: flowers, photos, and kids' drawings sagged in the damp air. The lights inside were half off, leaving the front section of the space in the dark, the desks and chairs there abandoned and empty.

I pushed through the glass door with Goldman following me like the tail of a comet.

"Sam!" DaShondra called out when she saw me. She was the only person in the outer office. "Who's this? You have a girlfriend now?"

Goldman choked a cough, and I shook my head. "No, D. This is Agent Rita Goldman of the FBI."

"We're here to see Mr. Dennison," Goldman said, showing her credentials.

"Of course. He's in his office." DaShondra waved a hand at a plain door in a bare sheetrock wall behind her. "We were just cleaning up some paperwork. Before we... you know... closed up the office." Her eyes were red and puffy. A tissue was bunched in one fist.

"Thanks, D." I patted her on the shoulder as I passed.

The plain door opened to an equally plain hall leading to four rooms, two per side. Two were offices—Trey's left, April's right—one was a conference room, and the last was a closet with network and phone gear. Trey's office door swung open at my knock, and the stubby campaign manager looked up from his PC screen when I ushered Goldman into the room.

"Cable?" he snapped. "And who the fuck is this?"

"Goldman, FBI," the frizzy-haired agent told him. "I have some questions."

"Huh?" Dennison's brow creased. His hands remained poised over the keyboard, like they didn't know where to go. "What kind of—"

"Did April Fortney discover the embezzlement? Is that why you killed her, Trey?"

"Say what? Killed her?"

Goldman planted her butt in Trey's visitor chair and leaned back like she owned the world. "Evidence shows you got off the elevator on the fourteenth floor of the Hyatt at 12:25 a.m. Where did you go?"

Dennison blinked. "Uh. To my room."

"Directly?"

"Yeah, directly. What the fuck is this about?" He glanced at me.

I shrugged and assumed a cigar-store Indian stance by the door. This was Goldman's show, and I let her call the dance.

"How long is the walk from the elevator to your room?" she asked.

"How long?"

"Roughly."

"A couple of minutes."

"Two minutes? Three?"

"Yeah, about that."

"You know," Goldman said, "that hotels record the time door locks are accessed by their guests' keys, right? So why was your room not accessed until 1:18 a.m.? That's a long two minutes. Want to re-consider your answer?"

Dennison shrugged. "It musta been broke."

"Broke?"

"The lock, I mean. Got the time fucked up."

Goldman nodded and said nothing. Twenty seconds of silence could sound like a lifetime during an interrogation. After the first twenty, Goldman waited another ten before speaking. "Did you access any other part of the hotel? Say, the stairwell door?"

"Umm, what? I don't think so, no."

"Did you meet anyone in the stairwell?"

"Meet anyone? What are you sayin' here?" Dennison had both hands on the desk now, clenched into fists. His gaze shifted from Goldman to me, then back.

"Who at the campaign headquarters was responsible for media buys?"

"Media buys?"

"Paying for advertising and PR firms to place advertising."

"Uh, mostly me." Dennison blinked, clearly confused at the change in questioning. "Maybe one or two others."

"Who are the others?"

"Fuck, I don't know right this minute. You got me so shook up, saying did I do away with April Fortney."

"Do you own any PR firms?"

"Me? Why would I—"

"OneTouch? STS Services? Global Ad Agency? Any of those ring a bell?"

"I... I, uh..." Dennison's face drained of color. He looked like a man who wanted to shit a pig.

"Our research indicates you own these companies, Mr. Denni-son. Here's the documentation, just so you know I'm not bluffing." Goldman pulled a sheaf of papers from her satchel.

Dennison glanced at the top sheet. "I... Yeah, okay. I guess I do."

"We have learned that you also drafted, signed, and issued checks to these three companies from the Fortney Campaign operational account, over which you had sole control. Specifically, $217,486 worth of checks."

Dennison's mouth worked, but no sound came out. Goldman let the silence drag for another twenty count.

"Further, Mr. Dennison, none of these companies ever made a single advertisement buy or did anything on behalf of April Fortney, did they?"

The campaign manager mumbled something unintelligible.

"Say again? I didn't catch that."

"No comment."

"So I ask you again, did you kill Judge Fortney because she uncovered the fraud?"

"Hey, look, I didn't kill nobody," Dennison said with a rush. "Yeah, I got, you know, behind on some debts, so I borrowed some cash. I was gonna pay it back, soon as I got even."

"How did you get in debt?"

"I, y'know, I place a bet now and again. I've just been on a losin' streak is all. I'll make it back."

"Mr. Dennison, do you know an individual by the name of Jason Byerly? Also goes by Snake?"

I thought Dennison had gone pale earlier, but I learned the definition of pale. White as a cotton sheet.

Goldman leaned forward and pitched her voice to carry loud and clear. "Did you pay Mr. Byerly to stage the murder of Mrs. Fortney because she threatened you with exposure and said if you didn't pay her back, she would get—and I quote—'her pet Ranger'—unquote—to arrest you?"

Dennison swallowed a golf ball. "I want a lawyer."

Goldman sat back and cast a look at me over her shoulder. "Ranger, would you do me a favor and place Mr. Dennison in hand-cuffs?" She smiled. "Pretty please?"

I grinned and unsnapped the cuffs from my belt. "My pleasure, Agent Goldman. Trey, stand the fuck up and turn around. You have the right to remain silent..."

Epilogue

"Country boy ain't got no blues." – Johnny Cash, "Country Boy"

Sam

"So Dennison made a deal?" I tipped the last of the Shiner Bock down my throat and set the empty bottle on the table. Across from me, Agent Goldman sat next to Delman Taylor. Matt was on my left. Goldman looked like she needed a booster seat with the three of us around her.

"He tried," Goldman said. "Snake beat him to it."

Delman leaned forward. "How did this Dennison hook up with a pair of low-life crooks? Guys willing to kill a judge and involve a peace officer?"

"He was in so deep," Goldman said, "with his gambling debts, the syndicate boys sent over Snake and Tyler because Dennison told 'em he needed help keeping the lid on. He cooked up the whole thing, start to finish, with his two best buddies."

Matt interjected, "What he didn't count on was Snake Byerly keeping the evidence and blackmailing him to keep the faucet open on the money pipe. Finding the GHB and the other stuff in Byerly's place—man, that was some good luck for you, Peanut."

"Good police work." I saluted Goldman with my beer bottle.

The way it had gone down that night, according to Byerly's testimony, Dennison connected with him and Tyler Ritterman in the stairwell then got into Fortney's room. They hit her with the GHB first, knocking her out, then Trey used her room phone to call me. He told me to get over to Fortney's room, fast. When I showed up, the two felons ambushed me with another syringe of GHB. From there, it was all window dressing and staging. Something Dennison was good at.

"Look at that," Delman said. A chuckle burbled up from deep in his chest. "No racial agenda at all. It was just about the money."

"Hah. Yeah, funny."

"Anyway," Matt said. "He's going down, buddy." Matt signaled the waitress, who came over. "Another round."

"Make mine a Jack Daniel's," I said. "Double. Straight up."

Delman laughed and waggled his empty mojito. "Don't be angry, Sam. This could have gone real bad for you."

"Did you hear?" I told him, "JC Fortney hasn't missed a beat. Now, instead of the white cop who killed her, it's the white political operative that did it."

"Politics, baby. It's what makes the world go round."

"So what's next for you, cowboy?" Goldman sipped white wine and watched me with her dark eyes.

"Captain Marshall says he's gonna send me back home for a while. Back in East Texas, where I can't get into any trouble."

"Yeah, sure." Goldman snorted. "Good luck with *that*."

Also by Scott Bell

An Abel Yeager Novel
Yeager's Law
Yeager's Mission
Yeager's Getaway

A Sam Cable Mystery
April's Fool

Standalone
Working Stiffs

Watch for more at snapshooter4hire.com.

About the Author

Scott Bell has over 25 years of experience protecting the assets of retail companies. He holds a degree in Criminal Justice from North Texas State University.

With the kids grown and time on his hands, Scott turned back to his first love—writing. His short stories have been published in *The Western Online*, *Cast of Wonders*, and in the anthology, *Desolation*.

When he's not writing, Scott is on the eternal quest to answer the question: What would John Wayne do?

Read more at snapshooter4hire.com.

About the Publisher

Dear Reader,

We hope you enjoyed this book. Please consider leaving a review on your favorite book site.

Visit https://RedAdeptPublishing.com to see our entire catalogue.

Don't forget to subscribe to our monthly newsletter to be notified of future releases and special sales.